ANNIE HARLAND CREEK

EVERNIGHT PUBLISHING ®

www.evernightpublishing.com

THE ART OF SEDUCTION

Copyright© 2017

Annie Harland Creek

Editor: Katelyn Uplinger

Cover Artist: Jay Aheer

ISBN: 978-1-77339-477-0

ANNIE HARLAND CREEK

ACKNOWLEDGEMENTS

The Art of Seduction almost wrote itself. While writing Kiss of Death, my youngest daughter, Brooke, fell in love with the secondary character, David, and my eldest, Pamela, reminded me that he wasn't the hero of the story so I shouldn't focus on him. Despite my efforts, David refused to stay in the background of his brother's story so I was forced to give him a book of his own. Fortunately, I had my daughters to bounce ideas off so it was relatively easy. Thank you my gorgeous girls. I couldn't have done it without you.

My family means the world to me. They are my muses, my loves, my reason for getting up every morning and my last thoughts before sleeping. Dave, Grant, Brooke, Pamela, Travis, Lorelei and Angelica, I love you guys.

A big thank you to Kerry, my beautiful sister-in-law who beta reads my books and gives me great feedback. My gorgeous friends Efthalia and Chelsea, who are always there with advice and support. My gratitude to Stacey, Katelyn, and all the staff and authors at Evernight for their continuing faith in me. Kisses to Jay Aheer for the fantastic cover and, once again, a huge thank you to my readers. You're the best!

ANNIE HARLAND CREEK

THE ART OF SEDUCTION

Blood Brothers, 2

Annie Harland Creek

Copyright © 2017

Chapter One

Meaghan stared at the blank page on her sketch book and tried to concentrate on the task at hand rather than the erratic beating of her heart. A bead of sweat trickled from her brow, followed the contour of her cheek down her neck, and finally came to rest in her cleavage making her even more self-conscious. Over the course of her twenty-five years, she had learned to hide her insecurities but today she struggled with emotions she had never before experienced and she had no idea how to deal with them. Her training at the academy didn't cover this type of scenario. Why would they? *Focus on the task at hand. You can do this.* Another look towards the center of the room and she came undone. A tremor shook her body and the charcoal pencil in her hand dropped to the vinyl floor with a clunk.

She stooped to the floor to retrieve the pencil, ignoring both the glances from fellow students and the compulsion to take another peek at the dais. The overhead fans—switched to high speed—offered little respite as her body temperature soared. Perspiration soaked through her clothes. She turned to the young woman sketching beside her and asked, "Hey, Lilith, is it hot in here or is it just me?"

Lilith answered without making eye contact. Her focus on the platform in the center of the art room. "Oh it's hot in here all right. Smoking hot."

"Shhh. He'll hear you."

"I don't care if he does. The way he's been staring in our direction for the last twenty minutes, he's interested in one of us and I call first dibs."

Meaghan *had* noticed. It was his attention causing her the anxiety. Since the moment he positioned himself on the platform, the model's gaze had been focused on her, and to her horror, she realized that she couldn't take her eyes off him either. The most perfect specimen of a man she had ever seen, reclining on pillows—naked except for the replica Spartan helmet covering his manhood—and he stared at her as if he could see through her cotton dress. She shook her head. "He's just facing this way … he isn't allowed to move until the teacher directs him."

Lilith rolled her eyes and sighed. "I think I've drawn enough naked men to understand how it works. This dude is definitely watching us." She took another long look at the model and whispered, "Pretty big helmet, do you think his *actual* equipment is big?"

Heat rushed to Meaghan's cheeks. She stared down at her feet. It was hard enough concentrating on drawing the parts that she could see, without imagining the parts that were covered. She took a deep breath, and raised her eyes. *Oh God, he's smiling.*

****

David Corel struggled to stop his lips from curling into a grin. Despite their whispers, he had heard the two women discussing him and found the reactions of the blonde amusing. She was a delicate little thing, he guessed around five feet five inches tall, and compared to his six feet two she seemed tiny. He tried not to laugh as he watched her sneak looks at him from around the oversized sketch pad on her easel. Other than noting that she had long blonde braids and dark rimmed glasses, her face and figure were relatively obscured by the easel. He deduced that she was reasonably athletic. Her calves were toned and her ankles trim. Pink toenails poked from the white sandals. He found the little daisies on the shoes cute.

For the last ten minutes he had remained perfectly still, waiting for the teacher to instruct him to change positions. Watching with amusement as the blonde stole quick looks at him from behind her drawing pad, without ever appearing to draw. But there was something more. He felt compelled to see her face. *Perhaps she was the unsub? The murderer he had been assigned to destroy.* There was a definite pull in her direction, something drawing … no, demanding his attention. Something connected to the case. He could feel it in his very core. So he watched and waited, knowing that by the end of the class, he would make a point of introducing himself and find out all he could about the little blonde.

****

"Time."

The art director's announcement shocked Meaghan back to attention. In the last few minutes she had been feverishly drawing in an attempt to have at least something on her page before the model left. She had been given a wonderful opportunity. A chance to do something she loved while getting paid to work undercover. Finally, her big break. A chance to show Terry that she had what it took to make a great detective. *Don't blow it over one naked man.*

None of the previous life drawing classes had

been a problem for her as the models were normally average looking, leaning towards the plump side. Handsome males tended to be self-conscious and less inclined to volunteer but not this man. This man looked as though he spent half his life in the nude and—Meaghan guessed—probably not alone. She examined her work, cringing with disappointment. The sketch looked rushed and rough, lacking in detail. A complete waste of a perfectly formed male specimen. *You can do this, Meaghan. Concentrate on the drawing, not the model.* She firmly decided that the next sketch would be better, especially because this time he would be facing away and she would not be bothered with the distraction of his eyes or his smile. *Oh, but what eyes* … she knew there was no color in her inexpensive box of paints intense enough to do them justice. Bluer than the deepest oceans, brighter than sapphires and clearer than glass. *Oh to swim in those liquid pools.* And his smile … Meaghan shook her head and flipped to a new page on the drawing pad, ready to begin, but the moment she looked back at the model, she was lost.

****

The pain hit David the minute he changed his position on the dais. Not so much a physical pain, more like a spiritual feeling of loss. He felt a tugging at his soul and wanted … no, *needed* to turn back so he could watch the blonde. But he couldn't allow himself the luxury of indulging his own desires. He was there—at the University—on a mission and as co-leader of his coven, he was obliged to put the needs of the others first. There to observe and only to interact with the humans in order to gather information that would help the case. Although he couldn't rule out a vampire attack, strangulation seemed more like human behavior. Despite only grabbing quick glimpses at the little blonde, she hardly looked strong enough to choke life out of a chicken, let alone another student.

Still, there was a pull in her direction. A gut feeling he couldn't explain. Perhaps she would prove pertinent to the case but he would need to bide his time. He held his pose and concentrated on remaining still for the last forty-five minutes of the class.

****

A rush of adrenaline hit her, soon followed by blind panic. It didn't make sense. The model had turned his back to her, now reclining on one elbow, his hand supporting the weight of his head and his other hand resting on his bent knee. His supporting leg was slightly bent under him revealing a hint of red fabric from the Spartan cape that had replaced the helmet. His broad shoulders looked even larger from behind and tapered down to his waist forming a vee shape that seemed to point to his tight buttocks. Meaghan tried to concentrate on drawing but she could barely breathe. Her hands itching to trace the contours of his body and the thought of touching him sent another wave of heat through her body. When the sudden and completely foreign impulse to squeeze his butt cheeks hit her, she knew it was time to leave. Hastily, she gathered her art supplies, tucked her oversized sketchpad under her arm, and dashed from the room without offering the teacher an apology or daring to looking back.

****

David watched the blonde rush past him and it took all his will power not to call out for her to stop. She held the sketchpad under her arm, angled high enough to cover her face from view as she left the room, leaving him with his plans foiled and an emptiness that he could not comprehend. Somehow, she had taken a part of him with her, leaving him confused, agitated, and somewhat frustrated. He had been conscious of her eyes on him, aware of her arousal and although he had—on more than one occasion—sensed the desire of young artists, he had never physically reacted to their attraction. This little blonde affected him physically, viscerally. He imagined her delicate hands tracing the contours of his body and his body reacted as though she were physically stroking him. Thankfully, the red cloth of the Spartan cape hid his erection.

How was she doing that? His gut twisted in protest to her departure, and the blood in his veins boiled, begging for her to return. Holding his position on the dais became painfully difficult. Nevertheless, he was obliged to both the class and his coven to see the lesson through to the end so he remained still, disappointed in the knowledge that by the time he dressed and left the room, the mysterious blonde would be long gone.

Chapter Two

As if the shame and humiliation of her panic attack hadn't been enough, the final straw came when Lilith rang on the pretext of checking up on her. Theirs was a friendship of convenience. Lilith needed someone to gossip with and Meaghan needed to learn all she could about the other students without drawing attention to herself. Without revealing her true purpose for attending the classes. Previous attempts by the police to question the students had proved fruitless so, posing as one of their own seemed like the best way to gain information. Unfortunately, she had little in common with Lilith besides their love of art.

"We so have to get you laid," Lilith teased. "Maybe we should give Leonidas a call and organize a threesome. I have a feeling he would be up for it."

"If you're referring to tonight's model, I'm sure he gets offers like that all the time. Besides, I'm not interested in a twosome let alone a threesome." Meaghan had often wondered about Lilith's sexuality. It wasn't the first time she had mentioned threesomes and Meaghan was pretty sure that Lilith wasn't even her real name. She recalled Lilith as being Adam's first wife and the mother of vampires or something similar. It was probably chosen to represent her fascination with the macabre. They had met in night classes and after hearing about Lilith's interest in the recent murders, Meaghan had encouraged a friendship, of sorts. She had never seen Lilith around in the daytime, but to be fair, she herself was rarely there during the day as her work schedule only permitted her to attend night classes. So far, Lilith hadn't done anything *too* out of the ordinary.

"Anyway, gotta go. Meeting some people tonight

who are gonna hook me up with some good shit."

When Lilith hung up the phone, Meaghan shook her head and reminded herself that she had to ignore the drug reference. She wasn't there to arrest drug dealers or users and she had to be careful in case she ran into any undercover narcotic agents. They might blow each other's cover. She had worked too hard to get this particular job and knew that she wouldn't have been given the chance if it wasn't for her youthful looks and mediocre artistic talent. Torn between her love of art and her desire to succeed in the police force, she jumped when this opportunity presented itself.

She picked up her large sketch pad and flopped into her only chair, a big overstuffed armchair that she had found at a second-hand store in town. Flipping through the pad, she stopped at her most recent sketch and sighed. For the first time this semester, she actually had a model worth drawing and all she could manage was a mediocre sketch that would hardly get her any recognition as an artist. Not nearly good enough for her portfolio, especially if she hoped to get a High Distinction. *What a waste of time*. As she considered her behavior in class, she suddenly became aware of the fact that—for the second time today—she had been absentmindedly tracing the drawing with her index finger, running her hand over his body and face with the intimacy of a lover. A ripple of electricity ran down her spine, the hair on her neck prickled. She tossed the pad across the room as she yelled, "Who the hell are you anyway?"

****

"David."

The name was repeated, this time louder. "David! Earth to David."

"What?" David answered. He had hardly noticed

when his sister-in-law walked into the room. He was forced to quickly step behind the kitchen counter to hide his erection. His body felt sensitized, as though soft hands gently stroked his skin. He had experienced the same sensations during the art class when the little blonde seemed distracted by his backside, unaware that he was facing a mirror and could see her actions. He was grateful that Anna had made her presence known before the daydream went any further. "Oh, sorry, Anna. I didn't hear you come in."

"You *did* seem deep in thought," she agreed. "Is everything okay?"

"Fine." He sighed, disappointed that his fantasy was cut short. "Was there something you wanted?"

"I was wondering if you had discovered anything at the University yet."

"The students are talking plenty, but everything is hearsay, no eye witnesses that I have found."

Anna sighed. "Maybe I was wrong. It's been a week since I had the premonition."

David touched her shoulder. "You were right about the first murder, it happened where and how you said it would. I have no doubt that your second premonition will be just as accurate."

"I wish that these visions would at least give me a time and day. Something like that would be rather helpful. I feel so useless."

"You're still developing your powers, Anna. The last couple of months have been a nightmare. I don't know how you coped with everything that life threw at you."

"Fortunately, I had you and Derrick to guide me through."

She rewarded him with a smile, but he knew she had been to hell and back. It would take time to process and heal, but he had every confidence in his new sister.

"Give it some time."

"But what about those poor women in the visions? Their time has run out."

"David will be at the University again tonight, watching and waiting for the killer to show up. Isn't that right?"

David turned to see his brother enter the room. Derrick picked up his bride and kissed her. As the kiss heated and Derrick's hands began to wander over Anna's body, David objected.

"Will you two get a room?"

Anna blushed as Derrick put her down. He reminded David.

"We have a room. A very nice room in fact." He pulled Anna towards the stairs and called over his shoulder, "If you need us, we will be in that very nice room," then after a moment's consideration he added, "try not to need us."

****

David poured himself a drink and looked out the window. Years of experience had already warned him the sun was close to coming up, but he knew he had time to relax for a while before retiring to his darkened room. Besides, he had a feeling that sleep would elude him or at the very least, his dreams would be filled with visions of braids and daisies and, if he was lucky, more sensations of being touched.

Chapter Three

Meaghan covered her yawn with the back of her hand as she sat in one of the front seats of the 6.30 p.m. bus to Uni. She had spent the day sorting through mug shots and researching some of the teachers in case there were any suspects at the campus. A pointless, waste of her time but part of the job. To top it off, she had lost sleep to the wailing of some strange animal outside her bedroom window. She considered feral cats in the area but if this was a cat, it must be huge.

Lilith boarded the bus and joined the other Goths in the back row rather than take the empty seat beside Meaghan. Not that it bothered her. Typically, Lilith ignored her when the other Goths were around and only spoke to her if they were alone. She assumed that being seen with her would ruin Lilith's image. When the bus stopped and Meaghan alighted, Lilith followed.

"Hi," she called, acting as though she hadn't walked straight past her on the bus.

As usual, Meaghan played along with charade. She suspected that there was more to Lilith than her strange garb and body piercings. "Hi."

"I guess we'll be stuck with Mr. Huge arse again today. We always get him on Fridays."

"I guess so," Meaghan agreed, hoping for her art's sake that this would be the case but nevertheless, disappointed that she would not be seeing the Spartan today.

"And you shouldn't call him that, it's mean."

"Can I help it if his arse is so big it needs its own postcode?"

Lilith seemed to be still buzzing from the previous night's drugs, so Meaghan decided not to bother arguing. Instead she fished for information, "Did you hear about the girl found dead outside the library last week? They say she was strangled."

"I heard she had puncture marks on her neck. I hope there are vampires around, I'd love to meet one, maybe even offer my blood." She lifted the heavy chain on her neck, exposing her throat and the tattoo of a small bat.

"Don't be ridiculous." Meaghan scoffed. "There are no such things as vampires."

"Until I met you, I wouldn't have believed there was such a thing as a twenty-five-year-old virgin either."

The smirk on Lilith's face infuriated Meaghan but she resisted the urge to retaliate. Unfortunately, Lilith continued tormenting.

"I can't believe you are saving yourself for Mr. Right."

"I don't see what's so weird about that."

For the umpteenth time, Meaghan regretted admitting to Lilith that she was a virgin. It just slipped out one day while Lilith was discussing another one of her one-night stands. Now Lilith took every opportunity to rub it in Meaghan's face. She was sure that Lilith had spread the news around campus. She had been the recipient of many winks and noticed young women giggling and whispering as she walked by.

"It's time you realized, Miss … I'm a twenty-five-year-old virgin and proud of it, that there is no such thing as Mr. Right, only Mr. Right now."

They walked in silence to the art department door. Meaghan took her usual place by the window, grateful that Lilith chose to set up beside the new student. Dressed in similar garb, her lacy black dress, fishnet black stockings, and Doc Martins almost mirrored Lilith's clothes. *I bet she believes in vampires too,*

Meaghan deduced, noticing that the women seemed to immediately hit it off. The hairs in her neck prickled and she shivered. There was something about Lilith's new friend that alarmed her although she had no idea why. Meaghan didn't remember ever meeting her and judging by her appearance, it was unlikely that they visited the same stores or restaurants. *Where have we met?*

The model that Lilith had referred to as Mr. Huge arse walked in and began to strip behind the screen beside the platform. Meaghan sighed and felt a pang of disappointment. Despite the disaster of her previous lesson, she had still hoped for another chance to see the handsome stranger. As she set up her easel, she noticed that the teacher, Mr. Nagle, was making his way over to her. She steeled herself for a reprimand her for the previous night's behavior.

"How are you feeling tonight, my dear? You had me worried when you rushed out of class last night."

"I meant to apologize," Meaghan told him, biting her bottom lip. "I suddenly felt nauseous and needed to race to the bathroom but I feel much better now."

"Good, good. Meaghan, I have some wonderful news for you," he announced, barely able to contain his enthusiasm. Patches of pink tinted his pale skin and balding head. "I have shown your previous portfolios to a friend of mine who is a renowned artist. He is very impressed with your work and has agreed to mentor you. This could mean great things for you, my dear. He has many friends in the business and he travels in the right circles."

"That's wonderful," she told him, hiding her personal doubts behind a bright smile. "Thank you for having confidence in me. I promise to work hard and not let you down."

"See that you don't." He smiled. His attempt at a

wink looked more like a slight stroke. "Opportunities like this don't come around very often in this industry and I imagine most of this class will hate both of us. I might be reprimanded by my superiors if they found out, so let's keep this mentorship our little secret, okay?" He touched a finger to his lips.

Meaghan pinched her fingers together, drew them across her lips in a zipper reference and nodded. As he shuffled towards the door, she absorbed the news. It didn't make any sense. Why would a prominent artist offer mentorship to her? Her work was mediocre at best. Why her? There were many students more deserving of a mentorship program than her. Distracted by the sound of giggling, she turned to see Lilith and her new friend staring in her direction, no doubt discussing the earlier conversation. She bit her lip and looked away. *Geez Louise. Who knew that virginity was such a crime?* Concerns over Lilith disappeared when the teacher returned with a companion. *Oh, you've got to be kidding me.*

****

The moment David entered the room, he forgot all about his mission. The little blonde faced him, her mouth agape, and her eyes as wide as saucers. Even before his eyes recognized her, his heart acknowledged her. There was no doubt in his mind. *It's her*. No wonder the previous night's class had been a strange, new experience for him. While his mind had been slow to identify her, his body had no hesitation. His skin prickled and warmth rained down over him like a hot shower. He paused at the door, unable to move, while his old friend made the introductions to the class.

"Class. I believe you remember Mr. Corel from yesterday." The students mumbled and giggled acknowledgments until they saw the frown on their teacher's face. "As well as being an excellent model, David is a well-respected artist. He has graciously offered to oversee today's class, share his experience, and offer suggestions. You should take advantage of this opportunity and learn as much as you can. I hope I don't need to remind you to be respectful to our guest." He directed his last remark to a couple of girls, one of which David recognized from the previous class. Her dark clothing and makeup conspicuous in a class full of casually dressed students. He made a mental note to keep an eye on her as the teacher finished addressing the class.

"Mr. Corel will be making the rounds, giving each of you the chance to ask questions, so please do not interrupt him, you will each have your turn with him." David suppressed a smile when the students reacted to Mr. Nagle's unfortunate choice of words with laughter. The joke lost on the teacher who finished his address with, "Ah, I see our model is ready, class, please begin."

David knew he was expected to show interest in *all* the students, but it took every ounce of his willpower to control himself. So many years of waiting and now she was here, close enough to reach out and touch. More beautiful than he had imagined. More seductive than his raging hormones could handle, more … everything. Perfect.

He approached the closest person to the door and feigned interest in his work until he felt he should move on to the next. The students ranged in ability, some were good, others not so much. Considering the model, they had done well. Skin folds proved challenging to an experienced artist and this model provided a wealth of difficulty. In his peripheral vision, he could see the little blonde poking her bespectacled face out on the side of the easel, her braids swaying as she worked feverishly on her drawing. He couldn't help but wonder if her passion was restricted to her art. Tonight she was wearing jeans that hugged her body like a second skin, accentuating every beautiful curve. The filmy red blouse she wore almost transparent under the bright overhead lights revealing the scrap of pink lace covering her breasts. He watched as her chest rose and fell under the shirt and knew she would be his undoing.

****

Meaghan tried to focus on her drawing but the closer it came to her turn with the visitor, the more anxious she became. How could she work in close proximity to this man without making a total fool of herself? *Think about something else, think about the murders.* Before yesterday's disastrous class, she had thought of little else and she felt ashamed that her own raging hormones had taken her concentration away from the death of those poor young women. She was there to use her unique ability in order to identify suspects. Hopefully discover the killer without the risk of ever putting herself in real danger. Not there to lust after every good looking man on campus. But she hadn't lusted after every good looking man. Hadn't even noticed any other man. Until—

"Hello." A voice as sensual as hot chocolate whispered into her ear. Strength left her legs and her knees bent of their own accord. She staggered a little, he caught her elbow, supporting her weight and saving her from an embarrassing fall into the easel.

"Are you all right?"

"Fine, you just startled me."

"I imagine I did." He stepped close to the sketch and took his time before mentioning, "I saw you madly sketching and realized that you're passionate about your craft. Looking at this sketch, I can understand why." He scratched his chin. "You have talent … Miss?"

"Lamb. Meaghan Lamb." She extended her hand and was surprised when, rather than shaking it, he raised it to his mouth and kissed her knuckles. A shock of electricity zapped through her body. Her voice quivered as she accepted the compliment. "Thank you, Mr. Corel."

"David. Please call me David." He looked around the room before leaning close to her cheek and whispering, "We should be on a first name basis if we are going to be spending so much time alone together."

She could feel his breath on her neck and the sensation made her feel both uncomfortable and yet, strangely exhilarated. *What did he mean by that?*

"Excuse me?"

"I'm sorry." He apologized, but the cheeky smile on his face made her doubt his sincerity. "Pierre told me that he'd discussed my offer with you. If you give me your address, I'll send someone to collect your belongings."

Meaghan noticed that David spoke with purpose and with a confidence that suggested he was accustomed to having his instructions obeyed. He wasn't asking her; he was telling her. She became wary of his intentions. It would be very easy for a man like David Corel to lure a woman into a dangerous position. Any woman could easily fall for his charms and be vulnerable to his suggestion. This may be the unsub she was looking for. She regarded him warily as she confessed, "I don't understand. Where am I going?"

"Besides my painting, I have numerous other responsibilities. If this mentoring is to work, you must be available to work whenever I find a spare moment. This may mean late into the evening at times so it makes perfect sense for you to move into the flat on the property I share with my brother and his wife. It's only ten minutes from the University and I assure you it is quite comfortable."

Meaghan shook her head. *Not so fast buddy.* "I have my own responsibilities, Mr. Corel. I have a part-time job in town and so I need to be near public transport for both work and classes."

"I must insist on your entire focus for this mentorship to work," he told her.

Her entire focus? She could barely think with him around.

"Now just wait a minute!" Meaghan realized she had raised her voice and attracted the attention of a few members of the class. She faked a smile and lowered her voice to barely above a whisper. "I can't afford to give up my job, it pays my bills."

"Didn't Pierre inform you that this mentorship program comes with a scholarship?" He looked in the direction of the teacher and shook his head. "Sorry, Meaghan. I can understand your reaction to what must have sounded rather rude. This isn't just a mentorship. It's also a job offer. You'll be paid to work as my assistant while you complete your degree. Your room and board is part of the salary."

You've got to be kidding. "I'll need to think about it." It seemed like a dream come true but how could she accept it while she was working the murder case? *What are you thinking, Meaghan? You barely know this man and he expects you to move in with him?* She studied him closely. David seemed like who got his own way, a man of means and connections. If she accepted his proposal, what sort of payment would he expect from her in return? The thought of him making sexual advances or demands made her feel uncomfortably aroused. There was no explanation for the way he made her body react to him but she could barely think when he was standing so close. *Why does he have such an effect on me?*

He rested his hand on the small of her back, slowly sliding it down to the curve of her bottom. She wanted to object but the words caught in her throat. The heat of his hands burned through her jeans and melted her panties. She glanced around the room, certain that someone would see the intimate way he touched her, but no one seemed to be looking.

"I've just placed my business card in your jeans pocket," he informed her. "Please don't make me wait too long."

She watched him walk away. Walk? No, that man didn't walk. His movements too predatory, too fluid to be considered anything but sensual. Her heart skipped a beat.

After a quick word with Pierre and a farewell to the class, David Corel left. Meaghan could hardly concentrate on the remaining half hour. Too much to consider. *How could she accept his unusual business proposal? How could she not?* When the class finished, she gathered up her equipment and ran for the bus stop, knowing that if she missed her bus, she would be waiting an hour for the next. The bus was practically empty, usual for this time of night. Her neighborhood was not a safe place to visit and even the bus drivers were reluctant to travel that way at night.

On the journey home, she fished out the business card from her back pocket and stared at the gold embossed writing on the plain white card. Other than his name and mobile number, there was nothing to identify his business or give her any details to search online. She had met his kind before during police interviews and knew his type. Rich, self-obsessed playboys who treated the law with disrespect and more often than not, contempt. Their business cards kept deliberately vague to cover the fact that they had no actual qualifications and lived off the money they had inherited from their parents. Meaghan knew that on some level she was jealous of, not only their prosperity, but the reality that they had parents who loved them enough to leave them financially secure for the rest of their lives. She, on the other hand, never knew her parents or the circumstances that led to her being abandoned at the orphanage as a baby. Her life had been an uphill battle to survive in an environment that treated her as a pariah, never to be adopted, never to know the love of a family.

She shook the painful memories from her mind and considered David Corel's offer. The prospect of living rent free and close to the school tempted her, but the idea of living with a stranger—even if he was a handsome stranger—was daunting. She didn't know David Corel or anything about him. She considered calling Terry. Besides being her superior, Terry had been her only friend at the orphanage. *He'll know what to do.*

The brakes squealed as the bus came to a halt at her stop, ten minutes' walk from her tiny flat. She tugged her light cardigan closed over her chest as she stepped off. The nights had become colder and darker which would not have been too serious a problem except for the recently broken street lamps which made the journey home fraught with danger. The tree fringed darkened path provided cover for anyone who sought to pounce on unsuspecting victims. Meaghan had learned the compulsory self-defense techniques that came with her basic training but knew that it would never be enough to protect her from the low-lives that populated this area. She hurried her steps as she walked through the section of footpath almost completely hidden from view of the road. The area had slowly become more run-down thanks to the drug dealers who'd set up shop in the vacant house on the corner of her street. One by one her nicer neighbors had fled, leaving her almost alone in the street. Heavy shutters covered the windows of the houses she passed, the streets seemed deserted. Tonight she felt more isolated than the day she discovered she was the only child left in the orphanage. The only one no one wanted.

She clutched her purse to her body taking comfort in the weight of the hand gun that she carried for safety as she warily made her way home through the almost deserted street. She should be happy. She had finally managed to talk Terry into giving her the undercover job using her ability and youthful appearance as leverage and now, she was finally being recognized for her talent as an artist. But, there was something strange about David Corel's offer of mentorship. She shook her head. *Nothing in life is free.* Everything comes at a cost, and if she had learned anything from her days on the force, it was that if something seems too good to be true, it probably was.

Despite her better judgement, she let her thoughts meander to the restless night she had spent after her first encounter with David Corel and the dream that haunted her ever since. The dream of running her hands over his naked body, a dream so real, it felt more like a memory than a fantasy. She had awoken feeling restless, her body over-sensitized and damp. *Why does he have this effect on me and why was this man—a stranger—offering me his time and a home? Does he have an ulterior motive?* Meaghan stopped in her tracks. *Could he be the campus killer?* Her cop mind went into overdrive. If she was staying on his property, she could keep a close eye on his activities and monitor his comings and goings. This could be the big break she had been looking for.

Unless he killed her? She shook the thought from her head. He was hardly likely to kill her on his own property with the art department aware of the scholarship, and she suspected that he was too smart to try something as obvious as that. Meaghan continued walking. While she considered her options a car filled with drunken potheads turned the corner and called out the usual vulgar remarks and obscenities. She hurried her steps. Even living with a serial killer was probably safer than staying on *this* street.

Once safely inside her flat, she locked all three deadbolts and checked for any signs of a break-in. It had become a habit since the first night she had heard the strange howling. At first, she had wondered if it had been some sort of signal to inform someone that she was home alone but nothing came of it. Not then anyway. After throwing her bag onto her bed, she began to undress for the shower until she heard a noise that sent a shiver down her spine. The howl sounded closer. Whatever made the noise seemed to be right outside her window. Her hand shook as she cracked the curtain slightly and looked out into the darkness. What she saw made her jump back in shock. She tried to convince herself that it was her imagination, that she hadn't seen glowing red eyes staring back at her from the cover of the trees. She tweaked the curtain again, almost afraid of what she might see. The eyes were gone but the sensation of being watched remained. Frantically, she checked all the window and door locks before she pulled out her mobile and dialed the number on the card.

"Hello, Mr. Corel? This is Meaghan Lamb. Yes, okay… David. I've considered your proposal and I've decided to accept your generous offer. Do you have a pen and paper handy?"

Chapter Four

The limo arrived to pick her up at 7 p.m. which seemed to her like a strange time to be moving house. David had instructed her to only bring her personal items as her accommodation would be fully furnished. Meaghan handed the driver all her worldly goods, which fit neatly into two second-hand suitcases. As they drove out of the run-down street, she came to a decision. No matter what happened, she would not be returning. She would work hard and make use of all David's advice as her mentor so that her next move would be into a nicer area. She wondered what type of accommodation she would be living in at David's house but was not particularly concerned as anything would be a step up from this place. As the limo passed the University, she noticed that there appeared to be more security hanging around the carpark. A sensible idea, considering the recent murders. She reminded herself that once she'd met with David and worked out the plans for the next day, she needed to get back to the campus and look for more clues.

Just as David had promised, the drive to his home lasted ten minutes past the campus. Her first indication that living with David would be an experience was the great brick wall surrounding the property. Behind the impressive cast iron gates that opened as the limo approached, she could see a long road and, besides the lush foliage, there wasn't a house in sight. Meaghan gazed in wonderment as the car slowly made its way up the steep paved road. A travel brochure advertising a tropical holiday destination would not have done the property justice. Palm trees swayed with the breeze and when she wound down the tinted window for a better look, the fragrance of frangipani filled the air. As she neared David's home, she realized that *house* was an understatement. Mansion suited better and, if her keen hearing and sense of smell were correct, it was close to the beach.

When the limo finally stopped, David opened the door and took her hand to help her out of the car while the driver saw to her luggage. "Welcome to my home."

"I didn't realize you lived near the ocean, David."

"Do you like the ocean?"

"Very much so, although I don't get the opportunity to go often. Work and study keeps me indoors most of the time."

He offered her his arm and they followed the driver around the corner of the house and along a pebbled path. "I've always considered the ocean as a perfect subject to paint. I already know that you can draw, Meaghan. Do you also paint?" His smile disarmed her.

Meaghan nodded and diverted her eyes from his face hoping the beautiful landscaping surrounding the house would quieten her erratic heart. "Watercolors mostly."

"You don't like oils?"

"My salary at the supermarket is minimum wage so, after paying the rent, I have a choice between quality materials or food." During the night she had formulated the supermarket job as a ruse but, unfortunately, her real job as a cop didn't pay much better.

"Personally, I'd go for the quality materials."

Meaghan didn't respond to his comment, but felt as though she had already failed some sort of test, thinking that her answer should have conveyed her love of art. His expression changed. His smile wavered and he kicked a loose stone with the tip of his shoe, sending it careening down the path. She felt as though she'd disappointed him. Maybe he already regretted his offer to mentor her. They continued their walk in silence.

"What do you think?" He asked when they reached a small cottage nestled in between some huge, fairy light decorated palm trees. "I hope it will suit your needs."

He opened the door and stepped inside, pulling Meaghan by the hand as he led her into a living room. The small gesture sent ripples of goose pimples down her spine. It felt genuine, comforting. She found it difficult to take her eyes off him as he gave her more information.

"As I mentioned on the phone, you should have everything you need for your comfort. The television has cable, the landline has been linked to my bill so feel free to use it as often as you like, there is a laundry at the end of the hall…" He pointed to a small room. "There's an en-suite bathroom connected to your bedroom and an office slash art studio through here although you will be doing most of your training in my studio."

When David opened the door to the office, Meaghan gasped. Shelves overflowed with brand new art supplies including sable brushes, both oil and watercolor paints, blank canvases of different sizes, pastels, drawing pads, an easel, a computer and printer plus materials that Meaghan had only ever seen in expensive art stores.

"David, this is too much. I appreciate your generosity but these things must have cost a small fortune."

David shrugged. "Let me worry about that. You concentrate on producing good quality work." He casually took her hand again—causing her heart to do another jig—and led her through the sliding door adjoining the living room. "I believe that you'll find inspiration in this view although it's a little hard to see at night."

They stepped out onto a terrace overlooking the ocean and Meaghan breathed in the salty air. When David stepped close to her, placing his hands on her shoulders, he stole that breath from her lungs.

She felt his cheek against her own as he whispered. "Beautiful."

"Uh-huh," she mumbled as heat rushed to her cheeks. His hands left her shoulders and slid down her arms. The solid muscles of his body pressed firmly against her shoulders.

"I know that we haven't known each other very long, Meaghan, but I think that we both feel the physical attraction." He turned her around to face him. "There's something that I must tell you."

She felt her body warm to his touch, her skin prickled with anticipation and she subconsciously moistened her lips with her tongue. He sighed, lifted her chin with one forefinger and leaned closer. "But first…"

His lips parted, she mirrored his action, waiting for the kiss, which never came.

"I must go," he suddenly announced. "Have a good night's rest and I will see you in my studio around 10 a.m."

He abruptly turned and walked back into the cottage with Meaghan following behind.

"I don't know where—"

"I'll send someone to collect you and bring you to me. Goodnight, Meaghan." He called over his shoulder as he dashed through the front door and disappeared into the night.

****

"Great timing, bro." David announced as he met his brother in the kitchen of the main house. He headed straight for the liquor cabinet and poured himself a glass of scotch, downing it in one gulp.

"Bro? That's a bit out of character for you isn't it, David." Derrick chuckled.

"What can I tell you, I'm trying new things?" He held up the bottle, offering his brother a glass.

"So I've heard." Derrick shook his head, declining the drink. He winked at Anna who had just joined them before turning his attention back to his brother. "How's your little prodigy working out?"

"None of your business." David turned abruptly to Anna. "Tell me about this new vision that needed my *immediate* attention."

"It's actually the same vision I told you about yesterday but it feels more urgent. I believe it'll happen tonight."

"Any idea where this time? The campus *is* rather large."

"Sorry, David. I wish I could tell you more."

"I'll check it out." He turned to leave but Derrick called to him.

"I'll make sure your new little friend is taken care of while you're out."

David turned abruptly. "You look after your own woman and stay away from mine."

Chapter Five

Meaghan leaned on the wooden rail of the balcony and sighed. *Why did he rush off like that?* She was sure that he was about to kiss her. She could feel the warmth of his breath against her lips as he leaned towards her and she'd closed her eyes in anticipation. His hurried departure made her wonder if was all in her imagination. His slight accent convinced her that he was English and according to Mr. Nagle, he was well-travelled. *Maybe he was merely being polite and about to offer her a friendly peck?* She shook her head. Her experience with men may be limited but her intuition rarely led her astray and her instinct told her that he wanted more than a friendly goodnight kiss. He'd looked as though he'd wanted to whisk her into the bedroom. His hooded, "come to bed" eyes were beckoning, and his lips looked as if they'd devour her. Why did he suddenly change his mind? "Have a good night's rest," she mimicked as she carried her suitcases to the bedroom. *Not bloody likely.*

****

The ten-minute drive to the campus gave David time alone with his thoughts. He could easily have crossed the distance faster without the car but he couldn't risk running into one of the teachers and explaining how he had travelled there on foot. Besides, the journey gave him the opportunity to compose himself. Meaghan would be working with him, living close enough to touch. The prospect equally terrifying and thrilling. After all these years of searching for her, he now found himself unable to think clearly around her and he discovered that being away from her was even worse than before. It took all his will power not to turn the car around and head home, but he knew that somewhere in the darkness of the almost empty campus, lurked a killer. It was his duty to stop him.

Light rain began to hit the windscreen and the car's automatic windscreen wipers reacted as David turned into the car park. A few students ran for their cars, trying to beat the impending storm. He waited until they left before exiting his own vehicle, zipping his leather jacket closed. The gesture less to keep out the cold—as he no longer felt the bite of winter winds or the sting of rain—and more to protect his designer clothes. *You really are a pretentious prick*; he accused himself as he walked stealthily along the path leading to the art studios. He shook his head in disgust. Meaghan must have thought him arrogant and indulged when he informed her that art was more important than food. He inwardly cringed. How cavalier his statement would have sounded to a struggling artist. He had never known the pain of poverty and—thanks to his investments and inheritance—he likely never would. His statement tactless, but unintentional, merely stating a fact. Art was his passion. It was a hard habit to break and besides, he hadn't lied. It was a no brainer choosing art materials over food. His body functioned perfectly well without food.

****

David smelled the blood before he even turned the corner. He ran towards the source, assessing the other smell. *Blood and ... what was the other fragrance?* He recognized the two other scents as Bergamot & Black Pepper which seemed like a strange combination, especially in a musty University corridor. The reason became clear as he rounded the corner and accidentally kicked over a couple of large black candles.

As they fell, the candles extinguished, leaving the

area cloaked in darkness which would have been a problem for someone without David's keen eyesight. He, however, saw, not only the body of the young woman lying motionless on the ground, but also the macabre setting. Someone had taken their time after the murder to surround her body with Echinacea flowers. No need to feel for a pulse. He had seen enough dead humans in his long life to recognize death. Instead, he studied the area for other signs or scents, something that could help him discover the identity of the killer. Like the last victim, she had been strangled with bare hands. No claw or teeth marks to suggest a supernatural predator. *Why the scent of blood?* He inspected the area and discovered the dead body of a bird. The poor creature's neck had been broken, the head barely held on by a small piece of sinew. Stranger still, the use of black candles and flowers implied a ritual sacrifice. *Could there be satanic cults practicing in the area?* He knelt down and studied the dead girl. She was dressed normally for a student, nothing to suggest her being a member of a group of devil worshippers. She didn't appear to have been sexually assaulted unless the killer took the time to dress her after the assault. While searching for some form of identification, he sensed someone close. Someone in the bushes behind him. He turned quickly and caught a glimpse of blonde braids and daisy sandals before the woman disappeared into the night.

****

Don't panic! Meaghan paced the living room floor of her new accommodation, wringing her hands and trying to think of a good reason to stay despite the horror of what she had seen. *David was standing over a dead body. What was he doing at the campus in the middle of the night with that woman?* There were no classes scheduled for tonight. He had no reason to be there unless … he was there to kill. Meaghan flopped into the nearest chair. *Why this girl? Were they having an affair and she wanted to end it so he killed her? Maybe he wanted to end it and she wouldn't accept it. You didn't actually see him do anything,* she reasoned with herself but doubt niggled in the back of her mind. *If he wasn't there to kill that woman, why was he there? Now let's just think about this for a moment. There are at least a few rational scenarios. One … he just happened to be there picking up something he left in the storage room. Okay, that's reasonable enough. Option Two … he gets rid of his old students by strangling them.* Her hand shot to her throat as she considered, *Oh, my god. I'm living with the Bluebeard of the art world.*

Chapter Six

"Are you sure it was her?" asked Derrick after he'd heard David's story. "Surely she's not the only blonde at the campus."

"It was her. I know it was, only…"

"Only what?"

"She was different somehow." He scratched his head. "I felt the same physical reaction I usually notice when she's around but it seemed … diluted."

"I think you've beaten your own record for time taken to lose interest in a girl, David."

David took a menacing step towards Derrick who raised his hands in surrender. "Sorry, go on. What do you mean by diluted?"

"I'm not sure. I guess … it's like the difference between looking at the real person and a photograph. I still felt that emotional tug, but it wasn't as strong. It was a though she was only there in spirit."

"You believe she is a ghost?" Derrick stifled a chuckle.

"If you can't take what I'm saying seriously, Derrick, this conversation is over." He turned to leave the room.

"Wait!" Anna rose from her seat in the corner of the room. "We're all tired and should have gone to bed hours ago. David, you know Derrick is just pulling your leg." She turned to her husband and shot him a "behave yourself" look before asking David, "Do you really think Meaghan may have something to do with the murder?"

He frowned and shook his head. "No. She couldn't possibly be involved."

"Why David?" Anna asked, gently touching his arm. "Because you're in love with her?"

"Wait, did you say love?" Derrick's grin spread

from ear to ear. "Is Meaghan *the* blonde?"

David nodded. He turned to address his new sister-in-law. "Being in love with her has nothing to do with it, Anna. I just know she couldn't hurt anyone."

"You don't really know her at all. Have you tried reading her mind or planting a suggestion to answer your questions?"

"It didn't work. Maybe those glasses she wears are thicker than they appear or her vision is worse than she lets on."

Anna shrugged. "If she didn't kill the woman, why did she run?"

"I don't know but she'll be here soon for her first lesson so I'll try and find out."

Anna looked at her watch. "It's daylight, David. You should be resting. Aren't you worried that you'll be vulnerable to an attack?"

David laughed. "I may be slightly weaker during the day, but I think I can still fight off a little thing like Meaghan. Besides, I'll make the time to have a rest during our class by keeping her busy at her lessons. She'd get suspicious if I was only available at night."

"He's a grown man." Derrick reminded his wife. "Leave him to his fantasy woman while I take mine back to bed." He whispered something in her ear and she responded with a slap across his arm and a flush of color to her cheeks.

David watched them run up the stairs to their bedroom before he descended the stairs to his basement art studio. He envied their happiness. Theirs would be a happy ending. Was it too much to ask for the same fate? If Meaghan was indeed the killer, he would be forced to… No. He refused to accept that she had anything to do with the murders despite the evidence to the contrary. He'd lived among humans for centuries and his instincts had never failed him. There must be another explanation.

****

Meaghan waited patiently outside the cottage, enjoying her coffee in the morning sunshine when she noticed an elderly man in a weathered suit slowly making his way towards her. He introduced himself as Evan—although Meaghan thought the name Methuselah suited his age better—and he led her to the main house. Once inside, he showed her to a door leading to the basement and advised her that she would find Master David working downstairs. She got the impression from the "master" reference that Evan had been serving this family since David was young. After opening the basement door and switching on a light, he quickly closed the door. The action startled her. *Was this a trap? Was Evan an accessory?* One way or another, she had to find out. She took each step slowly, unsure of what to expect. By the time she was halfway down the stairs, she had convinced herself... *This is the part in the movie where the killer grabs your legs and trips you so you break your neck.*

"What are you looking for?"

Meaghan realized that she had been trying to look through the gaps in the staircase as she descended. She looked up to see David staring up at her.

"Oh, hi."

"I assure you there are no monsters under the stairs," he informed her, chuckling to himself as he covered the painting that he was working on with a sheet and placing it against the wall in the corner of the room.

"What are you painting?" she asked, trying to change the subject to avoid the topic of monsters. She reached out to touch the painting. "May I see it?"

David stepped between her and the artwork. "No." He made no explanations and the stern quality of his voice left her in no doubt that there would be no changing his mind. He handed her a sketch book and a box of pastels. Holding her elbow, he escorted her over to an overstuffed chair where he instructed her to sit. She studied the room while he set up a fold-up table with a tablecloth, a bowl, and some fruit.

"Is this your room?" she asked when she noticed the corner of the huge basement was divided by a large screen. From the angle where she was seated, she could see a large bed. Its sheets tangled as though someone had recently spent a restless night. *Or got lucky.* His answer was as abrupt and absolute as the last.

"No."

"Does someone else live down here?" Meaghan wondered out loud. Maybe the murdered brunette had spent her last night between those satin sheets. Now she lay on a cold slab at the morgue.

Despite the lack of windows and the strong smell of paint and turpentine, the large room looked quite comfortable. A computer and printer sat in one corner of the room beside an intercom and phone, suggesting that David used the room as an office as well as a studio. She made a mental note to fish through the computer's history as soon as she got the chance.

****

"I live upstairs," David told her. His back still turned to her.

Her proximity made it hard to remain aloof. She radiated heat and he could hear the erratic beating of her heart. He fought the impulse to kiss her. *Stay disconnected David. Focus.* "Would you like to start your lesson or do you have more questions concerning my personal life?"

"Sorry."

"I am sorry too, Meaghan." He turned to face her.

Her bottom lip protruded in a pout. Cherubic bow shaped lips. He stood transfixed to the spot, mesmerized and when she ran her tongue between those luscious lips, he almost came undone. He closed his eyes. *Focus, David. Focus.*

"I had a rather unpleasant experience last night which left me feeling agitated. I had no right to take out my mood on you." *Unless you are the killer.* He forced a smile. "In answer to your questions… I occasionally sleep here when I work late and lose track of the time. You are welcome to use the bed whenever you wish."

Meaghan's eyes widened. A blush painted her cheeks a slightly darker shade of pink. She looked away as she told him. "I'm perfectly happy with the bed in the cottage."

David cleared his throat. "Good. Good. Then let's get on with it." He noticed her glance back at his covered paintings. *Inquisitive little thing. She's going to be a handful.*

"I don't like to show my paintings until they're finished so I hope you understand and respect my need for privacy. I trust that I can rely on your word that you won't be tempted to look when you're alone in here?"

****

David worked at his computer for most of the day, occasionally stopping to check Meaghan's drawings and offer suggestions. Every half an hour or so, he rearranged the fruit in the bowl or changed the tablecloth and then went back to his own work. At one stage, Evan sent down a tray on the dumb waiter and Meaghan enjoyed a lunch of roast beef and onion sandwiches and fruit juice before being instructed to go back to her sketching.

When she asked for a toilet break, she was directed to an en-suite adjacent to the bedroom. She opened the door and gasped. En-suite be damned. This bathroom was huge. She bit her lip. A sunken spa bath. *Wow. How good would that feel after a hard day on the beat*. The shower had a rainforest shower head. It looked as though three people could fit comfortably in the recess. She bit her bottom lip and suppressed a giggle. *Did he like threesomes? Maybe Lilith was right*. Like the studio, there were no windows in the room.

As she passed the mirror, she did a double-take. Her reflection looked pale. Dark shadows circled her eyes. Her nightly activities were taking their toll on her health. Until the case was closed, she would probably continue to look like one of the "living dead" dolls sold in novelty stores. She leaned in, closer to the mirror. Her gray-green eyes as big as saucers on her small heart shaped face. As she pinched her cheeks, she wondered—not for the first time—which parent she may have inherited her features from. She ran her fingers through her fringe and tidied up her braids, grateful that at least her hair looked healthy before she returned to join David.

As she passed the bed, Meaghan noticed that David had evidently decided to take a nap. *Wonderful. What a great mentor he turned out to be*. He lay on top of the disheveled sheets, shirtless with his designer jeans slung low on his hips. She paused, seizing the opportunity to get a closer look at his long, heavily muscled body. He looked less like an artist and more like a work of art. As though chiseled from marble, his body rippled with muscles from his mountainous shoulders, bulging pecs, down to his well-defined almost eight pack abs. Longingly, her eyes lingered on his hips and the way they seem to draw the eyes down to the waist band of his jeans and beyond. She swallowed the lump in her throat and forced her eyes back to his upper torso, concentrating on the subtle way he flexed his biceps during sleep.

His arms were huge and she wondered—if he ever decided to hug her—if his embrace would crush her small frame. *My polar opposite.* When he stood beside her, he towered above her, despite her being of average height for a female. His dark, neatly cropped hair a stark contrast to the pale blonde hair that reached half way down her back, even in braids. Her heart-shaped face created an illusion of youth despite her twenty-five years, while his square jaw and strong features gave away no secrets, told no tales. No wrinkles worried his brow. No crow's feet creased the corner of his eyes. *How old are you, David Corel?*

He murmured in his sleep, a warning that he might wake up at any moment so she returned to her fruit bowl. Glancing back at his masculine form, she wondered when or even if, she would be allowed to draw something besides food.

****

Despite her previous concern, hours passed before David awoke and, without a word to Meaghan, rose from the bed and disappeared into the bathroom. Meaghan checked her watch. It was already 6 p.m. and would be getting dark outside. Time to begin patrolling the university. She had to invent a good excuse for leaving. Something credible. She waited for a few minutes, expecting his return until she heard water running and realized that he was taking a shower. For a moment, she considered lifting the sheet on his most recent painting but thought better of it. If he caught her, there was no telling what he might do. *Bide your time, Meaghan.* Living in his guesthouse would give her the perfect opportunity to monitor his movements and she wasn't going to jeopardize this advantage just to satisfy her own curiosity. It turned out to be a wise decision because the door suddenly opened and David walked into the room, dripping wet and wearing only a towel wrapped precariously around his waist. Despite her shock, Meaghan found it impossible to look away as he rubbed at his hair with a second towel, seemingly oblivious to the woman gaping at him behind the fogging lenses of her glasses.

Her head warned her that there would be repercussions but her eyes remained transfixed on a particular droplet of water as it trickled down his chest and disappeared under the makeshift loincloth. *Oh, my god. He looks like Tarzan.* Breathing became difficult. Her throat tightened. Her eyes followed the concave line that separated his abs from his belly button up to his solid chest. His muscular shoulders drew back and she heard a sharp intake of breath as she lifted her chin to look into his eyes. *Oh, god. He's looking at me.*

He smiled and she knew he had caught her staring at his near naked body. She turned back to her drawing as she felt the heat rush to her cheeks. She cleared her throat.

"When can I draw something other than fruit?"

"Some artists would be grateful to have a piece of fruit to draw." He informed her with a gleam in his eye that she acknowledged with an eye roll of her own eyes.

"Fine, have it your way," he said as he lifted the table, fruit bowl and all, and moved it to one side of the room. He dragged what appeared to be a heavy pallet from across the room, not only impressing her with the demonstration of his strength but also giving Meaghan a good look at his long, well-developed hamstrings and tight arse as he backed towards her. When he reached the center of the room, he threw a blanket over the pallet and began to remove his towel.

"What are you doing?" Meaghan squealed, her

voice sounding embarrassingly shrill as she jumped to her feet.

"You wanted to draw something else," he reminded her, apparently surprised by her reaction. "I thought you were accustomed to life drawing?"

"No I, well yes I guess … but—"

"Oh, that's right," he teased. "You ran out of the class last time I modelled."

"I wasn't well." The heat of her cheeks fogged her glasses.

"All right then." He stripped off his towel and threw it on the floor before reclining on the pallet. "You now have the opportunity to catch up with the rest of the class."

Meaghan looked up at the ceiling, trying to avoid the full frontal nudity that confronted her. "You had a helmet between your legs in the classroom," she protested.

"Not for the entire class. If you'd stayed, you would have known that."

"I don't think this is appropriate for a mentor and his student," she argued. Her chin down as she stared at her feet. "Doesn't this fall under sexual harassment or something?"

"Maybe if we were in an office." He sat up, and swung his legs over the edge of the pallet. "I don't understand you, Meaghan. We're both adults and you're here to learn how to paint. I know that you've drawn naked men before and, as you're not a teenager, I expect that you've spent time with naked men before."

"I've got to go." She dropped the sketch book as she bolted for the stairs.

David stood up and intercepted her. "Meaghan, I don't understand why you are so upset? Surely you…" He held her by the shoulders and looked down at her face. Suddenly his eyes widened. "You're a virgin?"

"I didn't know it was a crime." She argued, struggling to break free of his grip. When she tried to look down at her feet in order to avert his gaze, she was found herself staring down at an impressive erection. The experience was confronting, embarrassing but worse still, arousing. He held her against his body. She felt her womb clench and her breasts grow heavy with desire as he held her tight against his solid frame. His damp skin pressed against her. Wetness crept through the thin material of her dress, soaking through the lace of her bra. The sensation of the water like fingers lightly skimming her breasts. She leaned into his chest, unable to move. Unwilling to move. His skin smelled wonderful. He smelled of musk and cedar wood and sex.

"You misunderstand, Meaghan," he told her, "I find your confession both refreshing and enlightening." He lifted her chin with his finger. Their bodies still touching. She could feel his manhood pressing against her stomach. "Now it makes perfect sense why you reacted the way you did. I apologize for my behavior."

"It would be easier to accept your apology if you weren't poking me with that … thing." Meaghan stepped back. "I have to go."

"Wait!" he called after her. "We should discuss this further."

"I have an appointment," she told him without turning around. "We can talk tomorrow."

She was halfway up the stairs when she heard him again. "Don't give up on this mentorship program. I believe now, more than ever, that there's a lot I can teach you."

She wanted to answer, to say something witty that would give her the upper hand, but her physical reaction to the double entendre warned her that if she stayed a minute longer, he would be teaching her the art of making love. She took the last stairs two at a time, narrowly missing a young woman who was entering the room. She froze. *Who was this woman? A girlfriend? Lover? Potential victim?* Her hand shot to her mouth. *Bastard.* He had apparently planned on seducing her knowing full well that another woman was on the way over. The sheets would still be warm from making love to her as the new woman took her place on the bed.

"He's all yours." She told the pretty woman with the unruly copper hair as she hurried past. She kept the pace until she found herself back at the cottage. *You just dodged a bullet*, she informed herself as she entered her bedroom but the reality did nothing to soothe her soul or quench the fire of her desire. *Damn him.* She still wanted him.

****

David heard the light footsteps on the stairs and ran to meet them.

"Oh, good grief, David." Anna yelped, covering her eyes with her hands, "Put some pants on."

"Sorry, Anna." David retrieved his towel and fastened it around his waist. "I was expecting someone else."

"And you were obviously very pleased at the prospect." She continued as she descended the stairs. "But there are certain things about a brother-in-law that should remain a mystery."

"Don't tell Derrick," David joked. "He'll be jealous."

"Your brother has nothing to be jealous about." She retorted with a wink. Their eyes met and they both laughed. "Can we please change the subject? I was coming here to ask you if you were going out to the campus again tonight. Your protégée almost bowled me over. What was that about anyway?"

"A stupid misunderstanding." He shook his head. "She said she wanted to draw something other than fruit so I—"

"Thought you'd show her your banana?"

"Very funny, Anna," he complained, although he held out his hand for a fist bump. "She left the life drawing class early last week. It didn't occur to me that she ran out of the class last week because she was embarrassed to see a naked male."

"So the braids, pretty frocks, daisy sandals and heavy rimmed glasses didn't give you a clue about her sexual innocence?"

"Now that you mention it ... I'm a dumb arse."

"No. She's just very different to your usual type of female. This one is special but..." her eyebrows knit as her mouth tightened into a grimace.

"What is it Anna?"

"There's something about her that disturbs me. I can sense that she has power but I can't quite put my finger on the source of it. She has secrets David, and as much as I hate to put a damper on your love life, as leaders of our coven, it is yours and Derrick's responsibility to find out what those secrets are."

"I know my responsibilities." He turned away as if by concealing his face he could block out his thoughts from his witch sister-in-law. "But, what if she's the killer, Anna? If she is—and I truly believe her to be—human. I'll have to turn her in to the authorities. If she is supernatural, I'll be forced to deal with it myself. How can I bring myself to hurt her?"

"I guess we'll deal with that if it comes down to it. In the meantime, go after her and makes things right. If she leaves, it'll be harder to keep track of her comings and goings."

"You're right." David started up the stairs before Anna reminded him of his state of undress.

"David. For heaven's sake, put some pants on."

Chapter Seven

Meaghan responded to the knock at her door

"Come in, David," she called as she continued to place her belongings into the suitcases.

"There's no need for you to go," he told her. "I promise that from now on, I will confine my nudity to the *campus* classroom."

She turned to look at him and felt slightly disappointed that he'd changed into a white t-shirt and jeans.

"I don't think this will work out. Surely there are others who you can choose to mentor, that woman I just ran into for instance."

"Anna?" David laughed. "I've seen her drawings. Her buses look like turtles. Besides, I believe my brother keeps his wife on a pretty tight leash. They are, after all, still on their honeymoon."

"Oh." She felt her shoulders relax. Despite her reservations, she was relieved. *Why*? She stood motionless, staring at him, trying to find the right words to explain how she was feeling but in truth, she didn't know *what* she was feeling. *Lust? Fear?*

"I was disrespectful," he told her. "I can't hide the fact that I am attracted to you and I got the impression that you felt the same. I made a stupid mistake and it would be a real shame if you threw away a chance for recognition in the art world just because I came on to you. I promise that in future I'll keep my hands off you."

"No." Meaghan found her voice. "That's not what I want—"

David raised an eyebrow. "But I—"

"If you'll let me finish…" Meaghan interrupted.

"I don't think I want you to keep your hands off me," she confessed.

She lowered her eyes. Her confidence fading. It was now or never. *Tell him.*

"I *think* that I want to experience *everything* you can teach me. But, I am afraid I will disappoint you."

David's lips parted slightly. The edges curled into a smile. He slowly approached her but she held out her arm, palm out, to signal to him that she had more to say.

"I don't understand why I feel this way about you. I've only seen you a handful of times and barely know you but, as you said last night, we seem to have an undeniable physical attraction which—to tell you the truth—terrifies me."

"You're not the only one who's terrified, Chérie . This is a new experience for me too."

Meaghan raised one eyebrow.

"All right, I admit that my playboy reputation is not completely unjustified but this is different. I'm your puppet. You pull at my heart strings and there is nothing I can do to stop the physical urges I get whenever I see you." He pulled her into his arms and kissed her, gently at first but once she became pliant in his arms, he cupped the back of her head and deepened the kiss.

When he reached down to lift her, cupping her bottom with his large hands, she facilitated him by wrapping her legs around his waist. He moved closer to the bed, bending his knees as he gently lowered her onto the thick quilt. When he lifted her thin cotton dress up to her hips, positioning himself so his jean covered erection rubbed against the crotch of her silk panties, she gasped and stiffened in his arms. He shook his head.

"I just want to be close to you, no more than that for our first lesson. This time we will both keep our pants on."

He kissed her again and something deep inside her told her to trust him. Her muscles relaxed while he slowly eased his hips up and down between her legs. The crotch of his jeans stimulated her through the thin silk of her panties and her heart pounded hard against the fabric of her bodice. She became aware of the warm, moist sensation spreading over her body, pooling between her legs. When his hands crept over her breasts, her nipples strained against the lacy fabric of her bra. His lips traced the outline of her face, lingering at the junction of her neck and shoulder, his teeth gently nipping at her skin. A shiver of pleasure shook her body. Her hips kept time with his thrusting movements.

A low groan escaped from her lips as she felt her womb clench. Her insides wound tighter and tighter, building to the point where she felt that she might explode from the pleasure. When his fingers eased under the elastic of her panties and dipped into her moist entrance, she gasped. He was not the first male to try this maneuver but he was the first one who she allowed to continue. There was no stopping now. She was past the point of no return. Her body shuddered as a tsunami of pleasure crashed over her, shattering her senses. She moaned her appreciation into his open mouth.

When the room stopped spinning, she broke contact with his lips long enough to tell him, "I guess I'll be staying."

He kissed her and rolled onto his back pulling her with him so that she was now on top. She snuggled into his chest and he kissed her forehead.

"That was lesson one," he informed her. "When you're able to cope with a naked male model without running from the room, we'll move onto lesson two."

"So, lesson two will cover…"

David shook his head and smiled. "No, Chérie .

In lesson two, I plan on there being *no* covering."
****

When David finally excused himself for the night and left Meaghan to attend to his family business, she felt a tug at her heart, but reluctantly let him go. She checked her watch. *Damn.* She was already late getting to the campus. *Priorities, Meaghan. Focus on your duty as a cop.* After all, finding the killer was the reason she had accepted scholarship. Although … her body still tingled from David's touch, making it harder to focus. She giggled and bit her bottom lip. David's kiss was her first *real* kiss. Sure she'd had other dates over her teenage years and kissing was mandatory after a couple of dates, but those kisses didn't even compare with what she experienced with David. She shook her head, determined to get on with her work and forced the thoughts out of her mind. Her body, however, would take longer to persuade.

****

As she suspected, no one lingered after their classes, leaving the campus relatively empty. The murders had frightened most of the students into leaving for their homes immediately after classes. Many had taken to walking to the carpark in pairs for added safety. She doubted that the murderer would strike in the same place again but, as she had to pass the area anyway, she headed towards the art building. No signs of movement around the vicinity. She headed towards the lights of the library and peered through the glass. Three people inside, a librarian and two students. One utilized the photocopier, the other researched information on a computer. Meaghan stepped away from the window and started towards the canteen which was located behind the closed convenience store. The sound of voices made her turn around and she saw two figures moving behind a tree, both too deep in conversation to notice her. She backed into the shadows of the nearest corridor before they had the opportunity to see her.

"Meaghan?"

She recognized David's voice without turning. *Shit*! She had to act quickly. She dashed out of the laneway and ran into the nearest building with him close behind but not fast enough. By the time he had rounded the corner, she was gone.

Chapter Eight

"How the hell did she get away?" Derrick half questioned, half demanded after hearing David's unlikely story. "No one is faster than you."

"I used to think so." David sighed as he poured himself another drink at the kitchen bar. "This doesn't make any sense."

"I hate to throw another spanner in the works," added Anna as she approached the brothers. "But according to Evan, Meaghan didn't leave the estate all night."

"Could you have been mistaken?" Derrick asked. "Maybe it wasn't Meaghan."

"No bloody way it wasn't her." David cursed. "She was wearing the same dress, the same shoes I left her in this evening."

"Well, according to Evan. She was here in the kitchen borrowing some milk about five minutes before you got home. I doubt that she could have run home faster than you drove."

David shook his head before swallowing another large gulp of his drink. "It doesn't make sense, Derrick. How is she doing this?"

"I don't know, but I think I've come up with a way to find out." Derrick walked into the study, searched for something in his desk, and returned with a business card. "While you and Meaghan are at the University tomorrow night for your usual session, I'll have camera's installed in the cottage."

"That seems a bit extreme," David protested.

"Relax. I won't have a camera installed in the bedroom or bathroom, only the living rooms and exterior of the cottage. That way we'll see when she leaves."

David nodded his agreement. There didn't appear to be any other way of solving the mystery. Somehow, Meaghan had been able to be in two places at once. *How was that even possible?* He thought back to the night of the previous murder. The blonde hair, the daisy sandals. She'd been there too. His instincts had never forsaken him before and they screamed at him. She was somehow involved. His gut twisted. His chest ached. For the first time in his life, he wanted to be wrong. *Could the love of his life be a murderer?*

****

Meaghan waited on an uncomfortable wooden chair inside the small musty office, confident that using Evan as her alibi had successfully thrown David of her scent. She knew that beginning a sexual relationship with him was playing with fire as he still appeared to be the number one suspect in her case but he was so worth the burn. She physically ached for him and she knew that killer or no, she wouldn't be able to resist him for much longer.

Last night, while he rubbed himself against her, his hands working their magic on her body, she had been close to asking him make love to her. She knew that the next time he posed naked for her, she would have trouble concentrating on anything besides how well she imagined they would fit together. Hadn't he even insinuated their next lesson would involve sex? His words haunted her. *"No,* Chérie. *In lesson two, I plan on there being no covering."*

She blew out a deep breath and fanned herself with her hand. *You're in deep shit, Meaghan.* Last night's patrol had complicated things further. This was the second time he'd caught her at the campus and she was sure that this time he'd recognized her. He would know that she was on to him and may question her about her presence at the campus after hours. The thought suddenly occurred to her. *He was in no position to accuse*. He had no excuse to be hanging around the empty campus at night, while she was there on duty. Unfortunately, she would have to keep that information to herself.

"Thanks for coming in, Megs."

"I don't mind," she told her superior as he entered the room and took his seat behind the coffee stained desk. "I don't know if my phone line is bugged so it is probably better this way."

"So, what's the skinny on this Corel guy?"

"I'm not sure yet," Meaghan told him as she watched him flipping through some paperwork on his desk. "He seems clean but..."

"But what?"

"I don't know, Terry. There is something secretive about him. He works in a windowless studio below a mansion. He poses as a nude model for my art class despite being a billionaire. I haven't seen him outside in the daylight since I moved in a few days ago and every time I search the campus at night, he turns up. I saw him hovering over the second body."

Terry looked up from his paperwork. "Did you see him kill her?"

"No."

"That's a shame. We can't arrest him just for finding the body. When I questioned him last time, he had a perfectly legitimate alibi."

"You know very well it's easy to invent an alibi, Terry." She stood up and paced the room. "I was forced to fabricate one myself for last night."

"Did he believe you?"

"He had no choice. I made sure I was seen by his trusted butler."

"Butler? Wow, you're really living the life aren't you? A big step up from our days at the orphanage."

"I know. I feel guilty accepting his hospitality considering I'm there to find evidence to convict him. He seems like a really nice guy, Terry. His whole family is really nice."

"That may be so but until we catch a killer, I want you to find out all you can about him but don't put yourself into a situation where he could hurt you, capiché?"

"Yes, sir." She made a mock salute and headed for the door, but stopping at the doorway she asked, "What do you make of the windowless rooms and only coming out at night?"

"I think you should be careful," he said sternly, but his mouth twisted into a smile then he burst into a soft chuckle. "You're probably living with a vampire."

She flipped him off and left.

****

Meaghan hurried to meet David in the arts building at the pre-arranged time. Butterflies had taken flight in her stomach and she bit her bottom lip in anticipation of seeing him sprawled naked in the center of the classroom. Her smile faded when she noticed that his place on the platform was already occupied by another male. After their last encounter, she had steeled herself for her second lesson. One that he had insinuated would be in the nude. The new male model was indeed naked and rather good looking but not even in the same league as David. She set up her gear and waited for the teacher's instructions, noticing that Lilith had taken up a permanent position across the room with the other Goth girl. Tonight they were joined by a male who also wore the obligatory black garb and makeup. The weird trio were discussing something that, by the looks on their faces, looked serious. She was still watching them when David walked up behind her, his cheek almost resting on hers when he whispered. "Are you ready for lesson two?"

"Here?" she stuttered, her body already reacting to proximity of his body.

"I have no idea what you mean." He teased with a wink that was intended for her alone before he stepped into the middle of the room to address the whole class. "We will be working in oils today, class. I have taken the liberty of setting up a small range of colors on your easels, a small gift so you can continue to practice at home. Choose a flesh color from your palette and paint a rough outline of Mr. Moir. Don't worry about the details, just work quickly to establish a base. You can add features and shades as you go. This will be an exercise on brush strokes and speed so you will not be judged on accuracy. If you get into difficulty, wave me over and I'll be happy to assist."

He walked in the opposite direction to Meaghan, leaving her confused and unsure of herself. He'd promised to teach her a lesson, insinuating one of a sexual nature but she had expected the lesson to be private. *What is he playing at?* Reluctantly, she located a tube of flesh colored oil paint and began working on her canvas although she had no idea if she was even using the correct brush. Her only experience with paints was watercolor pencils as art materials were expensive and her real job as an undercover cop paid only slightly more than her sham supermarket position. She jabbed at the canvas with her bristle brush hoping to get the paint onto the canvas as fast as possible in order to impress David. It didn't work. Her brush strokes clumsy and messy.

"No, no, no." David protested as he came up behind her and took the brush from her hand. "For a start, this is the wrong brush." He exchanged the bristle for a sable brush and delicately dabbed it onto the palette. "Think of your brush as a tool." He said as he put the brush in her hand and held her hand to the canvas. She could feel the hard muscles of his chest on her shoulders as he leaned over her, moving her hand like a marionette. Together they stroked the canvas.

"When you hold the tool, I want you to make slow, seductive movements like this…" he demonstrated downward movements, "the oil makes the paint slide easily, making your brush strokes more fluid."

It took Meaghan only a few seconds to realize his double entendre. "Control the tool. Move your hand slowly up and down, adding linseed oil when your movements begin to catch. Ah, that's good." He pressed against her, his erection rubbing against the small of her back as he continued his play on words. "The tip is very sensitive. Use a featherlike touch for optimum effect. Pay careful attention to the reactions of the canvas. You will sense when to add oil and when you should apply more pressure. That's very nice. You're doing well … keep up the pressure … yes, yes … that's it." She heard his low, quiet groan and she gasped in response. "As the pressure builds, move faster, faster Meaghan … oh, that feels good doesn't it." His voice breathless, ragged as he moved her hand furiously over the canvas.

"Faster … until you can sense that the canvas is at the point where it can take no more, then … add a bit more for good measure." David stopped abruptly. The painting finished. Meaghan could hardly believe what they had created in such a short amount of time. She stood admiring the work. Her body exhausted as though she had been put through a wringer. Damp heat soaked her dress. She shuddered when David asked her.

"Was that as good for you as it was for me?" He

released her hand and whispered, "I know *I* will appreciate your continued practice of these techniques and you, in turn, will be rewarded for your efforts."

By the time he left to finish his rounds of the class, Meaghan nipples felt hard enough to rip through the bodice of her dress.

****

David's game of tormenting Meaghan backfired. He found himself uncomfortably aroused, his tight jeans strangling his erection. He excused himself and left the class to stand with his back against the wall in the empty corridor to compose himself and adjust the crotch of his jeans. It took every ounce of his resolve, not to run back into the room, throw Meaghan over his shoulder, and carry her to a secluded area where he could continue their "private" lessons. The pheromones she secreted left him in no doubt as to her own arousal and even blind Freddy could notice that her nipples peaked and strained against the cotton fabric of her dress. He shifted his position, tilting his head in order to peer into the classroom window. He expected to see Meaghan struggling with her own arousal but when he looked in the direction of her easel he gasped. She was gone.

In that same moment, a gust of wind blew down the corridor carrying the pungent smell of incense and a scent very familiar to him … blood. He ran towards the source of the smell. Was the murderer one of his kind? Worse still, a member of his coven? Either of those suggestions would be preferable to believing that Meaghan had something to do with the murders. As he turned the corner, he slipped. His supernaturally fast reflexes stopped him from falling in the slick red substance that covered the floor and spotted the walls of the laneway. Arterial spray. The victim a young male. His throat cut from ear to ear. Judging by the look of shock frozen on his face, David deduced that he had died quickly and his killer had been someone he had known.

There were no signs of struggle and—as it was the middle of the laneway with nowhere to hide—the killer didn't have the element of surprise. With the exception of the burnt down black candles, *this* murder was different. While the first two murders had been by strangulation which alluded to a rage killing, this one had been fast, efficient and executed with confidence. Classes were still in progress so the killer knew that he could be discovered at any point but this did not deter him. *Did the killer use a knife because the intended victim was male?* He stroked his chin. Strangulation would have been difficult, had the killer been female or a small male. Judging by the quantity of blood on the ground, the victim had bled out. A vampire wouldn't have wasted a drop of the precious substance. If there was one thing David knew without a doubt … this was the work of a human.

Chapter Nine

After the police were notified and word had circulated about the third victim, the art class abandoned for the night. Students gathered around the crime scene jostling to get a better view, despite being warned by the officers to remain behind the yellow tape. As he was the person to discover the body, the police questioned David for around one hour, most of which he spent subtly trying to spot Meaghan in the thickening crowd that gathered near the taped off crime scene. The routine questions didn't bother him. He knew that if they became too suspicious he could easily enthrall the officers and convince them that he wasn't a threat. It wouldn't be the first time. His ability worked well unless he tried it on the blind or vision impaired. He assumed that Meaghan fit into that category despite her attention to detail on the canvas, because he'd tried on more than one occasion to compel her, to no avail.

One policeman, an inspector by the name of Palmer, seemed particularly interested in his whereabouts this evening. What disturbed David more than the officer's interest in him was his pre-occupation with Meaghan who had suddenly appeared at the front of a crowd of students. Terry Palmer stopped questioning mid-sentence and looked directly at her, his attraction obvious to David who heard the distinct change in Palmer's heartbeat. He sensed the rise in blood pressure. The cop lusted after her and David experienced the overwhelming compulsion to tear him limb from limb. Despite his effort to remain calm, tension built in his muscles. His hands clenched and unclenched by his sides and he was aware that the tone of his answers had become noticeably terse. She was *his* woman and this man had no right to be staring at her with such obvious interest. He cut interview short.

"I have nothing else to add. Perhaps you could badger someone else for a while."

"Taking that tone with me isn't going to speed up the questioning process, Mr. Corel."

"I've told you all I know, Inspector. I fail to see how asking the same questions ad nauseum is going to help your investigation. I assure you, my answers will not change despite your failed attempt to confuse me into altering my story."

David noticed his interrogator still peering over his notepad in Meaghan's direction; she appeared to be embarrassed by his attention, keeping her head down and looking around the crowd.

"If that's all…"

"I haven't finished yet, David. I may call you David?"

"No. You may not."

"Fine … *Mr. Corel*. I'll need a number where I can reach you."

David reached into his inside jacket pocket and handed Terry a business card. "This is my lawyer's number. If you have any more questions, I suggest you set up an appointment."

"At this stage, you don't need a lawyer, Mr. Corel, but if I have any more questions, I'll definitely give him a call."

It had not escaped David's attention that while the inspector addressed him, he did not take his eyes of Meaghan. The officer's pulse raced, his heart practically beating through his shirt as he watched her maneuver through the crowd. David tapped into the inspector's thoughts which made matters worse when he heard the man think, *oh god she's beautiful* and when Palmer's thoughts became lascivious, it was more than he could bear. His inner demon screamed at him. *Destroy this man.* Unbidden, his incisors lengthened. He kept his mouth shut until the anger subsided long enough for him to regain control. Taking another approach, he told the inspector,

"I'm sorry, Inspector Palmer but it's been a long and distressing night. Finding dead bodies is not a habit I enjoy despite the sudden regularity." He offered his hand and a firm handshake. "If you'll please excuse me, I'm anxious to take my fiancé home."

"Your fiancé?"

David noticed a hint of pleasure in Terry Palmer's voice. Was it possible that he had misread the man's reactions?

"Yes. She's an art student here and I'm sure the experience has upset her. I'd like to get her back to our home and tuck her in for the night, if that is all right with you?"

David didn't wait for an answer. He rushed past the crowd of students to where Meaghan waited behind the yellow tape. In one fluid motion, he jumped the tape, cupped the back of her head in his palm and kissed her. He took his time, holding her tight despite the mortified look on her face. Her eyes as wide as saucers. Students wolf-whistled. Some whispered. He knew he'd made a foolish mistake. In one act he had publicly humiliated her, his kiss tantamount to placing a scarlet letter on her clothes. It insinuated a mentorship based purely on sexual attraction. He'd acted in jealousy, laying claim to her as though she was a coveted possession. From the crushed expression on her face when he released her, he knew he may have thrown away any chance to be with her. Although she allowed him to take her hand and lead her to his car, he realized that she only tolerated this last act of intimacy to prevent a further scene. His heart warned him. It's the beginning of the end.

****

For the entire drive home, Meaghan had sat silently, although at times David sensed that she was on the verge of telling him off. Her body trembled, her cheeks flushed. Her mouth would open slightly, only to close again without uttering a word. She sat, hands in her lap, her body language warning him that she was out of bounds. She shut him out emotionally and physically. His insides turned to knots, twisting until he felt nauseated, empty. *Hungry?* The moment they reached home and he stopped the car, she flung open the door and made a dash for her cottage. He ran after her, catching up within seconds and held her shoulders by the shoulders. She spun around and slapped his face. He could tell by Meaghan's facial expression that the strike had been intended to cause him some physical pain. She seemed disappointed by his lack of reaction.

"How could you?" she screamed in frustration. "You've ruined everything!"

"I'm sorry. I know what I did was unforgiveable but by the end of the week the class will have forgotten all about the kiss."

"No." She shook her head as she wrung her hands. There was more to her anger than he could comprehend. He listened while she vented. "I've spent the entire semester trying to blend into the background so people won't notice me and now … now you've made me the center of attention."

David tried to understand why assimilation was so important to Meaghan. It didn't make any sense to him. *Why would a woman as beautiful as Meaghan not want attention?* He watched her as she appeared to have some type of meltdown. She was wringing her hands and tugging at the elastic that held her hair in neat braids.

"Do you know how stupid I feel wearing braids at my age?" she dragged her hands through her hair until the braids disappeared. Waves of pale blonde cascaded down her back. Her words seemed to less aimed at him and more to do with some inner turmoil. "Forced to wear these ridiculous glasses when my eyes are perfect."

Suddenly she stopped, as if she realized that she had said too much. Her hand shot up to her mouth and her eyes widened in horror.

****

"Wait. Let me get this straight. You wanted to look young *so* no one would notice you? Why would you do that?"

"I … I just wanted to concentrate on my art without any distractions," she mumbled, inwardly cringing at her feeble excuse. Even worse, her stomach lurched. She'd noticed an odd smell in the air back at the campus and it became worse in the car despite the air-conditioning. It affected her viscerally, making her nauseated and she swallowed the copper tasting lump in her throat.

"Meaghan. I may be a fool for you but I'm no idiot. What's going on?" His voice sounded firm but gentle as he reached for her.

She stepped away.

"Oh, I don't know what I'm even trying to say anymore," she answered, trying to distract him from his line of questioning. "I'm upset, that's all. Doesn't it even bother you that the whole class thinks we're sleeping together? We haven't even had sex yet."

The moment the words left her mouth, Meaghan knew she'd set herself up. The *yet* reference did not go unnoticed. David smiled and moved towards her. She tried to make a speedy escape.

"I can't discuss this with you. Besides, I'm upset and I want to go to bed."

"Do you want some company?" The touch of his hand on her cheek shot a surge of electricity through her body, reminding her of the lesson he had promised to teach. She wanted, no needed to accept his offer. *Get a grip girl! You're angry with him.* She followed the line of his gaze as it drifted from her face, over her breasts. *Be strong.*

She watched his expression change. His hooded eyes tightened as his eyebrows narrowed into a scowl.

"Meaghan, this looks like... How did you get blood on your skirt?"

Meaghan looked down and, to her horror, noticed a large blood stain on the hem of her dress. Bile rose in her throat. She covered her mouth with her palm.

"I have no idea how that got there," she told him honestly, but this time, she could tell that he was less inclined to believe her. His expression hardened. He looked not only disappointed but furious. Something inside warned her of the danger.

"I want to go inside now." She tried to leave but he snagged her by the wrist.

"What were you doing at the murder site?"

"I wasn't," she protested. "I was in class the whole time."

"No more lies!" The volume and tone of David's voice terrified her. She tried to pull away but his vice-like grip cut off circulation to her hand.

"Let go of me. You're hurting me." She informed him to no avail. He neither released her nor lessened his grip.

"Where did you go tonight?"

"Nowhere. I never left the class. Let me go, David!" She struggled against his grip. Pressure built around her wrist. She heard a loud crack and then came the pain … the pain was excruciating.

"That's a lie!" he bellowed. His voice resonated across the driveway. Neighborhood dogs barked. "After I left you, I looked in the window and you were gone."

Meaghan tried to think. Had she left the building? Her heart pounded with fear, her wrist throbbed and she struggled to breathe. She gagged every time she looked at the stain, a reflex she had developed back in the orphanage. Suddenly she remembered.

"The only time I left the room was to use the ladies room. I was only gone for a few minutes."

She knew the answer didn't explain the blood on her dress. David opened his mouth to question her further when they were joined by Anna and Derrick.

"Is there a problem here?" Derrick asked.

"Yes." Meaghan took advantage of the opportunity by pointing out, "Your brother has broken my wrist."

David released her. His angry expression changed when he looked to her waist where she cradled her swollen, bruised and misshaped wrist with her other hand. He lowered his chin, ran his fingers through his hair, and when he looked back up, she could swear she saw tears in his eyes. He reached for her. She pulled away.

"Come inside and I'll ice and bandage that for you," Anna offered, but Meaghan waved her off with her good hand.

"I'll be fine. I just want to be left alone."

She ran to the small cottage before anyone could argue, locking the door behind her. As she stood with her back against the solid wooden door, she remembered the strength of David's grip and wondered if it would be enough to stop him if he decided to attack her during the night. *Got to get away*. But how? Without a car, she had no way of leaving besides she could still hear voices outside. David and his family were still standing in the driveway discussing her.

She considered ringing Terry for help. No. He would already be upset that she had drawn attention to herself at the campus. Telling him that she'd now blown her cover and probably alienated their lead suspect, would force Terry to pull her of the case. Tears threatened behind her eyes. She'd worked so hard to prove that she had what it takes to make an undercover cop. Now she was sure that all she'd proven was her own incompetence.

The pain in her wrist distracted her from her thoughts of being murdered in her sleep. She headed for the bathroom to run her hand under cold water and remove the bloody dress. To her horror, she realized that the blood had soaked through, her legs stained pink with the victim's blood. Her body heaved and she barely made it to the toilet. She struggled out of her dress and turned on the shower faucets, anxious to remove the stain from her skin. The dress would be dispatched to the garbage as there was no way she would be able to remove the mark. Besides, how could she scrub at the blood when she could barely face it let alone touch it.

Now you listen here. She told herself as she showered, scrubbing her skin with a loofa until it was almost raw. *It's not over till it's over. There has got to be a way to turn this around.* She remembered the look on David's face as he gripped her wrist. The throbbing pain reminded her of his anger. Could she muster the courage to continue with her charade? Would he even give her the opportunity?

Washing her hair proved difficult and she suspected that he had indeed broken a bone when she noticed how black and distorted her wrist looked in the harsh bathroom light. Wrapping a towel around her body as best she could, she located a first aid kit in the well equipped kitchen and bandaged her wrist. She applied an ice pack over the bandage to reduce the swelling. A rumbling in her stomach directed her to the well-stocked kitchenette. Unfortunately, the only thing she could find and manage to eat with one hand was a banana, so she ate it, washed it down with a glass of milk, and retired early, taking her side arm to bed. Just in case.

During the night, she tossed and turned, pondering her mistakes and unable to tolerate the physical and emotional pain. *How could I be falling in love with a man who I now know for sure is capable of being a killer?* She cradled her injured wrist to her chest, torn between self-preservation, duty and the completely idiotic reasoning of her heart. The internal dialogue between her brain and gut relentless. *You only think you love him because you lust after him. He could be the killer. Be smart. What if he attacks you again? Could you draw your gun fast enough to protect yourself? Why risk your life for a case, even if it's your only chance for promotion? Get out of here before he kills you too.*

She held her hands over her ears, squeezed her eyes tight shut and tried to block out the voices of reason. *I just don't get that killer vibe about him. I can't imagine him deliberately hurting anyone.* Her wrist throbbed in protest giving her brain ammunition to use against her. *That's because when you're around him, all you can imagine is his talented hands on your body. Try imagining those same hands around someone's neck, squeezing the life out of them.*

A howl pierced the silence of the room, drawing her attention back to her surroundings and the gun beneath her pillow. She reached for the cold metal and wrapped her fingers around the handle as another wail shook her to the core. How was that even possible? *The animal followed me here?* Sliding her body across the bed, she broke into a run the moment her feet touched the floor. After taking a deep breath, she drew back the curtains, scanned the dark garden and gasped. A pair of red, unblinking eyes stared back at her from behind the heavy foliage of ferns. She closed her eyes tight, wishing the creature away and when she opened them, it was gone.

****

By the time the sun began to rise next morning, she had reached a decision. Rather a flesh and blood killer than risk being attacked by whatever the hell had followed her here. Living close to David not only gave her the opportunity to either convict or exonerate him, it's heavily fortified grounds offered more protection than her run down, gang run neighborhood. She sighed and lay back on the bed. *Who are you kidding?* She already loved this place with its beautiful gardens and view of the beach. Living here, close to David was a dream come true. No ... more than a dream. A fantasy come to life. Especially if he followed through on his next lesson plan. He had promised bare flesh and she had a feeling that he was a man of his word. Worse still, after all that he had done to her: the damage to her wrist, the humiliation at the campus in front of her classmates, teachers and even her boss ... *damn it,* she still wanted him.

Chapter Ten

David sat on the end of the studio's bed imagining Meaghan packing to leave him. He had spent the night there, rather than his own, more comfortable bedroom, hoping she might come to him there. She didn't. Now it was time for their regular lesson and he had convinced himself that she was on her way back to her old neighborhood, but he was helpless to stop her if she chose to leave him in the daylight. He pulled at his hair, berating himself for his behavior at the campus. Inconsiderate, reckless behavior but worse than that, his aggressiveness towards her when they arrived home … reprehensible. The blood on her clothes had convinced him of her involvement in the murders, turning his world upside down. There was nothing he could do to change the way he felt about her. *What's the expression? The heart wants what the heart wants.* He loved her, probably always had and he would gladly walk into the sunlight if it could change the way the previous night had transpired. Make her stay.

The door at the top of the stairs opened and he heard the creaking of the steps leading down to the studio. The lightness of the tread indicated a woman and he fully expected to see his sister-in-law coming to tell him that Meaghan had caught a taxi back to town. His heart skipped a beat when he saw, not Anna, but Meaghan at the foot of the stairs. *She's forgiven me. She's … oh my god! Her arm.*

"Meaghan. I'm so sorry."

"I would say it was okay but actually, David, I'm in a fair bit of pain. Your well-equipped first aid kit didn't contain anything stronger than paracetamol and that hasn't helped at all."

"Come over to the bed and let me have a look at it." He put his arm around her to lead her, overjoyed when she didn't pull away from his touch. She had every reason to hate him, nevertheless, she allowed him to guide her to his bed. As gently as he could, David unwound the bandage and immediately realized the extent of the damage. Damage he had caused.

"Why didn't you come to me last night? I could have taken you to the hospital."

Meaghan's accusing stare reminded him that he had probably terrified her. *Why would she have come to him for help?* He'd acted like a brute. She shrugged but said nothing.

"I need to make a call." He grabbed his mobile phone from his bedside table and pushed a number that he had on speed dial. "Hello, Michael? This is David Corel. I need you to come to the house and bring your mobile imaging device. Yes, I suspect a broken bone so could you please bring the necessary equipment for casting? Thank you, yes. Your discretion would be appreciated and I'll make sure you are compensated for any inconvenience."

After hanging up, he depressed the button on the intercom and informed Evan that a private ambulance would be arriving shortly and that he was to direct the paramedics down to the studio. He hung up the phone and sat down beside Meaghan on the bed, gently cradling her mangled right wrist in his hands. He gently turned her tiny hand to examine the bruises. Bruises corresponding with his fingers. Fingers that had gripped her wrist so tight, they broke her delicate bones. For the first time since his transformation, he felt tears well behind his eyes and unashamedly allowed them to fall. As the droplets fell on her hand, he wished with all his heart that he possessed healing powers. Powers that would mend the broken bone. Alas, his powers were limited to *breaking* bones.

"It's okay, really," she told him softly. "We all have our unattractive moments and, after all, I drew first blood … so to speak." She smiled but her attempt at humor only served to make him feel more ashamed. *He was a protector of humans, a leader of his own kind, not a misogynistic bully.* Bad enough that he had harmed a human woman but she was *his* woman. He knew that for sure now. The woman he had waited for, longed for. The other part of his soul. His job to protect her and place her on a pedestal, not tear her down and cause her suffering. *Monster.* He raised her damaged hand and kissed it, his tears welling in her palm.

****

Meaghan gazed down in fascination at the back of David's head as she felt his tears fall onto her palm. It didn't make any sense. A murderer, crying like a baby because he had broken her wrist. During the course of her training—and then the practical experience of working a beat and undercover work–she had seen many tears. She could easily tell the fake from the real. These tears *seemed* so real. *But, how could they be?*

"Master David?" the crackling voice on the intercom broke the awkward silence in the room. "The paramedics are on their way, sir."

"Thank you, Evan," David answered, wiping away the tears with the back of his shirt sleeve just in time for the paramedics to make their entrance. They lugged their heavy digital equipment and bags down the stairs. David introduced them and lowered his chin as he explained her injury.

"She was attacked by a madman last night."

She raised her eyebrows at David as Michael—the first paramedic—examined her wrist and agreed with

David's layman diagnosis.

"As usual, you're spot on, Mr. Corel. This looks like a serious break but I would like to take an x-ray to confirm."

He waited for Meaghan to give her consent and set up for the shot by donning his protective apron and directing both his partner and David behind the portable shield.

"Distal radius fracture," Michael confirmed as he studied the film. "Would you mind if I set up the casting equipment in the bathroom?" David pointed the way to the en-suite as the other paramedic offered Meaghan something for the pain, which she gratefully accepted. David refused to allow the paramedic to escort her into the bathroom where Michael had made preparations. He scooped her into his arms and carried her into the room while she sucked happily on the green penthrox whistle. It worked quickly towards relieving the pain. By the time her cast was in place and her wrist was supported by a sling, she was oblivious to *any* pain and she even giggled when David carried her back to the studio and placed her gently onto the bed.

Fighting to stay lucid, she strained to hear what David whispered to Michael as he reached into his jeans and handed the men a wad of notes from his pocket. They accepted the money with huge smiles and many thanks before heading towards the stairs. When Michael was halfway up, he suddenly stopped and called down to her.

"You should report the attack to the police, Meaghan. Your attacker may be involved with the recent murders. I heard that the first two were strangled and whoever broke your wrist had some serious strength."

David excused himself and bolted up the stairs after the paramedics. Meaghan could hear him talking slowly and deliberately to the men who seemed to be agreeing with whatever he was telling him. In her drug induced stupor, she couldn't help but giggle as she thought to herself. *Hey, Officer Lamb, I'd like to report an attack on myself. Yes, I was attacked by someone who could be the University murderer and who also happens to be the man I am falling in love with.*

"Did you say something?"

Somehow, in what seemed like only a split second, David had returned and stood beside her. Despite her addled state of mind, she realized that she may had said out loud rather than thought the words. *Shit.*

"What?" The pain medication overwhelmed her. She could barely keep her eyes open let alone think of a good excuse. She lay back on the pillows, fighting the effects of the medication, hoping she would not be killed in her sleep. If sleep had not taken her, she would have noticed David lie down beside her, stroke her forehead and cheeks with the tips of his fingers before whispering. "I love you too."

****

Meaghan opened her eyes, shocked to find herself in the dark, lying in the dirt behind a gravestone. *I'm in a cemetery?* She'd heard of sleepwalking people trying to drive a car while asleep, but this was ridiculous. *How did she get to a cemetery? More importantly, why?* A mist formed around the graves, its cold tendrils reaching like fingers for some unseen presence in the dark. In the distance, a car alarm went off. A dog howled in response to the terrible wail of the siren.

When she heard voices approaching, she curled up into the fetal position behind the stone and watched as eight people wearing dark hoods passed close by but oblivious to her proximity. From her hiding spot, she observed them as they sat cross-legged in a circle on the ground, each of them lighting a candle and uttering words that she didn't understand. It sounded like an ancient language or possibly one that they invented themselves. Whatever it was, she had never—in all her years in the force—heard anything like it. As the smoke from the candles rose, the chanting became louder, more frantic, culminating in the appearance of a ninth shape that suddenly materialized in the center of the circle. Meaghan didn't understand what she was witnessing but her intuition warned her. *Time to leave.* The *shape* turned to look in her direction. It raised a wispy arm and pointed towards her. The group jumped to their feet. She closed her eyes, willing herself to disappear and by the time the hooded individuals reached her hiding spot, she was already gone.

****

"Meaghan. Wake up!"

Before she even opened her eyes she recognized David's arms wrapped around her. The warmth of his skin against her body and the comforting heaviness of his arms as he held her tight against his chest.

"You were having a nightmare."

She knew better. "It must have been the drugs."

"And the broken bone," he added. "You were moaning in your sleep. I think the pain medication might be wearing off."

"It does hurt quite a bit," she admitted, supporting her freshly made cast with her good hand. "I'm also feeling hungry. Is there anything to eat in this studio? I'd even settle for a piece of that fruit you kept forcing me to draw the other day."

"I'll have a tray sent down for you." He gently propped some pillows behind her shoulders before ordering up for some food on the intercom. When he returned, Meaghan was deep in thought.

"Are you all right?" he asked.

"Oh. Yes. I was just trying to work something out." Her trip to the cemetery had left her confused. She had never travelled in her sleep. This deviation to her usual pattern left her feeling vulnerable. *She could end up anywhere and if she fell asleep in a public place, her body would be vulnerable to attack.* A chill ran down her spine. Worse still, those hooded figures may have had something to do with the murders and tonight, they came close to discovering her.

"I can't tell you how sorry I am about this, Meaghan." David sat beside her on the bed and took her left hand in his. "I'll do everything in my power to make it up to you."

"Well at least I'll have a good excuse not to attend classes for a while so maybe the gossip will have died down by then." She forced a smile. *Like that's going to happen.* "I hope you won't expect me to supply you with a doctor's certificate, considering it's going to be a bit difficult to draw for a while."

He drew her hand to his mouth and kissed it. "I'll make sure you see the best physiotherapists and specialists," he told her. "I promise you, I'll do everything in my power to ensure that you don't lose any dexterity in that hand."

Meaghan shook her head and laughed. "I've had broken bones before. The staff at the orphanage had a running tab betting how long it would take for me to break another bone. For the moment, I'm more concerned with how I am going to be able to use the bathroom or even feed myself."

His expression softened. "You were an orphan? I didn't know."

"How could you? It doesn't matter anyway. I manage fine on my own." It was a lie she had told herself most of her life. Sometimes she almost believed it.

For a split second, she sensed him access her memories. How was he doing that? David broke through the barrier protecting her thoughts. He saw the frightened little girl alone on a cot in the empty room of the orphanage, crying into her pillow. Their eyes met and for a moment, she considered mentioning the mental connection but the moment passed. Besides, any revelation would be an admission of psychic ability. Her advantage would be lost. There was still far too much at stake. How far could she trust him? Could she trust him at all? She broke the uncomfortable silence.

"Do you have any plastic bags or bubble wrap lying around?"

He raised an eyebrow as his mouth curled into a cheeky grin. "Why?"

Her heart skipped a beat. *Focus, Meaghan.* "To keep the cast dry while I shower."

"I promised to help you with that too," he told her, the twinkle in his eyes suggested more than she was able to cope with in her present state. "The bath in the en-suite is large enough for two people. It would be my pleasure to take care of all your bathing needs. I believe we still haven't had lesson three." He nuzzled her neck with his cheek sending a wave of Goosebumps down her spine.

She felt the flush of color to her cheeks as her skin warmed in reaction to his suggestions. He was back. The charmingly, cheeky David who made her act as giddy as a school girl, while his body reminded her that she was every inch a woman. A woman with needs that only *he* could satisfy. The dumbwaiter pinged, heralding the arrival of her food. She was grateful for the distraction, motioning to the tray with a tilt of her head.

"Oh, good. The food is here. I'm ravenous."

"I'm ravenous too," David agreed. "But, I can wait until after you've eaten."

He winked before he left the bed to collect the tray. Meaghan was grateful that he couldn't see her hyperventilate. Her breasts felt uncomfortably heavy and liquid heat spread through her body, pooling between her legs. She may have been naïve when it concerned actually making love but she knew a sexual proposition when she heard one and David was an expert. Her better judgement warned her, *he'll devour you, Meaghan*, but she no longer cared. She wanted him to take her, body and soul. Damn the consequences. She wanted this man with every fiber of her being. Killer or not, at least she would die satisfied.

"Aren't you going to eat?" she asked David when he placed the tray on her lap and she realized that there was only one plate.

"I had a quick bite while you slept."

The memory of her last meeting with Terry and his parting comment made her flinch. *A quick bite?* She felt for marks on her neck as David buttered a roll relieved to find her skin unbroken. Terry's comment still bothered her. *Why were there no windows in David's studio or bathroom?* She looked around the room. Not a peep of sunlight could infiltrate the studio. It was sealed as tight as a tomb. A room such as this would be perfect for a vampire. It was impossible to tell if it was day or night. She looked at her watch and discovered that she had slept away most of the day. Eight p.m. When vampires were at full strength.

David looked up from the plate. "Is everything okay? You look a bit stressed."

"I'm fine. Just hungry."

"So am I." he teased as he held half of the buttered roll up to her mouth. "But you should eat first."

"I am quite capable of feeding myself," she informed him, taking the roll from his hand.

"Indulge me." He spooned a forkful of vegetables into her mouth before she could protest. She resisted the urge to argue while she ate, realizing that feeding her kept him occupied, which made him less likely to think of ways to tease her. She ate in relative silence, hoping that the food might help ease the grogginess. When the pain returned with heightened intensity she regretted wishing the wooziness away.

"You look pale. Are you in pain?"

"A bit." She nodded.

He furrowed his brow. "A bit?"

"Okay, a lot."

"Michael left some codeine for the pain. Would you like some now?" David asked.

"I want to get back to my place and have a shower before I take anything else." She told him. "Hopefully, they'll help me sleep. Last night was hopeless."

David removed the tray and empty plate, placing it on the bed beside her before he scooped her up into his arms and walked towards the bathroom. "No shower for you, young lady. You aren't allowed to get that cast wet."

"Then how can I wash myself?" Meaghan protested. "I can hardly balance to get out of a bath."

David smiled another cheeky grin and Meaghan didn't need to be a mind reader to understand what he had planned. "Now just wait a minute, Mr. Corel. I am in no condition to put up with any of your shenanigans tonight. I'm in too much pain and I'm too tired to be interested in anything physical."

"No shenanigans tonight," he agreed. "I promise I will even keep my eyes shut as I help you undress."

Meaghan swallowed the lump in her throat. *He wants to help me undress?* She hadn't been sure if she could cope with the embarrassment of being naked in front of him while making love. Having him undress and bathe her seemed a terrifying proposition. Humiliating but completely arousing at the same time.

David took a packet of painkillers from the vanity cabinet, removed two and poured a glass of water. He handed her the water and popped the codeine in her mouth. She swallowed the tablets before she realized what she had done. *What if they weren't painkillers? What if it was poison?* The thought of being naked in front of David was more frightening than having him strangle her to death. Look at him. So perfect. Michelangelo would have wept knowing that his David—despite being reputed to being a masterpiece— paled in comparison to her David. *My David? If only that were true*. She suddenly wished that the water had been scotch.

"Come on, Chérie. I promise I'll make this as painless as possible." He smiled and she couldn't help but return the smile. His eyes offered compassion, a promise of tenderness too honest to be misread. She allowed herself to ignore the doubts about his involvement in the murders, at least for tonight. For once in her life she was going to take a chance, risk heartbreak for a moment of pleasure.

Despite the excruciating pain in her wrist, the thought of a hot bath with David seemed like a fantasy come true. He sat her on a stool in the bathroom while he prepared the large bath with scented bath foam. He lit a few candles before turning off the lights. The light from the candles offered only a subtle light, barely enough to make out their silhouettes and the fragrance from the bath was inviting. As she inhaled the floral scent,

Meaghan realized that the subdued lighting had been for her benefit, to ease her doubts, protect her modestly. She made no attempt to stop him when he helped her to her feet and began to undress her.

****

Slowly, he lifted her arms so he could maneuver her t-shirt over her breasts, past her shoulder and finally off completely. He unzipped her skirt, allowing it to fall. The fabric billowed momentarily before floating to the floor like a parachute. Next, he reached behind her and unfastened her bra, pausing to rest his cheek against hers to steady himself before removing her panties. The temptation of her peaked nipples almost too much to resist but, as he'd promised to keep the bath purely non-sexual, he didn't want to risk making her regret her decision.

She stood in front of him, naked, perfect and innocent. Her cheeks flushed with color, her eyes modestly averted his gaze. *Completely unaware of her own natural beauty. Everything he had ever dreamed she would be and more.* The demon inside him stirred. *Taste her.* He pushed it down, closing off his mind to the sound of her blood pounding in his ears, knowing that even a drop would push him over the edge. He couldn't lose her. He wouldn't survive the loss, not after searching for her all these years. She was beautiful, vulnerable, pure of heart and body. His. He believed that with all his heart. His hand slipped behind her neck where he cupped the back of her head in his hand. She leaned into it, her silken hair soft against his skin. Resisting the urge to take her into his arms, he asked her.

"Do you trust me?"

She raised her eyes, biting her bottom lip as she nodded her answer. He almost came undone. Instead, he stripped off his own clothes and stepped into the comfortably hot water. There, he held out his arms, motioning for her to join him. She hesitated for a moment, modesty staying her movements. He knew she fought her own demons. He had asked for her trust after causing her pain. He'd given her no reason to believe she could trust him. His eyes beseeched her. *Please, Meaghan. Give me another chance.*

Reaching out her left hand, she allowed him to assist her into the water where he positioned her between his legs, her back against his chest, her damaged right hand resting outside the bath on a stool. She leaned against him, demonstrating the conviction of her decision, her head resting against his shoulder, her face turned towards his chest. He tilted his chin towards her and kissed her forehead, his lips pausing on her skin while he reached for the ladle that he had previously placed beside the bath.

She closed her eyes as he scooped a ladle full of bath water and, after gently easing her head backwards, poured the water over her hair. Rubbing a quantity of shampoo between his palms, he gently massaged the sweet smelling liquid into her hair, his fingers moving in small circles over her scalp, then down the length of her hair. He rinsed the shampoo, careful not to get any of the lather in her eyes then repeated the sequence before he conditioned her pale locks. When he stroked her hair, she shivered, her skin reacted with gooseflesh. She leaned back against his chest, breathing heavily. He closed his eyes and breathed her in, sensing her desire, wanting to give her more. He lathered a sponge with bath foam and began soaping her breasts with delicate but deliberate movements. She moaned when he dipped the sponge into the water between her thighs, finding the sensitive area between her legs and gently massaging her clit. She reached behind her, cupping his head, leaning into him as she cried out in climax. His cock jerked. He closed his eyes and held his breath. *Patience*. He eased her forward, lifting her silky hair and placing it over her shoulder so he could wash her back. Her satin smooth shivered beneath his fingers. She had said that she loved him. Perhaps it was the drugs. Perhaps not. He would give her time. Wait for her to fall in love with him. For the first time in a century he had hope.

****

The combination of the luxuriously fragrant hot water, David's talented hands exploring her body and his heavy erection pressing up against her back seemed like an erotic dream. A dream from which she hoped she would never wake up. When he eased himself out of the bath, she instantly missed the skin to skin contact. The bath lost its appeal. A yawn stretched her mouth and she covered it with her good hand. *If only I wasn't so tired.* He looked so damned hot as he quickly dried his body with a towel. Too quickly. After discarding the towel, he held out his hand, so confident in his nudity. He had every right to be. He was beautiful. His firm body, chiseled and bulging with muscle however something else stole her gaze. His heavy erection. Her body reacted with a shudder of anticipation. She accepted his hand and stepped out of the bath, her legs shaking with desire as he wrapped her up in a fleecy cotton bath robe and carried her to his bed.

She fought to stay awake but the sensation of David massaging her hair dry with a warm towel made her light-headed, sleepy. His chest pressed firmly against her back as they sat on the edge of the bed, her body once again between his legs, his hands in her hair, his breath on her neck, his naked skin within reach. She wanted to touch him in the way he had insinuated during the last art class, drive him mad with desire. *Sleepy*.

When David picked up a brush from his bedside table and began to brush her hair, the sensation sent shivers down her spine. It felt so intimate, so affectionate; *so tired.*

****

David sensed that Meaghan was close to sleep but her arousal was undeniable as she moaned in appreciation of the care he was taking with her hair. His lips kissed a path down to the base of her neck. *She wants you.* He shook his head. She was vulnerable in her present state and he could not, would not take advantage, no matter how her pheromones screamed at him. She'd trusted him to bathe her, groom her and although—from past experience—he knew she was likely to be intimidated by his nudity, she'd allowed him to wrap his legs around her in the bath and as they sat on his bed.

He leaned forward again, brushing her hair away from her neck with his hand and kissed her softly on the underside of her chin. She moaned. Her skin warmed at his touch. He maneuvered his head around to see her beautiful face, gauge her mood. Her eyes were closed, lips parted, waiting to be kissed. Giving in to his need, he kissed her. Her mouth melted into his. He supported her head in the palm of his hand, her body going limp at his touch. When he reluctantly withdrew his mouth, he noticed that her eyes were still closed, her mouth slightly open, a dribble of saliva hung on the corner of her bottom lip. She was asleep.

Despite his disappointment, David chuckled to himself. *Looks like you've lost your touch, old man.* Never, in a century of lovemaking, had he ever experienced a woman falling asleep while on the verge of making love with him. Meaghan was definitely one of a kind. He'd anticipated her arrival for what seemed like eternity, dreamed of her, painted countless portraits of her, but she'd kept him waiting, refusing to be born until she was good and ready. Now she was in his bed, in his arms, the woman of his dreams ... snoring.

The soft nasal sounds reminded him of a purring kitten, a precious, soft little creature in need of love and affection but capable of causing damage with her claws. He lifted her into his bed, removed her damp robe from under the covers so he would not be tempted to fondle her naked flesh, and he tucked her in for the night. As he looked down at her cherubic face, he wondered how it was even possible that someone so sweet, so innocent, could possibly be a cold-blooded killer.

Chapter Eleven

Meaghan awoke to the aroma of a cooked breakfast, shocked to notice that, not only was she naked in a strange bed, but she was not alone. David rested on one elbow, staring down at her with a big goofy smile on his face. "Good morning, kitten. How are you feeling today?"

"Fine." Meaghan answered as she pulled the sheets up to her chin.

David shook his head. "Nothing happened last night. You didn't happen to bring any nightclothes with you and I didn't want you to sleep in a wet bathrobe in case you caught a cold."

Meaghan noticed that David was lying on top of the sheets and he was gloriously naked. It shouldn't have been a surprise. "So why are *you* naked?"

"I always sleep naked," he informed her. "It didn't occur to me to change my sleeping habits."

Meaghan sat up, pulling the sheet with her. "I guess it also didn't occur to you that you could have loaned me a t-shirt to sleep in?"

David grinned and shrugged his shoulders. "Oops, my bad."

"You certainly *are* bad, David Corel," she said, trying to ignore the touch of his hand on her thigh as his finger traced a line down her leg. His deep blue eyes twinkled with mischief as he rose from the bed—in all his naked glory—to collect the tray of food that Evan had send down on the dumb waiter. She willed herself to look away when he turned, tray in hand, to face her, but she found the task impossible. Even when she saw his manhood quiver at the sight of her eyes on his body, she couldn't tear her gaze away from his rippling abdominal muscles, his narrow waist and hips and especially not his growing erection. *How could it get any bigger?* She was transfixed and, despite knowing that she blatantly stared at his manhood, she couldn't look away. Didn't want to look away.

David smiled. "I see we're making progress."

"Pardon?"

"A few days ago, you would have run screaming from the room, but now you seem to be appreciating the naked human form with barely a blush."

"You haven't given me much choice," she reminded him as he placed the tray of food on her lap. "You seem to find it hard to keep your clothes on." She turned her attention to the food. "Damn, that looks good."

"Thank you." David bowed his head slightly in appreciation.

"And he's back." She said the words out loud and instantly knew he would use them against her.

"What do you mean by that?" he raised an eyebrow and his lips curled in another cheeky smile as he began to cut up her English breakfast.

"Cheeky, David," she mumbled as he fed her a mouthful of fried egg. "I much prefer the cheeky side of you to the serious side."

"So do I," he admitted as he handed her a buttered slice of toast. "But sometimes I'm forced to deal with serious situations."

"Such as?" she took a bite from her toast and hoped that David would let his guard down long enough to provide information that would help with her case. After a restful night's sleep, she had awoken with a clear mind and the determination to concentrate on the case, despite David's attempt to distract her.

"My brother Derrick and I manage a company

which deals with community issues. Our business deals with … let's just say they aren't always people-friendly clients which can sometimes be problematic. It's our responsibility to ensure they don't cause any trouble, so this spate of homicides has us concerned."

That's why he's been around campus. "You think that one of your clients is the murderer?" *What type of people does he deal with?* "What sort of business do you run? David … are you doing anything illegal?"

"No, of course not." He rose from the bed, found some fresh clothes in his closet, pulled on a t-shirt and jeans, and returned to lie beside her on the bed. "Think of me as a kind of parole officer."

"I see that you like to go commando," Meaghan commented after noticing that he neglected to put on any underwear.

"What can I say?" he teased. "The boys like to be ready to go whenever the situation arises."

Despite his playfulness, she noticed his pensive expression as if he was trying to decide if he should ask her a question. Apparently he made his decision because he asked,

"I need you to be honest with me, Meaghan. How did you really get blood on your dress?"

Meaghan put down the fork she had used to eat a slice of bacon and swallowed before answering. "I already told you, David. I have no idea."

"Okay. I believe you, but let's work through this. You say that you didn't leave the art room, is that correct?"

Meaghan nodded and then paused to think, her eyes turned slightly up to the right. "Actually, come to think of it, I did leave for a few minutes. After your lesson—" she used air bunnies to emphasize her point— "I needed to splash some water on my face so I headed for the bathroom adjoining the main studio. The light bulb had blown so I couldn't see very well. I bumped up against the sink before I located the tap. I guess maybe there was blood on the sink?" The last mouthful of food threatened to be regurgitated as she tried to push the image out of her mind.

"Sounds feasible to me," he told her, nodding his agreement. "So I guess that means that the killer washed her hands in the ladies' room after the murder."

Meaghan raised her eyebrows. "*Her* hands? A male could just as easily have washed *his* hands in the ladies' room."

"Highly unlikely," he reasoned, dismissing her argument outright. "The class was still in progress and it would have been hard for a male to go into the bathroom unnoticed."

"You managed to disappear into the corridor unseen," she reminded him. "There is a back entrance to the ladies' room and with the bulb blown. It would have been easy to sneak in and out unnoticed."

"Enough about blood and murders for today," he told her. "We're behind in your lessons." He picked up the tray and took it back to the dumbwaiter.

"Ahem." Meaghan lifted her injured wrist, reminding him that she wasn't able to paint, but he shook his head.

"To be good artist, you must understand your subject."

Meaghan scowled. "Get to the point."

"The lesson for today will be understanding how it feels to model for an art class." Her stomach twisted. *I have a bad feeling about this*. What was he suggesting?

"Remaining still while others draw your naked body is a difficult and awkward skill, one that many artists fail to appreciate. Today's lesson, lesson three, is recognizing the difficulties of modelling and learning how to empathize."

"What?" Meaghan's body temperature rose. Heat spread over her body. "You don't mean … you can't expect me to … you want me to pose nude?"

"Yes," David told her without offering any more information. "Would you like me to help you to the bathroom before we begin?"

"I can manage that by myself," she argued. "If you would just hand me a towel or robe."

"Why?" he asked with a shrug. "You'll be taking it off in a moment anyway."

I'd prefer he attacked me with a knife or even try and strangle me … but stare at me while I'm naked? The idea terrified her. "I can't do this."

He narrowed his eyes but his lips curled into a smile. "Yes you can."

She tried to call his bluff. "I've never heard of an artist posing nude."

David grin grew wider. His full lips turned at the corners in smug satisfaction and she realized that he had her where he wanted. She had played into his hands.

"And yet, you've attended classes where the teacher becomes the model. Come now kitten, have you forgotten the nights I posed for you? Are you saying that I'm not really an artist?"

"I haven't seen any of your paintings."

"All sold."

"What about those leaning against the wall?"

"You can't talk yourself out of this kitten and you can't trick me into showing you my paintings until I am good and ready. Soon, I promise. But as for now…" He pointed towards the platform in the center of the room.

Meaghan stammered but couldn't find the words that would help her escape the reality of her situation. If

David felt it necessary for an artist to learn how to pose nude, who was she to argue. He was a professional artist and—from what she had heard and seen—a highly sought after model. But, how could she bring herself to pose for him when she could barely look at *herself* naked in the mirror? She assumed that he'd seen a great many naked women in the course of his career *and* in his love life. *How would her body fare in comparison?* A heaviness settled in her stomach.

"I need to use the bathroom," she told him, her statement giving no indication of her decision to pose for him. She hesitated, waiting for him to look away so she could leave the bed. "Could you please turn your back?"

****

David shrugged his shoulders but nevertheless, turned away. He heard the soft footfalls indicative of her running from the bed to the bathroom and then the slam of the bathroom door. He wondered if he had taken his game a little too far. She was naïve and innocent, of that he was sure, and he wanted to ease her into a sense of security around him. Sure, she had allowed him to undress her by candlelight, bath her and had even felt safe enough to fall asleep in his arms, but would she feel confident enough to allow him to admire her naked body in the light? He wanted so badly to explore every inch of her, touch and squeeze her breasts and taste her but more than that ... he wanted her to want those things too. If she learned to feel confident in her own skin, maybe she could learn to understand his way of life and his desire to live in her light. He'd lived too long in darkness. He wanted everything in his world to be bright and beautiful and illuminated. And to him ... Meaghan embodied all those things.

****

She used the bathroom's amenities and even

managed to wash her hands and face without assistance, much to her delight. The pain in her wrist troubled her but not as much as the thought of posing nude. Standing by the door with a towel wrapped around her body, she could hear David in his studio, preparing his easel and paints and dragging something that sounded like a couch around the room. A scene from the movie Titanic flashed across her mind and she pictured herself posing across a couch wearing nothing but a necklace. She scrunched up her nose but decided that Kate Winslet *had* looked quite beautiful as she posed and the drawing *was* very tasteful. Maybe modelling for David wouldn't be so bad, as long as he kept his cheeky remarks and his hands to himself.

She knew that David was aware of her insecurity but wondered if he would suspect the other reasons she felt reluctant to leave herself completely vulnerable and totally exposed. Would he deduce that she had suspected, and still hadn't ruled out the possibility, that he might be the serial killer? She would be naked and her injury would render her totally defenseless if he attacked her while she was inclined on the couch. But if he was innocent, and she hoped and prayed he was, she worried that her body would betray her, allowing him to see through her defenses and see her physical reactions to his proximity. She couldn't think around him, couldn't breathe. She wanted desperately for him to teach her the art of seduction so she could make love to him with her body, the way that he made love to her with his eyes. Yes, she sensed his eyes on her body whenever they were in the same room and she wished she could find the confidence to tell him to instead use his hands, his mouth and more, so much more. She rested her forehead against the bathroom door, took a deep breath and allowed the towel to drop onto the ground as she grabbed the door knob and prepared herself for whatever might happen next.

"Don't come out!" David called to her as she turned the doorknob. "We have company."

Chapter Twelve

After David had left with his brother Derrick, Meaghan dressed in her previous night's clothes and rushed back to her own apartment. She wasn't sure whether to laugh or cry. She should be happy; she'd dodged a bullet. Why was she disappointed? *Get a grip, Meaghan. Did you really want to parade around naked? What if he became aroused? Would you allow him to make love to you? Is your sexual desire stronger than your desire to catch the killer?*

She covered her face with her hands. *Yes*. Yes, to all those questions. Yes, yes, yes. She splashed cold water on her face, mindful not to dampen her cast and changed into fresh clothes before settling down onto the settee. As it turned out, the *breakfast* that Evan had cooked for her was actually brunch because she had slept most of the morning. The rest of the day dragged on without a word from David.

Dinner was delivered to her bungalow at six o'clock and Evan informed her that Masters David and Derrick were eating out, so Meaghan felt secure in the knowledge that she could safely check out the campus. After eating, she leaned back on the settee and closed her eyes, picturing the campus in her mind and deciding on a desired location. The last murder had been close to the art department so she focused on the corridor near where the body was discovered.

She'd practiced this technique since she first discovered her *talent* as a child in the orphanage. When the other children would leave with adoptive families, she would sometimes follow them in spirit, just to experience—even for a few minutes—the joy of having a family to love and cherish her. Unfortunately, she was spotted a few times and her sudden appearance would freak out the other children. Word got back to the orphanage and the buzz about the weird ghost-girl spread to prospective parents, so, not surprisingly, she was never adopted. Terry became her only friend. He thought her power—as he called it—was cool. Apparently he still thought it was cool because he'd assigned her to the case knowing she could inspect the campus without being in physical danger. As long as her actual body was in a safe environment, she was fine. Her incorporeal self could always come back safely.

Secure in the knowledge that David was away and therefore not a threat, she left her body and headed for the UNI. The University was—not surprisingly—empty. Classes had been cancelled in respect for the victims and the only people that Meaghan could see wandering around the perimeter were the security guards. *Damn. Not again!* This time she spotted David before he noticed her and was able to hide behind a cluster of industrial garbage bins. His presence prevented her from moving freely around the campus. *Another wasted night.*

When he moved on, she returned to her body feeling irritated. His constant presence at the campus reinforced her suspicious that he was somehow involved in the murders. If he wasn't, his clients must be some pretty nasty characters. *What are you up to, David Corel?* She couldn't think when he was around. Well, she did actually do a lot of thinking … thinking about what the next lesson would involve, what it would be like to make love with him, did they have a future together? Meaghan shook her head and sat forward in her seat, reprimanding herself for not seeing the big picture. Instead of fantasizing about love-making, she should be thinking about the case and trying to predict who would be next. *If you don't start concentrating on the job*, she warned herself, *the next victim could be you.*

****

After twice doing the rounds of the campus, David pulled out his mobile phone and called his brother who asked, "Any suspicious characters out tonight?"

"Not a one," David informed him as he walked back to his car. "Except…"

"Except what?"

"I'm sure Meaghan was here. I didn't spot her this time but I felt her presence again."

"Sorry, David, but that isn't possible."

"How can you be so sure? She could have caught a cab."

"Anna and I were bored so we started watching the closed circuit television." Derrick informed him, "Meagan has been sleeping quietly on the couch since you left. She has only just woken up in the last couple of minutes."

A sense of relief washed over him although he couldn't shake the feeling that she had been close enough to touch. Could his desire for her be so intense that he imagined her presence?

"David? Are you still there?"

"What? Oh, sorry. I was lost in thought. I'm heading home now."

David heard another voice in the background. "Wait. Can you hold the line?"

When Derrick returned he had instructions. "Anna just had a vision. She wants you to go back onto the campus and head to the science labs. She said she only caught a flash of a vision but it involved one of the security guards. Go now!"

David flipped his phone shut as he ran. His preternatural speed got him to the science lab in a matter of seconds but it was already too late. As he followed the smell of blood to the lab, he was stopped in his tracks by a security guard who instantly pulled his weapon and pointed it at David's chest. The guard shook violently. The gun unsteady in his hand as he ordered David to "Freeze!"

"Put the gun away," David commanded the nervous guard as he stared deep into the man's eyes.

"I said freeze, arsehole," the guard repeated, obviously impervious to the compulsion. David's brow furrowed in disbelief. His method of persuasion was usually effective, especially on a lone individual. Unless he possessed psychic powers or … *aha*. A pair of broken glasses lay in a smeared puddle of blood near the body. This victim was one of the guards, probably the nervous guy's partner. Blood soaked the back of his shirt and pants. He'd probably slipped in the pool of blood as he ran to help his partner. David stepped toward the terrified man, his hands up in surrender. "I'm not going to hurt you."

"Is that what you said to my partner?" the man argued, his voice quavering. "I've already called the cops. They're on their way, so you just stay right where you are."

"Calm down. I'm not the murderer and I'm not going to hurt you."

David hoped to pacify the man who was sweating profusely and turning ashen in color. He concentrated on the guard's pulse and picked up on the arrhythmia, recognizing the signs of an impending heart attack. When the man suddenly clutched at his chest, his suspicions were proven correct. There was no time to waste. The man needed urgent medical attention but he knew that any sudden movement would cause the man's heart to skip a beat, possibly throwing his sinus rhythm out and his movements were usually anything but slow.

David read the name tag pinned to the guards left shirt pocket and tried to connect with him on a more personal level. "Christopher. You're having a heart attack. I think we should get you to a seat and call for an ambulance."

"Oh, you think that do you?" Chris Glass mumbled. He hunched over, holding his hand to his chest, gasping for air as another pain tore through him. "Aaah."

As Christopher began to fall forward, David knew he could not waste any more time. He lunged, trying to catch the guard before he face-planted onto the tiled floor.

The guard misinterpreted his actions and fired his gun. He kept firing until he ran out of bullets. Then, he lost consciousness.

David felt the sting as the bullet entered his chest followed by the second, third, fourth, fifth and sixth shot. He fell back onto a wooden table which fragmented under his weight, a large section of the wood spearing right through his back and into his chest, narrowly missing his heart. Tempting as it was to try and escape before the authorities arrived, he was trapped, impaled by the largest remaining piece of table. He couldn't risk pulling the stake through as it appeared to be larger at the base and would more than likely rupture his heart on the way through. He couldn't reach back to pull it out as it was longer than his arms. There was no time to call Derrick for help, especially as he could hear the sound of heavy boots signaling that the police were running down the corridor. *Trapped*. There was no way he had the strength to compel all the cops at once and no way of escape. How would he be able to explain how he had survived not only six bullets to his body but also a wooden stake through his chest? There were no other options. It was time to play dead.

Chapter Thirteen

David heard the door of the autopsy drawer open and felt his body being slid out under the harsh light of the mortuary viewing room. He kept his eyes closed as the zipper of the body bag slid down to reveal his cold, lifeless body and heard Derrick tell the medical examiner, "I'd like to have a moment alone with my brother."

"Certainly, Mr Corel. I'll give you as long as you need. And please accept my sincere condolences." His footsteps faded away and the door clicked as he closed it behind him.

"How on earth did you get yourself into this mess?" Derrick asked him.

David used their psychic connection to ask, *Are we alone?* He waited until his brother gave him the "all clear" before sitting up. "This has been one hell of a night." He looked down at his bullet ridden and perforated body and shook his head in disbelief. "I could use a drink."

"You and me both."

So, what do we do now?"

"It seems we have two choices…" Derrick informed him. "We could perform a scene from Frankenstein and I could scream out *he's alive…*"

David frowned his annoyance. "Next option."

"Actually, that was my only idea. You've certainly stuffed up this time, David."

"I hardly think this is my fault. You're the one who ordered me to hurry to the lab. Anna's premonition might have been a bit more specific and warned me that I was rushing to my doom."

"Don't bring this up with Anna," Derrick pulled

up a very uncomfortable looking metal chair and dropped into it. "She feels bad enough without you rubbing it in. Her visions are all over the place lately and the only answer we can come up with is a blocking spell."

A phone rang in the adjoining office and the brothers realized that they were running out of time to develop a strategy. David suggested, "I guess we could use this to our advantage. If the police believe that I was the killer and that they've taken me out of the equation, it gives me the opportunity to do a bit of poking around without having to deal with that bloody nuisance Palmer."

"Okay, that sounds like a plan, but what about your little protégé? How are going to explain your death to her?"

David lay back on his metal tray and shrugged his shoulders. "I'll figure that out while you work on getting me the hell out of here.

****

Meaghan caught a taxi to the police station and hurried to Terry Palmer's office. He had told her on the phone to get there ASAP but had not elaborated on the reason. She suspected that she might be about to be admonished for the very public kiss that David gave her at the murder scene. She braced herself for a severe reprimand but that would have been preferable to the news he relayed. What he told her was a complete shock, one from which she thought she might never recover.

"What do you mean he's dead?" She leaned back against the wall for support fearing her legs may give way.

"I don't know why you're getting so worked up." Terry caught her as her knees buckled and helped maneuver onto the chair. "You knew he might be the killer."

Meaghan looked up into Terry's eyes; her own filled with tears as she tried to find the words to tell him what she was feeling. She shook her head subconsciously, deciding that confessing her love for David would only complicate the case. It was better that she kept her emotions tucked down deep. After a lifetime of keeping her emotions, longings and dreams to herself, it should be easy. She took a deep breath, hoping that the action would steady her voice as she asked, "How did it happen?"

"We got a call from campus security saying that there was a man down in the science lab and when we arrived, we found the dead security guard and Corel shot and get this … apparently staked. A funny co-incidence considering our last conversation." He snorted at his own vampire reference and Meaghan blood boiled. *How dare he joke about David's death?*

"I don't find that remark remotely funny."

"Actually, I think it is, or would be if his death didn't implicate him to the murders." The curve of Terry's mouth turned slowly downward until his lips formed a straight thin line. His eyebrows too, turned downward into a frown and even his tone changed when he retaliated.

"Where were you when all of this was going down? You were supposed to be tailing him."

Meaghan held up her wrist. Her plaster cast revealing what she had yet to inform him.

"I had a bit of an accident the other night."

"Did Corel do this to you?" his face twisted in anger. He slammed his fist onto the desk. "If that bastard wasn't dead, I'd kill him myself."

Meaghan shook her head. "It was a misunderstanding. We had a bit of an argument after the murder outside my art room. He saw blood on my dress and accused me of being connected to the murders. I was worried that I might inadvertently disclose my identity so I tried to leave but he grabbed my wrist…" Meaghan paused, remembering how upset David had been after discovering how seriously hurt she was. He'd fed and bathed her. She felt totally safe in his arms. *Gone.* She would never feel his touch again.

"Probably trying to deflect suspicion from himself…" Terry suspected out loud. "I should never have assigned you to this case. For God's sake, Megs, you can't even stand the sight of blood, which makes your involvement in a murder case bloody ridiculous, excuse the pun. It's my fault. I shouldn't have allowed you to talk me into this. I was concerned that you were too inexperienced to handle this assignment. Judging by your wrist and your piss weak explanation, I guess I was right."

"That's not fair!" *I was doing a great job.* "He had a very strong grip and I was pulling hard to escape."

"Escape?"

"Don't twist my words Terry. You know what I meant. I was trying to avoid having to answer questions that might blow my cover. He is … was, built like a freakin' bodybuilder. Any one of your agents would have been hurt, and as for my problem with blood … you know very well why it affects me the way it does. I think you're mean to throw it in my face."

"Okay, I guess you have a legit excuse but it still poses a problem, especially if you work homicide. But Corel is a different matter. Not all my agents would have become emotionally attached to the suspect."

Terry's words were like a slap to her face. The sting more painful because—deep down—she knew it was true. She *had* been falling in love with David Corel. An unforgivable mistake for an undercover agent. Taking another deep breath, she looked into her boss's eyes and asked, "What happens now?"

"Now you take a couple of weeks off on compo."

"What? No! I can't believe you're taking me off the case?"

"The case is closed. The killer is dead."

"I'm sorry to disagree with you, Terry but I'm still not sure David was the killer."

"David?" Terry laughed, but his stony stare warned her that he was deadly serious and his tone sounded cynical when he added. "Yeah, I guess you would be on a first name basis with your fiancé."

Meaghan stared at him in disbelief. This was a side of Terry that she had never before seen, despite having known him since childhood. He almost sounded jealous.

"What the hell are you talking about?"

Leaning heavily against his desk, he told her. "The same night that Corel broke your wrist"—he pointed to her hand as a subtle reminder—"he informed me that you were his fiancé."

"Why on earth would he say that?" Although the idea was ludicrous, the information pained her. *Had he loved her?*

Knots formed in the muscles of Terry's forearms as he gripped his desk. "I have no idea why he would claim to be engaged to you, unless…"

"Unless what?"

"I imagine that Corel saw me notice you in the crowd. Maybe he was jealous."

"That's a joke." Meaghan laughed for the first time since hearing the terrible news of David's death. "Why on earth would he be jealous? As if there could be anything between us."

"Yeah … as if." Terry stood up and rounded his

desk. He kept his back to her as he told her.

"Well. That's all. I imagine you'll need to pack your bags now that your fiancé has kicked the bucket."

His words were cruel. So unlike the Terry she knew so well.

"I guess so," Meaghan agreed. She hadn't considered the fact that along with losing David, she had lost her accommodation. It surprised her to notice that Terry didn't make an offer to let her stay in his spare room, or even on his couch. When she lived in her old dump, he constantly tried to convince her to move in with him but she treasured her independence and always declined his offers. After waiting a few moments to see if Terry would turn around and face her, she finally gave up and walked to the door. Before she was halfway down the corridor, he called after her.

"I don't want to see you back here until that wrist is healed."

****

Before returning to the Corel mansion, Meaghan checked out the local real estate agents. All the rental properties were well out of her price range, even if she was still collecting the scholarship money. Her mentor was gone, her future uncertain, and her heart shattered into a million pieces. She wondered if she should swallow her pride and ask Terry if she could crash at his place for a few weeks but after the icy reception in his office, she dismissed the idea. Although it was already dark, as the cab turned up the steep driveway, she could see the silhouette of a tall, well-built man standing in front of her cottage. Her heart missed a beat as she leaned forward in her seat. *David*? She didn't care how he managed to cheat death, or even if he was the campus killer, she wanted to run into his arms and cover his face with kisses.

She held the door handle as she strained to get a closer look and was tempted to jump from the moving vehicle until the man stepped forward into the headlights of the cab. *Derrick.* Her stomach lurched as she slumped back into her seat and swallowed the bile that rose from her esophagus. Of course it would be Derrick. There was no possible way David could have survived the injuries that Terry had described. She had hoped to have at least a couple of days to stay on the property to absorb any lingering essence of David before she was forced on, but it seemed like all her hopes were to be dashed in the same day. Derrick's presence meant only one thing. She was about to be evicted. When the cab stopped, he opened her door, gallantly paid the driver and greeted her with the news.

"I'm sorry, Meaghan, but I have some unhappy news."

"I know." She answered, trying to control the tears that burned behind her eyes.

"You know? How could you know?"

Derrick's expression was a mixture of confusion and suspicion and Meaghan instantly realized her mistake. She should not have been privy to such information. Only the police and Derrick knew about last night's events.

"The radio in the cab mentioned that there had been another murder on the campus last night. That makes four now, doesn't it?"

"Five," he informed her, his face still a mask that she couldn't decipher.

Was he suspicious of her excuse or could he be David's partner in crime? When he placed his hand on her shoulder, she knew what he was about to tell her and began to unravel. She couldn't bear to hear the words again. *David is dead.*

"There is no easy way of telling you this, Meaghan. I'm afraid that David was also killed last night."

Meaghan's collapse was less an act and more of a delayed reaction. There was no getting around the reality. David was truly dead. Derrick caught her before she hit the concrete driveway and carried her into the cottage, laying her on the couch. He walked to the kitchen and brought back a glass of water, helping to raise her up to a seated position before offering her the drink. Her hand shook as she lifted the glass to her mouth and swallowed some of the cool water. She thanked him and asked for the details, despite already knowing the fundamentals.

"I'm not exactly sure," Derrick told her. "He was at the campus last night, picking up some supplies for your next art class and it appears as though a security mistook him for the killer and shot him."

"I heard that the victim was in the science labs. What would David be doing there?"

"I imagine that he heard something that drew him there." Derrick shrugged his broad shoulders. "He was probably trying to help."

"Yes." Meaghan nodded, although she suspected that if David had indeed been the killer, his brother may have been involved and therefore withholding information. She put the glass down on the coffee table and rose to her feet. Whether David was a hero or a killer, it no longer mattered. He was gone, torn from her life just as they were beginning a relationship.

"I'm so sorry for your loss, Derrick. I'll be packed and ready to leave as soon as possible."

Derrick's next statement took her completely by surprise. "Anna and I want you to stay."

"That wouldn't be right Derrick. I appreciate your offer but, without David, there is no scholarship. You shouldn't feel obliged to—"

"David was very taken with you." He told her. "And he would want you to stay and continue your work. The scholarship is part of a foundation that David and I ran together so his death makes no difference to the contract, other than we need to find you a replacement teacher."

"No one could replace David." The words came out before Meaghan had time to think but she was relieved to see Derrick smile as he nodded in agreement.

"He *was* one of a kind. But, you need a mentor so I shall organize it after your wrist has time to heal." He had begun walking to the door where he turned and asked, "If you wouldn't mind, I'd prefer if you didn't use the studio for a few days. It would be a bit upsetting for us to hear someone moving around down there. I understand that David set you up with a small studio in here?"

"Yes, thank you. And of course I understand and respect your wishes. It would be a bit strange for all of us."

She wasn't sure if she could ever go back to David's studio anyway. There would be too many painful memories. She pictured him reclining half naked on his bed, his cheeky grin teasing her. Tempting her. The image quickly disintegrated into a scene of a funeral home. David inside a mahogany coffin. A reminder of what was to come. *How would she be able to hold it together for the funeral?* Terry and the others would not understand the tears that would be sure to flow during the ceremony but she had to attend, regardless of the consequences.

"Oh, Derrick. I hate to ask but I was wondering when you plan on having the funeral?"

Derrick approached her and gently rested his

hands on her shoulders. "I'm sorry, Meaghan. As per the instructions in David's will, we had him cremated this afternoon. His ashes are already interred in the back garden, by the large frangipani. He didn't want a service and requested that no death notice be posted. Considering the circumstances and David's celebrity, we thought we should honor his wishes before the press descended on our home or the funeral parlor. Over the course of David's life, we've found the paparazzi to be relentless in their endeavors to take incriminating photos. He had a bit of a playboy reputation as I'm sure you'd know." He lightly flicked the underside of her chin and smiled, although she suspected he was in as much emotional pain as she was. "I'll have a tray sent to you and then I think we should all probably have an early night."

As hard as it was, Meaghan returned the smile and nodded, although she had no appetite. David was gone and there was nothing she could do to bring him back. She'd wasted precious time hanging on to her virginity when, all the while, she could have been making love with David. Now she suspected that she would die a virgin. How could any man compare to him either physically or romantically? He had brought her to the brink of womanhood and left her wanting. Murderer or not, she had come to a painfully clear understanding. She loved him.

Chapter Fourteen

David observed the lonely silhouette from the safety of his darkened room. The tinted windows and heavy drapes blocked most of the sun's rays providing sufficient cover from the midday sun to peek outside. He watched her stroll down the path and stop at the large frangipani where his ashes had been interred. At least she believed they were there. She was wearing jeans and although he had never seen her in anything besides dresses, he could recognize her anywhere by the sway of her hips. She had a way of walking that was truly mesmerizing, like watching the pendulum of a grandfather clock or a magician's watch. He was under her spell. She didn't even appear to be aware of her sexual allure or the fact that she almost glowed with ethereal beauty. This new look fascinated and aroused him.

Her skin-tight denim jeans hugged her body, accentuating every curve and the white t-shirt molded around her firm breasts. Her pale blonde hair hung wild, free from the childish braids but she still looked younger than her age. *Cradle snatcher.* He chuckled to himself. If only she hadn't replaced her usual sandals with a pair of runners, the new look would have met with his approval. There was something sexy about the daisy sandals. Maybe it was the way they drew attention to her cute little toes or the nails that were always painted with pink polish.

She bent down, her back to him as she placed something on the ground beside his plaque. Derrick had managed to grease a few palms and the memorial plate and receptacle had been constructed and put in place within hours of his *death*. It had been harder to convince the forensic pathologist that he had performed an autopsy. "That man's mind is like a steel trap," Derrick had told David. "I was exhausted by the time I left."

Once released from the morgue, David's body had been taken to a crematorium where the director had been compelled to believe that he had disposed of David's corpse and he had even supplied Derrick with an urn. The director would later find a substantial check in his jacket pocket, to cover his costs.

David hated deceiving Meaghan this way but circumstances had forced his hand. How else could he have explained surviving six bullets to his chest and a stake almost puncturing his heart? Even if surviving such terrible wounds was possible, the paramedic and later the medical examiner would have been unable to detect a heartbeat. Necessity had influenced his decision to fake his death and besides, Meaghan would be safer without him. He had physically hurt her and he knew that if he continued to stay in her company, he could inadvertently draw the killer to her. Worse still, if she *was* somehow involved in the murders, he would be forced to take action to stop her and the result would be fatal. Probably for both of them. If he was forced to kill her he would end his own life immediately after.

But … no. *Impossible.* There was no way she could be responsible for the deaths of those apparently innocent victims. *How could she be a cold-blooded killer?* He watched her as she sat on the ground, crying over his ashes and delicately touching the plaque, tracing her fingers over his embossed name and giving every indication that she had loved him. Hell, she had said as much. *Okay, she may have been sedated at the time but people are usually very open and honest while under the influence of drugs or alcohol.* If only he could find a way to tell her that he loved her too.

****

The vibration in her pocket warned her that her phone was about to ring, so Meaghan answered it before it could break the silence of the solemn moment.

"Hey, Meaghan. I hear you've broken your hand. Bummer."

Meaghan recognized the voice immediately although she hadn't spoken with the caller for weeks. She wiped her eyes with her handkerchief before responding, "Hi, Lilith."

"When are you coming back to class? I hear that your mentor is dead. Bad luck that. He was hotter than Hades. Hahaha, I just realized how funny that was, guess he's in Hades now."

Meaghan held her finger over the hang up icon but changed her mind. "What do you want, Lilith?"

"So-o-r-ry. I guess someone's a bit sensitive now that she's not getting it anymore."

"David Corel and I had a professional relationship and nothing more, so I would appreciate it if you keep your remarks to yourself."

"Oh. I thought that…"

"Well you thought wrong."

"So you're still suffering from Virginitis?"

"If that's the only reason you called then—" Meaghan prepared to hang up when she heard Lilith shout out an apology.

"I'm sorry, Meaghan. I guess I'm on still on a high. I've been up all night with some friends who brought some really good shit. I'll probably be up for a week. Damn girl, you shoulda been there. Anyway, I didn't mean nothing by it, honest. I just thought you might need a bit of cheering up and my friends and me are having a rave on the oval behind the campus tonight. Wanna come? There should be some good shit, and even a keg."

"Thanks, but I'm not in the mood for a party and, as I've told you many times before … I don't do drugs and neither should you if you are serious about your health and your degree. You can hardly produce your best work if you're stoned."

"Get real," Lilith argued, her laugh reminded Meaghan of a witch's cackle. "Name one great artist who wasn't stoned off his face when he produced his best work. Maybe if you loosened up a bit, you might get laid."

Meaghan hung up the phone without responding and began walking back towards her cottage. Lilith's words hurt deeply. Not the drug reference as she had no intention of ever taking drugs, but the suggestion that she was tightly wound hit a nerve. Anxiety about sex and nudity that prevented her from having a real relationship with David and now, it was too late. She thought about the insensitivity of holding a rave at the campus so soon after the recent deaths and shook her head in disgust. What type of person would attend a party so soon after the deaths? Especially so close to where a murders were committed. The answer hit her like a ton of bricks, stopping her in her tracks. *The murderer would.*

****

David watched Meaghan answer her phone and realized that whoever called had said something to distress her. When she rushed back to her cottage, he'd longed to go after her and offer her comfort but … he was dead. Actually, he had been dead for over a century but there was no way she could know that unless he stuffed up and gave her reason to suspect that he was a vampire.

He considered the turn his life had taken. Until now, he had been able to pass as a human for the most part. He could be seen in the daytime as long as he avoided direct sunlight or remained in a windowless room. He neither slept in a coffin nor underground—unless he was badly injured—and his blood was supplied by courier from the blood bank and drunk from expensive wine glasses. This recent chain of events had forced him to live like the stereotypical vampire, existing in the shadows, hiding from humans like a monster, a killer. Of course his family and his fellow vampires would be privy to the truth but he couldn't risk telling Meaghan and driving her away. None of the scenarios he played in his head offered him any comfort or hope. If she chose to be with him, he would be condemning her to a half-life spent in the shadows. On the other hand, if she rejected him, his cover would be blown and he would be forced to leave town forever or worse still, he would be playing into the hands of a killer. No. It was better for both of them if she believed he was dead.

****

Meaghan settled herself down on her couch and mentally prepared herself for another out of body experience. She knew that she would be forced to camouflage herself in the dense vegetation behind the campus. The last thing she needed was for some "pot head" at the rave to see her and broadcast that the University had a ghost. It was hard enough when David managed to magically appear on her previous stakeouts and almost blow her cover. She figured that if he hadn't been the killer, he must have had some type of power or gift. Possibly one like hers? Now she would never know.

Terry was convinced that the case was closed. Sure that David Corel was the killer but she wasn't so sure. She decided to go with her gut instinct, sure that there would be another victim. She would prove that David was innocent and that she *was* detective material.

Taking a deep breath, she concentrated on the task at hand. This time she had to be precise, she couldn't just concentrate on the campus in general. She had to focus on the grounds behind the main building. It was difficult remembering. Were there bushes or other structures that would provide adequate cover? Previous attempts had failed to take her to the exact spot she needed to be and recently, while dreaming, she had found herself in the graveyard. She had no intention of repeating that experience. *Wildflowers.* Yes, she remembered seeing wildflowers growing near a cluster of bushes behind the oval. Keeping the image in her mind, she concentrated on their location and size as she allowed her spiritual self to float free of her body.

Within seconds, she arrived at the oval, horrified but not really surprised to find that she had been deceived. No rave. No party. Only a group of people surrounding another individual who was kneeling in the long grass. The group, who she recognized by their attire as being the same figures she had encountered at the cemetery, were chanting and burning candles. The air heavy with the scent of black pepper and bergamot, a fragrance she recognized as an ingredient in a perfume she had once tried. It was not to her taste ... heady and too strong for her liking. As in the cemetery encounter, they all wore hooded robes but one member in particular stood out in the crowd. There was something malevolent about this character, besides the fact that he or she was holding a silver chalice under the chin of the kneeling woman. The woman was naked, gagged, and hog-tied. Her wrists and feet bound behind her. Despite the gag, it was obvious that she was sobbing and pleading with her captors. They paid her no mind, high either on drugs or possibly the scent from the candles. The heavy fragrance was slightly nauseating.

The ring leader—who Meaghan deduced by her height and outline to be a woman—raised her hand, revealing a large curved knife. The naked woman's eyes widened in fear. Meaghan watched in horror, unable to scream out for them to stop. Her incorporeal body useless against the flesh and blood killers. Instinct told her to look away but it was her duty to report the scene in graphic detail. She was forced to watch as one of the hooded worshippers grabbed the victim's hair, pulling it back to expose the victim's throat. With the knife in her left hand the Priestess paused for a moment, her arm raised diagonally across her body and her hand hovering above her right shoulder as she said something in Latin before striking.

The blade cut through the victim's throat, opening her neck from left to right. Voices squealed in delight. Meaghan gagged. The priestess held the cup under the woman's chin to catch the blood as it gushed from the deep slash. The blood quickly filled the goblet, much to the delight and cheers of the others. When the cup was full, the body was discarded like an animal carcass, no longer of any use to the group and soon forgotten as they began to strip off their cloaks and dance naked around the fire. Half of the contents of the cup were poured into a separate, more elaborate goblet studded with jewels and placed on a makeshift altar. Beneath the velvet covering, Meaghan could see a wooden packing crate. The contents of the first goblet then mixed with a liquid taken from the pocket of the killer. Meaghan guessed it was likely to have been a hallucinogenic or narcotic of some description. As they passed the goblet from one member of the group to another, they drank the blood and licked their lips with relish. Meaghan's stomach heaved. She fought the urge to turn away. *Can't do this*. It was bad enough watching the psychos kill the poor woman, now she was forced to watch them drink her blood. The smell of the blood reached her and she gagged, sickened by the stench of the coppery liquid. *Stay strong. Think of something else.*

She'd seen many murder victims but never seen an actual murder and it was something she never wanted to experience again. *That poor woman. How terrified she must have been.* The revelers, obviously high on adrenaline and the drug-laced blood, danced themselves into frenzy, spinning and squealing in delight. They soared higher and higher on whatever the hell they had ingested, danced around the body and finally, paired up to copulate. Their victory celebrated in a drug fueled orgy. Despite the lateness of the hour, the full moon illuminated the naked bodies as they writhed in the long grass, their moans and grunts made them sound more like animals than humans. Finished with one partner, they moved on to another, sometimes same sexual orientation, other times multiple lovers, but never appearing to be satisfied. Meaghan tried to understand the significance of the ritual but came up cold. She wondered why she'd ever felt embarrassed to look at David. His body was magnificent while this strange group were all manner of weird shapes, none especially attractive. *Who are these people?*

A loud roar pierced the air and the orgy immediately broke up, the revelers breaking apart to resume their kneeling positions. Submissives waiting for their dominatrix's instructions. A shadow arose from the center of the fire and a form began to take shape. The silhouette huge and cumbersome, like a beast or what Meaghan perceived a demon to look like. The head worshipper snatched up the ornamental goblet, offering it with both hands, her naked body facing in Meaghan's direction. Although the mist creature obscured her vision, there was something familiar about the woman's face that Meaghan could not quite recognize. *A student perhaps?* She had definitely seen her before, possibly in the corridors of the campus. Tattoos covered the woman's arms, snaking up from her wrists to her shoulders then continuing across her chest. *This could be a form of identification.* Although she imagined it was not unique, the design was probably uncommon. *If only I could carry a camera or phone.* It was a shame that she couldn't get close enough to get a better look at the design but she couldn't risk detection. To be honest with herself, she didn't want to get closer. The thought terrified her. The Academy didn't exactly train her for dealing with demons or blood. *So much blood.*

The incorporeal monster's shape quivered for a short time over the sacrificial cup, sniffed the blood, threw his horned head back, and bellowed in anger. Worshippers dropped face down on the ground wailing. Their offering had been rejected. The shadow monster roared again and they held their hands against their ears to block out the deafening noise. Meaghan blocked her own ears as—despite being incorporeal—she too felt the throbbing of her eardrums as the thunderous roar reverberated through the campus, shaking the foundations. She watched as it grew in size, hovering over the group like a giant fanged storm cloud, threatening to rain down vengeance. With a final resounding bellow, it disappeared in a whirlwind of dark smoke that wrapped around the group. The pungent aroma of sulfur wafted through the air. The worshipers coughed and spluttered as they covered their bodies with their hooded capes.

Meaghan was able to hear a few comments bandied around to indicate that her deduction had been correct.

"Why didn't the spell work?"

They had evidently made a mistake. It soon became clear when another goth elaborated.

"Master said that the victim was unclean. He sure looked pissed. We'd better not make that mistake again. I'm afraid of what he'll do to us if we make him unhappy."

So, the "master was unhappy." She, on the other hand was very happy. There was no way she wanted *whatever the hell that was* to become corporeal. Even the moon seemed to be afraid because it hid behind heavy clouds, blanketing the area in darkness. Flashes of light streaked the sky followed by the crack of thunder. An icy wind lashed Meaghan's face. Time to return to her body. She had seen enough to understand that the murders had been ritual killings and more than enough to make her blood run cold. She would take this new information to Terry and convince him that David had nothing to do with the murders. *Maybe she would be reinstated to the case?* The only problem was … would Terry believe her?

Chapter Fifteen

David met up with his brother in the kitchen of the main house to discuss their plans. Now that he was *officially* dead, it would be difficult for him to make the rounds of the campus without upsetting the already jumpy replacement security guards. While they were deliberating over their options, they were joined by Anna who was finishing a phone conversation. "There's been another murder."

David stared at her in disbelief. "You've got to be kidding me. I don't understand. Why aren't your visions helping us?"

Derrick interceded on his wife's behalf. "Give her a break, David. She's new to this game."

Anna smiled but David could tell that his remark had offended.

"Sorry, Anna. I guess being dead has made me cranky."

"Being newly dead myself, I can understand your dilemma. Anyway, I just got off the phone to Sofie and between us, we've worked it out."

"Worked what out?"

"Well, as you know, Sofie and I should have been able to predict the murders and send you guys there *before* they happened. Between us, we should have had more than enough power and ability, so we've come to the conclusion that we are being blocked by another witch, maybe many."

"A coven of witches?" David scratched his head. The last coven had been killed off by Torke, a rogue vampire who had also killed Anna's mother. Sophie had survived the attack and she was training Anna on how to use her inherited skills. "I didn't know a new coven had moved in."

"Neither did Sofie, but that's the only explanation we can think of. Also, a friend of mine who works down at the police station told me that the latest victim was drained of blood. Her throat was cut left to right and as far as they can tell, from the front."

"That would indicate a left handed killer." David rubbed his chin. "It's possible for someone to cut left to right with their right hand but the movement would be awkward. Their wrist would be forced into a strange angle which would detract from the power of the strike."

His eyebrows rose. A grin stretched his lips.

Anna looked first to her husband who shrugged his shoulders and then back to David.

"This makes you happy because?"

"Because I broke Meaghan's right hand."

"Oh, yes. That makes perfect sense to me." Derrick told his wife in answer to her puzzled expression.

"Meaghan is right handed. I don't believe she killed tonight or any other night."

He turned and hurried to the home office. "Are the closed circuit screens up?"

"Yes, why?" Derrick called after his brother who was already at his desk checking the computer screens. Meaghan appeared to be asleep on the sofa. Her head lay back against the headrest, her mouth slightly agape, her eyes closed. As he watched his sleeping beauty, happy in the belief that she was innocent of the crimes, David failed to notice his brother come up behind him. "She's a snorer."

"I know," David told him, "but it's barely a snore … more like a purr."

"Like a kitten," Anna interjected as she studied the screen.

"That's what I thought." David smiled at his sister-in-law. "I think it's cute."

"He's got it bad." Derrick teased, elbowing his wife in the ribs. "When you think snoring is cute, you must be in love."

"And what does it mean when you think snoring is irritatingly loud?" Anna asked as she rubbed her ribs in mock reaction.

"It means the honeymoon is over," David answered for him with a chuckle.

Movement drew their attention back to the screen so Derrick took the opportunity to change the subject. "She's up and moving around."

"I'll let Evan know that she'll be ready for her dinner," Anna volunteered but David stopped her before she reached the door.

"Don't bother. I'll do it."

Derrick grabbed his arm. "What do you plan on doing, David?" He knew his brother well enough to suspect his next move. "You can't risk Meaghan finding out that your death was a hoax. At least not until we find the real killer."

"I hate to rub salt into the wound," Anna added, "but unless you plan on revealing yourself as a vampire, I can't see any way of resurrecting you."

David opened his mouth to argue but hesitated. Anna was right.

"I'll leave the tray at the door and disappear, I promise. I just want to be close to her." He left the room before they had a chance to argue but heard his brother's observation. "He does have it bad."

****

Meaghan answered the knock on her front door and discovered the covered tray of food on her porch. David watched her turn her head left to right. She shrugged her shoulders, called out a "Thank you, Evan," and took the tray inside to eat. He moved around to the back of the house to a spot where he knew the trees would conceal him from view. It was taking a big risk but he had no choice. He desperately needed to be close to her, to smell her fragrance. It pained him to think that he would not be able to help her with her food. Her break was still fresh and he knew that using her right hand would be uncomfortable. Silently, he cursed himself for not having thought to cut up the food before leaving the tray, but realized that hindsight is twenty-twenty and there was nothing he could do now to rectify the problem.

When Meaghan slid open the sliding door and took her tray out to the porch to enjoy eating her meal on the patio, he smiled in satisfaction. He was close enough that he could almost touch her and she would be none the wiser. But the sweet taste of victory soured in his mouth when he watched the love of his life pick up the knife with her left hand and cut the meat with the precision of a surgeon. She wasn't right handed after all, she was ambidextrous. *Why didn't she tell me?* Why had she led him to believe that she was helpless with her broken wrist? *What else was she keeping from him?*

David stepped back into the shadows and made his way back to the main house, confident in the belief that he'd gone unseen but, had he stayed a while longer, he would have seen Meaghan's head snap up, her attention drawn to something beyond the terrace.

****

Meaghan picked up her tray and hurried into the house, locking the sliding door behind her. She'd felt the presence of something malevolent, something that wished her harm. Even more confusing, she could sense another force, that while equally dark, its aura had tinges of conflicting colors. This troubled her. Since moving onto the estate, her ability to pick up the colors in auras had proved increasingly difficult. Sure, she could easily see the colors but they conflicted both with the personality of the people and also the color itself.

Meaghan shook her head. Since the day she began to see auras, the ability had never let her down and now she found herself doubting her own assessments. She turned to face the large mirror that hung on the wall in the hall and observed her own reflection. As expected, her aura was muddy brown, signifying her self-doubt. Lately, the only time her aura glowed pink was when she imagined herself in the arms of David. Now, she suspected the pink would never return. Her life, as well as her aura, would be forever dull and void of any passion. *Oh, David.* His aura was the strangest of all his family and they were indeed a weird mob. A rainbow of colors painted David's black aura with streaks of gold, orange and green confirming Meaghan's intuition that with David, what you see is what you get.

He was creative, gregarious, charming and comfortable being the center of attention. The darkness troubled her. It was usually associated with evil and negativity, which was strange because none of those traits appeared in his nature. Anna, who wasn't a blood relative, had the same darkness about her as her husband and brother-in-law. Not black as such, but there was definitely a tinge of danger in her purple hue. Meaghan flopped down on the couch and considered the significance of Anna's colors. On the few fleeting occasions that they had met, Anna gave the impression that—like herself—she was a bit of a loner who probably only had a couple of real friends. Purple in her aura suggested that she probably had psychic abilities and also that she may have had a troubled love life before meeting her husband.

Derrick's aura was as dark as David's although it was streaked with silver lights, signifying a talent for teaching which explained why his Karate Dojo was reputed to be packed to the rafters with students. She'd done some research on the family and discovered that Anna's father had part owned the health club and she inherited his share after the death, being the only surviving family member. Anna and Derrick were only recently married after a whirlwind romance and since she only saw them on occasion, Meaghan assumed that the honeymoon was ongoing.

Jealousy shot an arrow into her heart and she instantly felt ashamed. Why shouldn't they be happy? Everyone deserves happiness don't they? *Everyone except you it seems*, she decided as she leaned back into the comfortable sofa cushions to wallow in self-pity. She sighed. Twenty-four hours ago she had been on the verge of striping naked and posing for David, knowing full well that—considering his passionate nature—he would attempt to seduce her. Why had she taken so long to make the decision? Their mutual attraction was palpable, sensual, and completely irresistible but somehow she had found the strength to resist. Once again her self-doubt had brought her undone.

Tears burned the backs of her eyes so she closed them, hoping to block out the pain and temper the regret that ate at her thoughts like a disease. David was gone … lost to her forever. She would never again feel the warmth of his touch on her skin, blush at his playfully naughty mind games or experience the joy of finally making love with him. While her thoughts focused completely on David, she barely noticed as her spirit left her body and drifted off into the ether.

****

David lay on his bed in the darkness of his bedroom. He had wanted desperately to venture to the studio and finish his latest piece of work but he knew he couldn't risk the chance of running into Meaghan. Derrick would have conveyed the message to her about avoiding the studio until further notice. However Meaghan had proven to be inquisitive. She may try to snoop around. *What secrets are you keeping, kitten?*

He should have been lingering in the shadows of the campus buildings looking for clues on the killer except he had lost all desire to leave his room or even dress for that matter. It all seemed pointless. He'd finally found the woman of his dreams. More beautiful than he imagined, seemingly purer of heart and body than he had ever hoped to find and… she was probably a serial killer. *How could I have been so blind?*

Since becoming a vampire, he had learned to fine tune his ability to judge body language and, usually, his mind reading skills were spot on. Except when it came to Meaghan. The memory of watching her skillfully slice through her meal using her left hand sent a shiver down his spine as he realized she could easily have switched the murder weapon to her other hand. Something puzzled him. The first two victims who were strangled. Meaghan may be deceptively strong but was she strong enough to strangle two women who were of equal size to her? Crossing his arms behind his head, David lay back on his bed, staring at the ceiling and contemplated his next move. *I should probably put on some clothes and head to the campus in case Meaghan is already there. I might…*

A wisp of a breeze brushed over his legs, floated there for a moment and then settled on his genitals. At first, he relaxed and closed his eyes, enjoying the light touch on his bare flesh as the draft of air teased his flesh until his balls prickled with goose bumps and his shaft rose to the occasion. As the pressure around his cock increased, he gasped. His eyes flew open. This was definitely not a dream. A figure took shape at the foot of the bed and although it stayed incorporeal, he recognized her at once. He tried to rise and opened his mouth to protest but the apparition shook her head. She touched her finger to her lips to indicate for him not to talk while she used her left hand to fondle his genitalia. Her touch was featherlight, almost surreal while she held his cock firmly but gently in the palm of her hand. Her movements slowly pumped him, teased his skin, her mouth hovering over the tip. He watched her lick her lips and realizing her intention, he reached for her, his hands passing through the ethereal mist and grasping at air.

She pouted, shaking her head in disapproval while she continued to stroke his hardening erection. He gasped and lay back on the bed, afraid that the fantasy would end before completion. When she extended her tongue, he held his breath, hoping that his fantasy woman would not be as shy as the real Meaghan. He was not disappointed. A bead of seed formed on the tip of his erection in anticipation of her mouth and she licked it up with a deft flick of her tongue, leaving him quivering and rock hard. He groaned as she took him into her mouth, tasting him, pumping him, driving him insane with desire. It was more than he could bear. He felt his orgasm building, his cock throbbing in anticipation of the release he was desperate to experience. Unconsciously, he reached for her again, needing to hold her while he came in her mouth. The moment his hands came close to her face, the apparition faded from sight, leaving him alone, bewildered, and extremely disappointed. *Idiot!*

****

Meaghan came back to her corporeal body with an emotional thud. For the first time in her memory, her spiritual identity had left her body unbidden and located a *person* rather than a place. This was the least of her worries. Not only was David still alive, her alter ego had actually seduced him and performed oral sex. *What is happening?* She had no control over her actions as she implemented the deliberately suggestive directions from "lesson two" in David's naughty instruction manual.

Covering her face with her hands, she groaned her embarrassment and wondered how long it would be before David teased her about her indiscretion. *Oh, God!* He would know her secret, realize that she had the capacity to leave her body and explore parts unknown. *Parts unknown.* She shuddered when her concentration drew her back to David's bedroom. At least she presumed it was his bedroom having never been there before. Days ago, she could barely bring herself to look at his naked body. Tonight her incorporeal personality found the courage to put her mouth where her eyes refused to go. She could still taste him despite her body never leaving the room. She remembered how he had reached for her, unaware that she was only there in spirit and how she had pulled her spirit back to her body before he had achieved orgasm. The involuntary action had served a purpose. She hoped that he had felt as frustrated as she had been on the day he left her at her easel, her body over sensitized, her mind racing with notions of naked flesh and writhing bodies.

She covered her face with her hands. Believing it to be a dream, she'd allowed herself to act with wanton abandon. There would be no consequences. But she was wrong. As she berated herself for her actions, reality sunk in. *David is alive? How is that even possible?* Terry had informed her that David had been shot six times and fell heavily onto a bench, impaling himself on a piece of broken timber. Derrick had removed the body from the morgue and buried the cremated remains in the garden. She had seen the plaque with her own eyes but, then again, she had also seen him in the flesh and very animated in his bedroom. *Maybe it was a dream? But, it seemed so real.* Terry's taunt about David being a vampire suddenly sounded disarmingly credible and Meaghan realized that, despite the incredible notion, it was the only possible explanation. It all added up. The dark aura, the windowless rooms, and the superhuman strength. He had broken her wrist with hardly more than a squeeze and he was only trying to hold her. She imagined what damage he could do if he were really angry and shuddered at the thought. *She knew his secret. He knew her secret.*

The clap of thunder outside her window made her jump. A feeling of foreboding warned her. It was time to leave. Throwing her belongings into her bags, Meaghan failed to notice the blur of moment as David entered her bedroom. When she turned to grab her handbag, she found herself almost nose to nose with him, the shock sending her reeling.

"What are you doing here?"

David stared into her terrified eyes. "I would have thought 'David, you're alive' would have been your first reaction." He motioned to her bags. "It looks like you're in a hurry to go somewhere."

"I *am* surprised, of course I am, it's just that—"

"Spare me the bullshit, Meaghan!"

The storm outside intensified. Lightning flashed, illuminating the room seconds before the thunder boomed over their heads.

"I don't know how you did it, but you're not going anywhere until you tell me." His voice hummed with power, his upper lip curled baring glistening fangs.

She gasped and took a step back, colliding with

the edge of the bed. Her legs lost their strength, and she dropped down onto the mattress. *He really is a vampire.*

"Before I tell you *my* story, I want to know how you're still alive. Are you even human?"

David's expression softened. He looked away, as if her words had hit a cord. "No, I guess I'm not human, not anymore. I'm higher on the food chain than a human. I am what the movies describe as a *creature of the night.*"

"If this is some kind of joke … I'm not laughing." she edged along the bed, putting distance between them. "You believe that you are a vampire?" *I think I believe you.*

In a heartbeat, he was on her, his fangs exposed as he grasped her shoulders, his mouth close to her face. "Does this convince you?"

Meaghan nodded. Despite her mind arguing the existence of vampires, her heart knew it to be the truth. She wanted to scream but who would come to her aid? If David *was* a vampire, it was likely that his house was full of them. "So, wh-hat now? Are you going to kill me?"

"It depends," he answered, still holding her by the shoulders.

She trembled at his touch. Terrified, anxious, aroused.

"Should I?"

"Don't be so cryptic, David. Did you ask your other victims if they should die?"

"I only kill people who deserve to die … killers, pedophiles, rapists and the like." He dropped his hands from her shoulders. "I'm going to ask you a question and I want an honest answer," he told her. "Did you kill those students?"

"No! I thought *you* did."

"Then why do I find myself constantly bumping

into you at the murder scenes?"

"I could ask you the same question."

"Touché." He sat beside her on the bed. They sat silently for a moment before David spoke. "Let's say that I believe you. How were you able to move around the campus at night and more importantly, how were you able to come to me tonight without even knowing I was still alive?"

Meaghan shrugged. "Since I was very little, I dreamed of leaving the orphanage and finding a real home. I would lie on my cot and picture myself leaving with an adopted child, going to their new home, playing with their new siblings. Then, one day, I realized that I was actually there, at one of the homes, not in the real sense obviously, just spiritually. One of the kids freaked out and my reputation of being a ghost girl was established. The kids still in the orphanage gave me a wide birth and even the staff avoided me. Needless to say, I never got adopted."

"Kids can be cruel." David wriggled his fingers between hers, holding her hand as she continued her story.

"Anyway, I practiced my skill until I could picture a place and go there. I concentrated on the photos provided to the orphans or places where I had previously visited on outings. Eventually I also learned how to be stealthier so I wouldn't be seen. I haven't been discovered … until you came along." She scowled. "Which leads me to my question. Why were you at the murder scenes?"

"In a minute," he argued, lowering his chin to face her. "First, I want to know how you were able to come to my room. You said that it was necessary for you to picture a place to be able to astral travel there."

Meaghan nodded in agreement.

"How did you know where my bedroom was and how did you know I was there, or even alive for that matter?"

Meaghan stared at her shoes, struggling to find an answer that wouldn't get her into more trouble. In truth, she didn't have an explanation.

"I don't know how I did it." She kept her eyes down as she continued. "I was … missing you. I was thinking about what little time we had together and the opportunities we missed because of my inexperience and inhibitions. Next thing I knew, I was watching myself acting out your fantasy and I had no control over what my incorporeal self was doing."

David raised one eyebrow. "Really, no control you say? For someone so 'out of control' you certainly had everything in hand … literally."

Meaghan felt the heat spread from her cheeks, down her throat and creep over her breasts and by David's lustful, wide-eyed expression, he'd noticed it too. He reached forward and with his thumb and forefinger, unbuttoned the first few buttons of her blouse tracing his fingers over the flushed skin between her breasts.

"I seem to remember that you promised to pose for me."

Meaghan allowed him to remove her blouse completely, exposing the lacy pink bra that seemed to be holding David's attention, before reminding herself that she still had unanswered questions of her own.

"Wait a minute buster. I've told you why *I* was there. Why were you there?"

"Spoil sport." Cheeky David reared his naughty head. "Okay, if we are going to play truth or dare, *first*. I, reluctantly choose truth."

Meaghan realized the significance of the word

first, squirmed on the bed until his next words caught her attention and brought her mind back to reality.

"As you know, Derrick and I are C.E.O s of a large company—"

"No whitewashing. We're past that. I want the whole story and don't leave anything out."

"Okay, fine, we are the co-leaders of a coven of vampires. Anyway, Anna foretold a series of murders at the campus and, because of my background in art, I was elected to survey the area and detect the killer. Unfortunately, her visions have been blocked by some supernatural force—we suspect witches—and I've been too late on each occasion. It's become increasingly frustrating and on the last occasion, rather painful."

"How did you survive the shooting? Or the staking for that matter?"

"Bullets can slow us down but not for long. The stake, on the other hand, came disturbingly close to my heart. Close enough to stop me in my tracks. I couldn't use mind control on everyone present as there were too many to influence and my injuries would have been fatal to a human. Besides, the paramedic would have been unable to detect a heartbeat. Dying seemed like the most logical thing to do. Now I'm off the suspect list and free to find the real killer."

"Who you suspected was me?"

David nodded. "I didn't want to believe it but you must admit that you kept turning up at the crime scenes and you had blood on your dress. Not to mention that after I broke your wrist, the killer changed hands. Tonight, when I saw you cut up your food with your left hand, it gave me cause for concern."

"You were watching me?"

"Being dead is boring." He shrugged. "And I wanted to be close to you." He unbuttoned his own shirt, threw it on the floor and smiled when he noticed Meaghan's eyes widen in response. She tried to keep her mind on the case but David was proving to be a big distraction, especially when he reached behind her and unhooked her bra. She forced herself to keep her arms by her sides although they itched to fly up and cover her breasts. *Not this time, Meaghan. Don't blow this second chance.*

"While you were watching me, did you notice anyone else outside?"

David dropped the bra and edged forward but hesitated. "Come to think of it, I did feel something." He wrinkled his nose. "I'm ashamed to admit that I suspected the dark vibe was an indication of your guilt." He rose from the bed and began to unzip his pants.

"Whoa. What are you doing?" Meaghan turned her head away when the pants slipped to the floor, revealing a spectacular erection and no sign of underwear. "I thought we were having a serious discussion about the murders?"

"We *are* kitten." He eased her back onto the bed, slid her jeans down her thighs, and threw them across the room, returning his concentration to the elastic of her panties. He hooked his fingers into the elastic and eased them off, smiling his pleasure when she bent her knees and lifted her bottom to facilitate him in his quest. When he maneuvered himself between her legs, she gasped and her voice quivered as she asked, "Don't you even want to know why I have been tracking the killer?"

David slid his hands over her thighs, tracing the contours of her hips, her waist and finally resting on her breasts. "Of course I do…" He told her. "Later." The words had barely left his lips when his mouth settled over her left nipple, drawing the firm peak into his warm mouth while he squeezed her breasts with his hands.

"If you're a vampire, how can your skin be so warm…" she asked as her head fell back in a gasp.

"I fed on the way over," he mumbled, without lifting his mouth from her chest.

****

David silenced her next question with a kiss. Her mouth melted into his and he could feel her body becoming pliant beneath him despite her previous inhibitions. Her knees parted to allow him access, and he kept his lips pressed firmly against hers while he subtly eased his right hand down her body to rest on her hip. She sighed her approval … her breath warming the inside of his mouth and giving him an indication of her arousal. Her moan permission to proceed. When he dipped his index finger into the junction between her legs he found her moist and wanting. His slipped a second finger and then a third while she arched her back and moaned in approval. The sensation of her body bucking in appreciation of his fingers drove him insane with arousal but he knew she wasn't quite ready for him. He wanted her first time to be perfect. He continued stroking, his mouth followed the contours of her chin, kissed down her beautiful long neck and came to rest on her left breast. When he flicked his tongue over the tip of her nipple, she mewed her approval and surprised him with her verbal request.

"Make love to me."

"Not yet, kitten," he told her, although his cock throbbed in acknowledgement of her request. "Not yet." He withdrew his fingers, stopping at the entrance to massage gentle circles over her slick swollen clit until she began to buck against his hands.

"Oh god, David." She groaned, her eyes closing, her jaw dropping. "Oh, David."

His body already throbbed with impatience to be

inside her, and when she called his name, it was more than he could stand. He gave in to his own desire, catching a wave of her orgasm in a quick, gentle thrust. The tip of his erection eased into her moist entrance, a little deeper with each push, stretching her until he felt the slight resistance of her maidenhead. He forced himself to remain still, allowing her body the chance to adjust to his size. She surprised him when she thrust her hips up to meet him, forcing him deeper inside and she continued to pulse beneath him, taking him deeper and deeper into her tight core. For a moment she grimaced as he pushed past both her physical and mental barriers and then she relaxed, her body accepting all of him, scorching him, loving him.

His fangs extended to full length, drawn to the pull of her blood as it pulsed just beneath the surface of her skin. Her flushed skin and warm body called to his blood lust and he imagined the taste of her blood on his tongue, in his mouth, in his cells. *No. It was too soon.* She had given him her trust. He could not, would not ask any more of her tonight. It was enough that she had trusted him with her body, he couldn't risk frightening her by showing her his true nature. His needs could wait. Tonight he would concentrate on attending to her desires.

She convulsed beneath him, her fingernails dug into the flesh of his back, her eyes hooded, heavy with desire and her mouth curled blissfully at the sides. Her moans came in soft mewing gasps, melting his heart. She was purring for him and he wanted to make this moment last forever. Whimpering, she threw back her head, exposing the soft, smooth skin of her throat, making his gums throb in reaction to the vivid blue of her veins. He needed a taste, just a tiny sip of her blood to keep a small part of her inside him. Leaning down, he kissed the skin on her throat above her carotid artery and allowed his fangs to extend, only enough to prick the skin, drawing a few drops of blood which he lapped up, his tongue instantly closing the wound. The taste was exhilarating. His body reacted to the nectar of her essence. He drove deeper inside her, again and again until he could feel himself coming. With a final thrust, he came in a tidal wave of emotions: lust, love, pure ecstasy.

Her body reacted to the throbbing of his shaft with a shiver that shook her whole body. She gave a final moan, shuddered, and sank sleepily into the mattress.

"If I had known that having sex was as good as this," she confessed, "I might not have held out for so long."

"Making love." David corrected her as he rolled over onto his back taking her with him so she lay across his chest, their bodies still intimately joined. "Having sex and making-love are very different."

Meaghan frowned. "Okay, explain the difference."

David's mouth curled on the left side and his eyebrows knit together. "Promise you won't stake me?"

She answered his question with a nod but her frown remained.

"Well, over the centuries I've had sex with many women." He paused when he saw Meaghan's annoyed expression. "Let me finish, kitten. As I said, I've had *sex* with these women … for fun. It was mutually pleasurable and usually one-night stands. I may be a vampire but I am first and foremost a man with male needs and I was beginning to doubt that I would ever meet you."

"Meet *me*? You were *expecting* me?"

David could feel his desire build up anew and judging by Meaghan's expression, she could feel his shaft swelling inside her.

"Again?"

"I have something I'd like to show you," he told her before cupping her head in his large hand and drawing her mouth to his lips.

Meaghan lifted her head. "I think I've seen it before," she teased, the smile spreading across her face.

Cupping her bottom, he drew her against his hips, thrusting into her as he held her for support. As she found her own rhythm; he released her buttocks, his hands reaching her breasts. Squeezing. Massaging. She rode him with the skill of an expert equestrian, her timing perfect as she leaned forward, allowing her right nipple to brush his mouth. He pounced on the stiff peak, sucking greedily at the nipple while kneading the breast, tweaking the left nipple in time to his mouth.

She threw her head back and purred, "What was it you wanted to show me?"

"Later," he told her, "much, much later."

Chapter Sixteen

"I was wondering when you were coming home. It's almost dawn," Derrick called as David opened the front door to the mansion. "You should be careful, Meaghan might—"

"See me coming in?" David finished the sentence and watched his brother's mouth drop open in surprise as he entered the lounge room, holding Meaghan's hand. He felt the familiar tug as his brother attempted to connect with him telepathically. "It's all right, Derrick. Whatever you have to say to me, you can say it out loud. Meaghan knows what we are."

"Are you out of your bloody mind?" Derrick cursed. His shoulders drew back, extending his chest and his eyes glowed with anger.

"Don't hold back," David answered but he also used their mental connection to warn his brother that he should choose his next words carefully if he wanted to avoid a fight.

Derrick shook his head. "For all we know, *she* could be the killer."

"That's the pot calling the kettle black isn't it?" Meaghan reminded him. "I, for one, have never killed anyone. Can you honestly say the same?"

"She got you there." Anna walked into the room carrying a tray of wine glasses and a decanter. "Would you like a glass Meaghan?"

Meaghan stared suspiciously at the decanter and then at David who fell back onto the sofa with a chuckle. When he regained composure he informed her, "Its wine, kitten. A crimson cabernet if I know Anna."

"Alcohol? I thought that vampires drank…" Her cheeks paled as she said, "…blood."

"We do, but that can become a bit boring and I do enjoy a glass of the *other* red. You two look very relaxed." Anna noticed as she handed Meaghan a glass of cabernet. A sly, knowing grin spread her mouth. "What have you two been up too?"

"We've been learning a lot about each other." David answered her as he turned his head slightly to wink at Meaghan. "There is more to my little student than meets the eye. For example, I've discovered that Meaghan is able to astral travel."

"Wow, really? I would love to be able to do that," Anna confessed as she grabbed Meaghan's good hand and dragged her over to a seat on the couch. She began to question her about her abilities. "How do you do it? Could you teach me? Can you do anything else?"

"You must excuse my wife…" Derrick interrupted. "She's recently discovered that she is a witch and, being an impatient little firecracker, she's trying to learn all she can in the shortest possible time." He smiled at Anna who screwed up her face and poked out her tongue in response to his teasing. "What *I* would like to know is, if you're not the killer, what is your interest in the murders? Why do you seem to turn up at the crime scenes?"

Meaghan turned to David who nodded his head in agreement to her decision to share her story. It occurred to him that *he* hadn't fully questioned her on her reasons for stalking him at the university. *Later* never came. But he did. Multiple times.

"I'm an undercover cop, sent to the University to locate and identify suspicious characters. My ability to astral travel ensures my safety while giving me freedom to explore the campus at night. I was the only officer at my precinct with artistic interests so I was pretty much the only choice they had."

Anna shrugged her shoulders. "Seems like a reasonable alibi to me, although I think that you're underestimating your artistic abilities. David tells me that you're a really talented artist. You do have a cherubic face, which I imagine would help you blend in with the younger crowds."

"How old are you anyway?" Derrick interrupted. "You seem a bit young to be a cop."

"I'm twenty-five."

"Excuse my suspicious husband." The corner of her Anna's mouth turned up as she made an observation. "I think it's great that you're twenty-five and can pass for eighteen, although, today you seem to have swapped your usual braids and heavy glasses for the bed tussled look. It suits you." She turned to David and added, "It suits *both* of you."

David grinned but Meaghan blushed and downed half her glass of wine in one gulp so he rose from his seat across the room and shooed Anna away, taking her place on the couch. "Go and sit with your husband and tease him instead."

He leaned in close to Meaghan, whispering in her ear, "Teasing you is *my* job, kitten." His thoughts raced with ideas of how he could torment her with images of naked bodies and warm flesh, until he felt the annoying probing in his mind and turned his attention back to his brother.

"All right, all right. Back to the murders. Meaghan tells me that she was encouraged by her superior to accept our scholarship in order to keep an eye on my movements. Obviously, I'm no longer under suspicion due to my untimely death."

"My boss believes that David proved his guilt by attacking the security guard." She turned to David who was about to profess his innocence. "The security guard *believed* you were about to attack him. Anyway, Terry has closed the case and nothing I said would convince him otherwise. He's withdrawn the extra guards and left the campus relatively unsecured with only the usual skeleton staff."

Derrick pinched his chin between his thumb and forefinger. "This complicates things," he thought out loud. "If the killer is smart, he *or* she, will use David's death to their advantage and begin taking the bodies away to avoid suspicion."

"It's a lot more complicated than you realize," Meaghan informed him. "We're not dealing with a single killer. There's a whole group of people involved in the murders."

"You saw them?" David cupped her face in his hand and stared into her eyes. *What if she'd been caught?* "Why didn't you tell me about this?"

Meaghan frowned and tilted her head slightly into his palm as she reminded him, "I tried to tell you about it last night but you insisted it could wait until *later*." She smiled and kissed his palm.

"Why on earth would you prevent her from telling you something as important as that David?" Derrick barked at him.

"Maybe I had more important issues of my own … did you think of that little brother? I seem to remember you recently allowing your hormones to control your better judgement."

"Oh." Derrick stumbled over his apology. "Oh, well. Yes, I understand your predicament." He glanced quickly to his wife, then at his feet.

Meaghan closed her eyes and bit her bottom lip. Anna saw her discomfort and reminded the brothers of the importance of Meaghan's previous statement. "Meaghan, how do you know there's more than one killer?"

Meaghan opened her eyes and directed her story to Anna. "Last night, I was invited to a party at the campus. Of course I declined." She gazed up at David. Her soft, pale blue eyes sensually framed by the longest lashes he'd ever seen. It took all of his concentration to focus on her story as she continued. "Considering David's…" She used air bunnies to make her point. "…Death. I thought the party was in bad taste. Then, it occurred to me that the rave was a perfect place for the killer to find a new victim. I was right, although I wish now that I hadn't gone."

"Are you telling me that you saw the murder take place?"

Meaghan nodded between sips of wine. "Unfortunately, yes. It was heartbreaking. The poor woman begged for her life as her throat was cut by a hooded figure. The rest of the group were chanting and having sex as if the whole murder slash ceremony was somehow turning them on. It was disgusting to watch them take pleasure in her death." She shook her head. "The poor woman looked terrified. There was nothing I could do to help. I've never felt so helpless."

David took her shaking hand in his. "There was nothing you could have done. Even if you'd been corporeal, you couldn't have survived a group of killers on your own."

"He's right, Meaghan. I've been in your shoes. I know how it feels to be powerless to help. My best friend was taken by a rogue vampire who not only fed on her but also shared her with his minions. By the time I located her, she was barely alive."

"How awful." Meaghan sat forward on her seat and reached for Anna's hand. "Did she…"

Anna shook her head. "She's alive but she's

changed. When I first met her she was outgoing, trusting, and vivacious. Since the attack, she's terrified to leave her home. I'm trying to convince her to move in with us but I'm afraid she's even wary of me now that I've become … well, you know."

Derrick put his arm around her his wife's shoulders. "We'll find a way to help her get back on her feet, mon amour. She'll get through this." He turned his attention back to Meaghan. "How many would you say were part of the group?"

"Eight people plus…" Meaghan shrugged her shoulders. "…I don't know how else to describe the thing I saw except that it looked like a demon."

"Derrick, you know what this means." David squeezed Meaghan's hand protectively as he came to terms with what she had just revealed. Derrick nodded his understanding of the situation but Anna and Meaghan looked confused.

"Are you guys going to fill us in on what you are talking about?"

"Devil worshippers," the brothers announced in unison.

"I thought you said they were witches?" Anna argued as she turned to her husband. "I thought Devil worshipping was an urban legend. I've read about cults but I didn't think they could actually conjure anything. Don't they just—"

"Listen," Meaghan interrupted. "I don't have a clue about witches or covens and I am only just beginning to come to term with the idea of vampires. Now you tell me that there are real devil worshippers on campus? What the hell is that about?"

Anna shrugged. "I have no idea. I'm only new to being a vampire and still learning how to be a witch. This is the first I've heard about demons."

Meaghan wiggled her hand free from David's grip. She held out her empty wine glass and asked, "Would you mind? I think I need a little more liquid courage. This has been a very strange night."

Anna filled the glass and poured herself another while Meaghan addressed her question to David.

"Let me get this straight … the killers are actually sacrificing the victims to the Devil?"

"The sacrifices are usually made to a lesser demon, one who wishes to return to live on earth in corporeal form."

"Why would anyone in their right mind bring a demon into this world?"

"Usually for greed or personal gain," David answered without hesitation. "The worshippers offer a sacrifice in exchange for wealth, happiness, power, and sometimes for unreciprocated love."

"How do they choose the sacrifice? I noticed that three of the victims were women while only one was male. Does it make a difference?"

Both the brothers cleared their throats. David chose to answer.

"The blood of a virgin is usually the key to sacrificial spell. I guess their previous choices weren't as pure as they would have liked but I'm sure they'll keep trying until they find one."

Meaghan swallowed. She leaned close to David and whispered into his ear. "I think you may have saved my life."

He smiled and whispered back. "It's only fair, kitten. By coming into my life, you saved mine."

Meaghan turned back to the others. "If I hadn't seen the sacrifice myself, I'd say you were pulling my leg. This *is* the twenty first century."

"Look, I'm not saying that *all* of this is real…"

David rationalized. "But obviously the people holding these orgies believe in what they are doing. They've probably taken parts out of the Malleus Maleficurum and bits out of horror movies, hoping that they'd get it right."

"Malleus Maleficurum?"

"The Hammer of the witches," Anna answered. "A book written in fourteen eighty-six as a manual for finding and persecuting witches. It makes me shudder to think about all the white witches and innocent people rounded up and killed in the name of religion."

"Well the instructions in the manual must have been helpful in some way or they must have done something right because I saw something … something big that was mightily pissed off when the blood wasn't the type it wanted."

"It doesn't make sense." Anna scratched her head. "The Malleus Maleficurum is not an instruction manual for witches, it's a manual for witch hunters. If they were able to conjure a demon, they must have found instruction from somewhere else."

"Unless"—David quickly rose from his seat and hurried to a large teak bookshelf. He searched for and found an old book which he held up for the others to see—"they wrote a curse or spell."

"Is that book about Devil worship?" Meaghan asked, unfamiliar with the title but impressed by the heavily jeweled leather binding.

"Not exactly," David answered as he sat beside her and thumbed through the pages for an example, "but it gives examples of ancient curses that call upon demons to help them blight their enemies."

"Curses? Not sure I like the idea of an instruction book for cursing but at least the binding is nice. What type of leather is that?" Meaghan took a sip of wine.

David grimaced, knowing that his answer

wouldn't go over well. "The binding is human skin, kitten and the paper is vellum."

Meaghan chocked on her wine, coughing into her hand. "Human binding and calf skin paper? Are you pulling my leg?"

"Unfortunately, no." Thumbing through the pages, David found one that made his point and he handed the book to Meaghan. "The Mesopotamians believed in daemons or as we call them, demons and believed that they could be conjured to help vanquish enemies or to fulfil curses. Modern worshippers seem to believe that they also grant wishes."

Meaghan read the text. "This spell comes with a translation. Is it for real?"

"The person who paid good money to the mage for that spell certainly thought it was."

"But *you* think it is a bunch of hokum?"

"Oh don't get me wrong, evil does exist. I'm just not sure that these people have any real idea of what they are doing. Demons have a way of using stupid people; they actually enjoy playing a game of deceit. This coven or whatever the hell they are … pardon the pun, will never get what they desire or if they do, it will be short lived. Demons don't play by the rules. It will expect its pound of flesh."

Meaghan's face paled. She looked into David's eyes. "How do you know all this David?"

"I'm sorry to interrupt but I do believe it's time we retired," Derrick announced as he took his wife's hand and helped her rise to her feet.

****

Before Meaghan had a chance to argue that there was no point in going to bed because it was already morning, she realized the significance of Derrick's statement. The reality finally struck her like a slap. She'd spent the night drinking expensive red wine and discussing the case with three vampires. The whole situation seemed so unreal but then again, so did the murders on campus. David's proximity didn't help her think clearly either. Whenever he was around, her mind seemed to vacate the premises. All she could think of was his touch on her skin. She knew she was falling in love. *No. Not falling.* She loved him. But could she really trust him? Even if he was the genuine and considerate man slash vampire he seemed to be, what future could she expect with him? She would be destined to grow old and die while he stayed eternally beautiful and ageless.

"A penny for your thoughts."

"What?" Meaghan asked as she turned to face David.

"You spaced out for a few minutes. Anna and Derrick have gone upstairs and I thought we should retire to the studio before I combust."

"Oh, my god. Is that likely to happen in here?"

David laughed. "Not in here, kitten but I would have major sunburn problems if I tried to walk you back to your cottage."

"As much as I'd love to join you downstairs, I don't expect that either of us would get any sleep and you look dead tired, so I think that I should go back to my place."

David pulled her against him and held her tight. "That jibe about looking 'dead' tired didn't go unnoticed. I may have to put you over my knee."

"Assaulting a police officer is a criminal offense, Mr. Corel, and that would be your *second* crime." She held up her cast to remind him. "Besides, I know your naughty mind and I need a few hours alone to recuperate."

"I'll make you a deal," David informed her with a

twinkle in his eye that alluded to more mischief. "I will allow you to go *this* time, but after your nap, I intend to collect on that promise of posing nude for me."

Meaghan swallowed the lump in her throat and nodded agreement. Despite their earlier intimacy, she still felt self-conscious about posing for him but she knew he would be relentless in his request. Better to have done with it. Besides, by the time he woke up, she would already be back on campus. There was something she had to discuss with Lilith.

Chapter Seventeen

When the cab pulled up in front of the University, Meaghan checked her watch. It was already ten o'clock and the campus buzzed with students who were gathering in small groups to discuss the cancellation of night classes. She kept her head down as she hurried to the cafeteria, hoping to avoid the questions and fake condolences concerning the death of her mentor. As the sliding doors to the cafeteria opened, she instantly spotted Lilith sitting with a group of around six other Goths. Their dark clothing and heavy makeup made them stand out in the crowd, especially since the other students seem to have given them a wide berth. As Meaghan approached, she could smell the pungent aroma of pot on their clothes. *Really? Right here under the noses of the security guards? Were they plain stupid or supremely confident?*

Lilith whispered something to the others and they all turned to face Meaghan. She focused on the dark auras that hung from each and every one at Lilith's table. Her instincts warned her to retreat but, as she had already been noticed, this would have caused more suspicion. She stopped directly in front of the table and was immediately berated by her Goth acquaintance.

"Where were you last night? You missed a great rave."

"Something came up," Meaghan explained "and besides, I couldn't remember where you said to meet "

"You really are a blonde." Encouraged by the laughing from the rest of the group she continued, "I would have thought that even *you* could remember that I said the party was on the oval behind the campus."

This information confirmed Meaghan's

suspicions but she needed to be sure. She risked further ridicule by repeating the question. "So the rave did go ahead behind the campus?"

Lilith raised her hands in the air and rolled her eyes as she joined her friends about laughing. "Okay, one more time for the dummy. Yes, the rave went ahead as planned on the oval behind the campus."

Gotcha. "So you were *there* when the latest young woman was killed?"

Lilith visibly paled which was surprising considering the quantity of white concealer that she was wearing. She looked to the others for support. A young woman who Meaghan recognized as Lilith's new classmate spoke up in their defense. "We don't know what you're talking about, you stupid bitch. Nobody said anything about another murder."

Meaghan tried to keep her expression calm. *How could you be so stupid?* There was nothing in the news about another body. The body must have been disposed of, or, as yet undiscovered.

"I thought I heard someone mention another murder. It was probably just a rumor."

Lilith's friend pulled out a Swiss army knife, flicked open the blade and began carving symbols into the wooden table. She kept her chin down as she asked, "Who told you that someone got murdered last night?"

Meaghan watched as the woman's carving took on the shape of a goat's head. A horned goat. "I don't remember who told me."

"Don't remember? Maybe you don't remember *coming* to the rave." She looked up. Her expression as cold as ice. "Maybe you *were* there, sticking your nose where it don't belong."

"Who gives a shit." A skinny male with multiple facial piercings snorted. "I don't even remember *leaving* the party." His smile quickly disappeared when faced with the same icy stare.

Meaghan concentrated on each member of the group, studying the colors of their auras in an attempt to discover more about them. As she suspected, they all had tinges of black to their auras but the darkest aura surrounded Lilith's new friend. Hers positively radiated malevolence and for some reason, her anger seemed to be focused on Meaghan.

"Was there something else?" the Goth woman asked, emphasizing the last two syllables in a snake-like hiss that sent shivers down Meaghan's spine.

"No. I just wanted to apologize for missing the party, that's all."

"Well you've done that so bugger off!" Skinny pierced guy cursed as he leaned forward threateningly, slapping his hands down on the table, his mouth twisted into a snarl.

Meaghan turned and walked away. She'd heard enough to know that she was on the right track and the demeanor of the entire group was downright aggressive. They were self-absorbed, anti-establishment pot-heads demonstrating sociopathic behavior. The lead Meaghan had looked for. Her unsubs. *Okay. Onto the next step. Find evidence to prove that this group are somehow involved in the murders or at the very least, had a motive for the crimes. What were they hoping to achieve? Did they commit these horrible acts simply for the excitement or had the demon offered them personal gain?* Meaghan thought about the woman at the table and surmised that either scenario could apply to her. Her pale face and kohl blackened eyes may have been a false face that she sported to offend the public, but Meaghan suspected that her soul would prove to be more frightening than the mask. She shook her head. *You may have blown your cover.* The leader had noticed her faux pas and called her on it. *How could you be so stupid as to mention the last murder?*

Halfway back to the taxi rank, she became aware of hurried footsteps behind her and she glanced sideways at a class window so as not to alert her stalkers that she was mindful of their presence. To her horror, she recognized Lilith's whole group rushing to close the distance between them. *They were on to her.* Even with her police training she couldn't take on a group of seven people, especially with a broken wrist. Her heart beat frantically as she tried to formulate a plan while quickening her pace. The cab rank seemed miles away. Could she make it in time? *Think! Think quickly!*

"Meaghan!"

She spun around and recognized her art teacher who stood in the doorway of his class.

"Oh, Hi there, Mr. Nagle."

"I have been meaning to call you and talk to you about David's untimely death. Such a loss, such a loss." He shook his head in dismay. "Do you have time to talk about your mentor program?"

Meaghan noted that the Goth group had stopped walking and were hovering around in the alcove near the art department, obviously waiting for the teacher to leave. She had to think quickly. "I'm on my way to the cab rank. Perhaps you could walk me there and we could discuss things as we walk."

"Of course, my dear." He hooked his arm in hers and as they headed towards the front of the University, Meaghan noted with relief that the others remained behind looking rather annoyed and very animated. By the time the cab arrived they'd left.

****

When Meaghan walked into the main house she

was surprised to see David waiting in the lounge room with Derrick and Anna, despite the sun being high in the sky. All three jumped to their feet when she entered the room but David was the first to speak. "How could you be so stupid?"

"David! I think you're being a bit harsh with Meaghan, I—"

"Stay out of this, Anna. It doesn't concern you."

Meaghan noticed that Anna took a step back, away from David. Derrick, on the other hand, closed the distance between himself and his brother.

"The way that you speak to my wife concerns *me*."

Meaghan wedged herself between the posturing brothers. "I don't understand why you're all getting yourselves so worked up. I just went to the campus to check out a lead. I thought you were all asleep."

"Anna had a premonition in her dream and woke up the whole house," Derrick told her without taking his eyes off his brother.

"We sent Evan to check up on you and discovered that you hadn't been to bed. I don't understand why you seem determined to get yourself killed. I thought we'd decided to work together on this? Why couldn't you have waited until evening? Do you even realize how worried we were?" David reached for her but she pulled away.

"I really don't see the reason for your concern. As you can seem I'm fine."

"No. You're just lucky." David's voice lowered in tone and Meaghan couldn't help but be aroused by the tenor of his speech despite feeling as angry with him as he seemed to be with her. What he said next came as a shock. "I dread to think what would have happened to you if we hadn't sent Pierre to intervene."

"*You* sent Mr. Nagle? I don't understand. How did you know?"

"In my dream, I saw the group of Goths following you and David used his psychological connection with Pierre to send him a message. He compelled Pierre to speak with you and made sure he didn't leave your side until you were safely on your way home," Anna explained.

Meaghan flopped onto the couch and David sat beside her. "I guess I should thank you all," she mumbled in gratitude. She hated needing help but was smart enough to realize that their interference had probably saved her life. "Did your vision happen to tell you what they wanted with me?"

Anna shook her head. "Only that they meant you harm. One of the women positively despises you."

Meaghan nodded. "I think I know the girl you're talking about."

"Is she a friend of yours?"

"Today was the first time I've spoken with her but I got the vibe that there's something about me that riles her. Maybe *she* wanted the mentorship? Was she the front runner?"

David took her hand. "The mentorship program was designed for you and you alone. There was never a question of anyone else being offered the position."

"This is all very confusing, David. Why did you do this for me? Did you suspect that I was on the case and wanted to keep an eye on me?"

"David," Derrick interrupted. "I think it's time you showed her."

"Showed me what?"

David rose from the couch and offered Meaghan his hand. "Perhaps my brother is right. It's time you knew the truth."

Meaghan took his hand and stood up. Anna smiled and nodded, giving her the impression that she should go with David who appeared to be leading her towards the downstairs studio. As she descended the stairs, her heart raced and she prepared her mind for any scenario. *Will David's revelation give me cause to regret sleeping with him? Could he be the killer after all and have more bodies stashed away in a cellar?* By the time she reached the last step, she felt compelled to run back up the staircase and keep running until she reached the road, but David held fast to her hand dashing her ideas of fleeing. She knew he could crush it with minimal effort.

He escorted her to a group of framed paintings that leaned against the back wall, covered with a sheet. The ones he had forbidden her to see. He reached for the smallest, turning it around and Meaghan gasped when she recognized the small child in the portrait.

"I don't believe it," she exclaimed, raising her hand to her mouth. "When did you paint this? Why did you paint this?"

David reached for another frame. "Around twenty years ago I suddenly became inspired to paint a cute little girl with blonde braids. Every year I felt compelled to do another painting as the child grew and last year, the urge grew to a point where I could think of nothing else but the woman she'd become. The woman that *you* had become." He turned each canvas over to reveal the child growing to womanhood.

"You were *stalking* me?"

"No. I'd never seen you. I thought you were a figment of my imagination until you appeared at the campus the day that I was posing as a favor for Pierre."

Meaghan studied the paintings. Growing up without parents meant that she had no-one interested in taking photos of her. There was no record of her childhood. It was slightly overwhelming seeing her life laid out before her. Worse still, in each and every portrait, the child's expression was melancholic, reminding her of how unhappy her childhood had been. It was as though David had seen into her soul and captured her desperate longing to be loved on his canvas. Tears rimmed her eyes as she moved from one painting to another, searching for just one smile, one happy moment but even the more recent paintings depicted a pensive, despondent woman void of hopes and dreams.

"You felt sorry for me?" She turned to David with tears in her eyes. "

"No! It wasn't like that at all," David argued.

"You forget that I'm a cop, David. The evidence here is quite clear. You saw a sad sack little girl who developed into a miserable lonely woman and, although I concede that your intentions were well meaning, you confused pity with attraction."

"Of course I felt your pain and your loneliness," David told her. "At first I did feel sympathy for the small child and her longing for a family, however, as you grew, I fell in love with you. Your pain became my pain."

"Love? You didn't even know me. How could you claim to love me?"

David shrugged. "The heart wants what the heart wants. I only had to look into your eyes to know the type of person you are and your capacity for love. You're beautiful, Meaghan. Inside and out."

Meaghan shook her head. "I don't believe in love at first sight. It isn't logical."

"But you do believe in lust at first sight?"

Meaghan's mouth dropped open and she gasped when she remembered their first meeting. She had been instantly attracted to David. For the first time in her memory, she had pictured herself naked with a man. No, not any man. David. She had barely been able look at him for fear that he could see the lust in her eyes.

"Do you really think that it was only lust, kitten?" David edged closer. "Of course I wanted to take you to my bed the moment I recognized you but it was more than that. I physically hurt when you ran from the class. It was as though you took a piece of my soul with you. I'm only complete when we are together." He reached down and pinched her chin between his thumb and forefinger, raising her face to look her squarely in the eye. "You were not the only lonely person in this scenario kitten. I've spent over one hundred years grieving for a love that didn't exist until the day I met you. You can't tell me that you don't feel the same. I hear your heart beating a mile a minute and I can see the flush of your cheeks. This is real, Meaghan. Our love is real."

"I wish it was real, David. I truly do, but I'm a realist and I gave up on dreams back in the orphanage." It pained her to lie to him. She had many dreams. Dreams of promotion in the force, dreams of finding her real family, and more recently and frequently, dreams of spending the rest of her life with David. However, the cab drive home had given her time to process all the information that David and his family had given her. She had time to take stock of all that had transpired the previous night and the reality was … he would never grow old with her. She would be forced to watch herself age while he remained young and beautiful. Watch while he fed on … blood. Even the word made her sick to her stomach. How on earth could she spend her life with a man who needed blood to survive? How would he react once he discovered her phobia? How long would it be before he left her?

"Give me a chance to prove my love." David

implored, snapping her out of her thoughts. "I don't expect you to love me yet. I've had twenty years to fall in love with you, while this is all new to you. We can take things slowly while we work this case together. My first priority is your safety. I've waited this long to have you in my life, I can wait forever for you to fall in love with me."

Meaghan reached up and touched his cheek. She longed to tell him how much she already loved him but it wouldn't be fair to give him false hope. When the case was closed, she would apply for a transfer and move as far away as she could, even though it would mean leaving her only chance for real happiness. She loved him too much to saddle him with a woman who couldn't tolerate his lifestyle. A woman who would grow old and die. She smiled and nodded, hoping he couldn't see the lie in her eyes. "We'll take things slowly."

****

"Good. That's all I ask, kitten." He kissed her gently on her forehead and rested his chin on the top of her head as he held her, but his heart sank. Her words promised patience but her eyes told him that emotionally, she was already pulling away.

"Come on," he urged as he led her to his bed, "you need to rest for a while before you tell us what you learned from your Goth friends."

She hesitated, and he forced a chuckle. "I promise to keep my hands to myself while you sleep. I could use a few more hours myself."

He lay on the bed and motioned for her to join him. As she crawled across the bed and into his arms, tucking her head under his arm in an attempt to hide her tears, he felt as though his heart would break. She'd let her mental guard down and, for the first time since they had met, he was privy to her thoughts. *Oh, my god. He's warm. He must have recently fed.* She shuddered in his arms. He hugged her tighter in response which made her feel even more claustrophobic. *I feel so powerless in his arms. He could easily crush me. What if he drinks my blood? I don't think I could stand it. What if we had children? Would he be tempted to eat them? Don't be stupid. A vampire can't reproduce. Oh god. That means I will never have a real family.* She shuddered again in his arms and, this time, her gasp was audible.

The painful reality hit him like a ton of bricks. He'd painted her forlorn face for years. He felt her pain and should have realized that she longed for a family of her own. A child's love was unconditional. How could he deny her the love that she'd craved all her life. He hugged her closer and steeled himself to the reality of their situation. There would come a time when she would leave his arms forever but not now. Not tonight while he held her tightly to him, her soft breath on his chest, his lips pressed to her forehead. No. Not tonight.

****

The ship had been anchored for hours before David had been able to leave the bilge and make his way onto the deck. Most of the crew had left for shore and the nearby tavern, so his departure went unnoticed. As previously arranged with one of his servants, his horse was saddled and waiting for him, although it was not pleased when he attempted to mount it. At first it recoiled, rearing up on its hind legs and whinnying it disapproval until he was able to use the power of suggestion that his sire had shown him. Unfortunately, that was all she had taught him. He'd barely been a vampire for forty-eight hours before she left the ship when it anchored at its first destination. But he couldn't waste time worrying about his ineptitude, his family needed him.

Once enthralled, Midnight took off for home needing little encouragement and David rarely needed to urge him with a kick to his flanks. He was grateful for his horse's enthusiasm and love for speed. Time was of the essence. He'd already wasted precious hours waiting for the sun to disappear beyond the horizon and he had no idea how bad things were at home. The letter from his sister informed him that she could no longer bear the brutal beatings at the hand of her husband and anxiously awaited David's return so she could present him with divorce papers. As the eldest member of the family— since the death of their parents—she had felt it necessary to ask for his help rather than burden Derrick who she feared was not strong enough to stand up to Nigel and the thugs he called friends.

Midnight had barely come to a halt when David vaulted off and followed the sound of the commotion. He recognized the scream—his sister Isabelle—and Nigel instructed someone to "finish the job" moments before he burst into the room to find his sister dead and Derrick fighting for his life. Four men stood over him. Weapons in hand. Derrick's blood on their clothes. Bruises on their faces. Derrick must have fought them off as best he could before they overpowered him.

"Hold on," David ordered his brother as he literally took Nigel and his crew apart. They barely knew what hit them. He tore the screams from their throats in a fit of rage, saving Nigel for last. The coward begged for mercy. Mercy? Isabelle's body lay feet away, her dress torn and hitched up to her waist. Thighs marbled with purple marks from where they held her down with calloused, rough hands. Her beautiful face hardly recognizable. Mercy? He grabbed Nigel's hair, forcing his head to one side as he sunk his fangs into the bastard's throat, draining him of blood, feeling the life

slip away. Deeper, until he felt sinew and tendons snap, the carotid artery tear. He bit harder, feeling the crunch of bone as the skull detached from the spine. Another clench of his jaws severed the head from the body altogether. Holding the head by its hair, he stared into the dead eyes of his sister's killer.

"How's that for mercy?"

With a flick of his wrist, he tossed the head away and turned to his brother who lay gasping for breath, his eyes swollen shut, his face ashen.

"I can save you. Derrick. But your life will never be the same."

"No. Let me die," Derrick whispered as his life faded away. "I couldn't save her David. I don't deserve to live."

"Don't be an idiot, Derrick." David tore at his own wrist with his teeth and held it to his brother's mouth. "Take my blood. Isabelle wouldn't want you to die too."

Derrick shook his head and tried to push David away but there was no strength left in his body. He was helpless to resist as the blood trickled into his mouth and was absorbed by his cells but his eyes warned David that there would be consequences.

"I'm sorry." David murmured as he held his brother through the change. "Forgive me ... forgive me."

****

"David! Wake up!"

David's eyes flew open and it took a few seconds to appreciate that he was in his own bed. Meaghan was leaning over him, her long hair falling softly on his face.

She stroked his cheek. "You were having a nightmare."

"I guess I was." He wiped the sweat from his

brow with the back of his hand.

"It must have been pretty bad. You look shaken up." Her pensive expression gave him hope. She looked truly concerned for his well-fare.

He eased himself up to a sitting position and kissed her lightly on the forehead. "Memories of time long ago, kitten, that's all." He shook his head. "I haven't had that particular dream for a long, long time. I used to dread falling asleep for fear of remembering that part of my past but it has been years since I dreamt it. I really thought I was over it."

"It must have been something really awful. You kept repeating, 'forgive me.' What was that about?"

He faked a smile and hugged her close to his body as he considered the ramifications of his actions in the dream. It had taken Derrick years to get over being turned against his will. Hell, he could understand Derrick's attitude. He hadn't really forgiven Josephine for turning *him*. Big breasts and a bottle of absinthe had been his downfall. A mistake that not only cost him his life but also that of his brother. After Derrick, he had vowed that he would never again make another vampire and he had kept that promise.

He stroked Meaghan's hair, envying her humanity and realizing that she had every right to pull away from him emotionally. Besides his love, he had nothing to offer her accept pain and danger. His life was a nightmare, even compared to that of a homicide cop. He faced evils that she could never understand. His ability to read minds allowed him to see into the darkest minds and glimpse the horrors that they wished to inflict on their victims. Meaghan could only see the tip of the iceberg while he knew the depth to which these monsters would go. No. He could not drag her into this life, no matter what it cost him.

"Earth to David." Meaghan maneuvered herself into a position where she could see his face. "If you don't answer my question, I may be forced to tickle the answer from you." She dug her fingers into the flesh below his armpits searching for a sensitive area until the ring tone on her phone drew her attention to the bedside table. She checked the caller ID and grimaced.

"It's Terry," she informed him. "I have to take this."

Chapter Eighteen

On the phone, Terry had sounded less than impressed that Meaghan had taken it upon herself to question Lilith and her group. He was downright angry that she had withheld the information about the recent murder. Nevertheless, he called her into his office to discuss the phone message she had left for him on her cab ride home from the campus.

"Sit!" he ordered the moment she entered the office. "Explain your cryptic message and why you believe there was another murder."

Meaghan did as she was told without question. Terry looked angrier that she had ever seen him, even in his youth, and something in his expression warned her not to argue. Not that she was afraid that he would cause her physical harm as he had always treated her with kid gloves. No. It was her job that was on the line, not her well-being.

"I'm sorry Ter—"

"Just cut to the chase Officer Lamb. What led you to believe there was another murder and why were you still questioning students? You are technically on sick leave."

Terry hadn't called her Officer Lamb since that day she graduated the academy. On that occasion the reference had been in recognition of her achievement. Today it felt like a reprimand. She cut straight to the point.

"Now don't get angry Terry…" She bit her bottom lip knowing it was already past that. "But the reason I know there was another murder is because, this time … I witnessed it."

"What the hell!" Terry slammed both fists onto

his desk, spilling his coffee and drawing the attention of other officers who were working near his office. He waved them off and walked over to close the door. "I specifically told you that you were off the case." He paused for a moment as if considering the significance of what she had said. His voice softened a little when he asked. "Did the killer see you?"

Meaghan shook her head. "No. I was incorporeal at the time and Terry … there is more than one."

"Body?"

"No. Killer. There's a whole freakin' group of them."

Terry sat back on the edge of his desk and Meaghan could see the tension raising his shoulders. He looked tired, but more than that, he looked worried.

"All right," he said. "You'd better give me the whole story."

Meaghan explained what she'd seen at the sacrifice and how she'd gone to the cafeteria in order to interrogate Lilith and her friends. When she told him how she had been followed and only narrowly escaped—thanks to Pierre—she noticed the strain on his face. His forehead crinkled, forming a thick line between his brows and he rubbed the back of his neck.

"Do you realize what could have happened to you?" Once again the volume of his voice attracted attention from outside the office and made Meaghan jump in her seat.

"I know, I know, Terry. And I've learned my lesson. I don't mind telling you, it gave me a bit of a fright. If it wasn't for…" She almost mentioned Anna's premonition which would have complicated matters further. Fortunately, she stopped herself in time to say, "…Pierre—the art teacher—asking to speak with me about my scholarship, I think I would have found myself in a bit of hot water."

"A *bit* of hot water? You think making yourself the target of serial killers is a bit of hot water?"

"Okay Terry. I get your point. I—"

"No. I don't think you get my point. I don't believe you understand the danger at all and, if you were going to say you won't do it again … you can hold your breath." He reached down, grabbing her roughly by the shoulders as he yelled into her face. "You got yourself into deep shit this time, Megs. You could have been killed!"

"I can do this, Terry, really I can. Just give me another chance."

"No! I'm responsible for you, both as your boss and your friend. You're off this case. I'll send a couple of officers to check the area behind the campus and see if they can turn up a body or any other evidence. In the meantime, you're to stay away from the campus, do you understand?"

"You can't make me stay away from the campus … *sir*." She emphasized the sir as she stood up, the speed of her ascent catching him off-guard. Her head almost connected with his chin before he stepped back. "I have a scholarship and I have every right to study there. You can't stop me."

"No, but I can fire you."

"You wouldn't dare!"

"I would if you push me." He paused for a moment and sighed. "Come on, Megs, be reasonable. Corel is dead. You *have* no scholarship and no reason to finish the art classes. If you are serious about being a cop, give up on the idea of being an artist and come back to work full time. I'll give you a nice safe desk job until you toughen up. You can move in with me until you find another place. No hurry, stay as long as you like."

He reached out to touch her but she backed away.

"So, you're saying that I can't be serious about police work *and* have outside interests? You are such a hypocrite, Terry. I know you play golf every Saturday and are in a bowling league. How are your outside interests more important than mine?"

"Come on, Megs, you can't tell me you're serious about your art? I thought it was a passing phase."

"My teachers tell me that I have real talent."

"Well, bully for them." He paused for a moment. "Actually, maybe that's not such a bad idea after all. Being a full-time artist might keep you out of trouble. Maybe you should give up the force altogether and concentrate on your art career."

Meaghan gasped. Terry had always been her ally. "You want me out?"

"If the truth be told … yes, I want you out. I want you safe, I want you…" He stopped mid-sentence and looked away. "And besides, what type of homicide cop pukes at the sight of blood."

"That's not fair, Terry. You know why I can't stand the sight of blood. You were there after I found Clarissa in the bathroom of our dorm."

"Okay, okay. I remember. It wasn't pretty."

"Then cut me some slack. I have proven myself as an asset to this case and proven that David was innocent."

"Oh, no, no, no," he argued. "Don't try and pass the buck. You may have found more killers but Corel was definitely guilty. He was killed at the scene of a murder for fu—"

"David was innocent and if the information I've given you already is not enough, I'm going to do whatever it takes to prove it."

"You listen to me Officer Lamb." Terry shook his

finger in her face, his cheeks crimson with rage. "You stay away from that campus and you stay away from the Corel residence."

"Or what?" she yelled back at him defiantly.

"Or … you're fired!"

"You know what Terry." She turned and headed for the door. As she turned the door knob and stepped into the corridor she added, "You can take your job and shove it."

****

Meaghan leaned heavily against the brick wall outside the police station and took a deep breath of cool night air. She had practically dashed through the corridors on her way out of the building and it was not until she stepped outside that the realization of what she had done hit her like a ton of bricks. *I quit my job.* Her body trembled but not from the cold mist that had suddenly enveloped her. She had resigned from the force, told Terry where he could stick his job and left without any idea of what she was going to do professionally or emotionally. She wondered if she should go back in and apologize. *No.* She had every right to lose her temper. *My information was accurate. I was an eye witness for Christ's sake. He should be the one apologizing, not me.* Terry was so hard to figure out sometimes. He could be considerate and thoughtful and then suddenly cold and hard, so different from the boy he had been in the orphanage. *That* Terry would never have thrown her blood phobia in her face so cruelly, especially knowing how it originated. That Terry had always encouraged her art.

She felt her mobile phone vibrating in her coat pocket and heard the familiar ping of the message alert. She checked the caller ID—Terry Palmer—and read the message. *You forgot to leave your gun and badge.*

Growling under her breath she responded. *Gun under my pillow, badge in my drawer. I'll bring them in tomorrow.* The phone pinged again displaying a cranky face emoticon then moments later another message. *I refuse to accept your resignation until you recover from your injury. Until then, we'll call it a leave of absence. Why is your gun under your pillow?*

She thought for a moment knowing she couldn't tell him the truth. She'd left the gun there since the night David broke her wrist. Shaking her head, she decided full disclosure was probably not such a good idea. Instead she typed… *To kill the monster living under the bed.*

Ping. *I thought I did away with him years ago.*

Meaghan smiled as she texted. *No. That was the monster living in the closet.*

Ping. *That's right, I remember now. Go home, Megs, go straight home and stay out of trouble. And carry that gun with you at all times!*

Meaghan snapped the cover of her phone shut and put it back into her pocket. A bitter wind had crept in while she was busy texting. She fastened the buttons on her jacket and pulled the collar up around her neck. It suddenly occurred to her that the fog had moved in quickly—probably pushed by the wind—and how unusually thick it seemed. She could barely make out her hand when she held it out in front of her and when she pulled her phone back out to call a cab, she couldn't see the screen. The street was deserted and the car drivers must have decided to stay at home because not a sound could be heard besides the nervous tapping of Meaghan's shoe on the pavement. A howl shattered the silence, shaking Meaghan to the core. *Oh, no. Not here.* She'd heard that noise before, outside the window of her old apartment and again at the cottage. But on both occasions she'd been locked safely inside her home. Now she was alone on an empty street, vulnerable and wishing her gun was where is belonged, in the pocket of her jacket and not under the pillow on her bed. *Damn it*. She hated Terry being right.

When the next howl shook her. It seemed closer, resonating through the glass in the window beside her. She looked inside, hoping to attract someone's attention but the few people still working within the station either didn't hear the guttural noise or chose to ignore it. Either way, she was screwed. She could hear the pad of paws on the pavement. Large paws. She remembered the glowing red eyes outside the bedroom window and swallowed the bile rising in her throat. The air hummed with electricity. No, not electricity. Growling. She leaned against the wall feeling the rough bricks through her jacket. The door to the station seemed miles away. Would she make it in time?

Simultaneously, she heard the footfalls of a large animal charging towards her and the screeching of tires. The car reached her first. David flung open the passenger door of the yellow Lamborghini and yelled at her to get in. She didn't hesitate, lunging for the car at the exact minute the unseen animal attacked. Meaghan felt a tug at the hem of her coat as she jumped into the passenger seat. She heard the sound of material tearing but didn't wait to face her attacker. Neither did David. He threw the car into gear and sped down the street with Meaghan trying and eventually succeeding to pull the door closed. A screeching noise assaulted their ears and she covered them with her hands and screamed as the beast swiped at the rear of the car with its claws in a last ditch attempt to stop them before they disappeared into the clearing fog.

David reached out and lightly touched Meaghan's hand as he kept his eyes on the road. He pushed 150 kilometers an hour with no sign of slowing but Meaghan had no intention of asking him to take his foot of the gas. If anything, she wished he would go faster. She would have made the request if she'd been able to find her voice. She turned to David and opened her mouth to speak but all that came out was a sob.

"Did it hurt you?" David asked. His voice sounded breathless. His face twisted in concern.

She shook her head. She had no idea if she was hurt. It was possible that the animal had torn her skin along with her jacket but she felt nothing but the cold sweat that was soaking her clothes. Her body going into shock.

****

David watched as Meaghan began to tremble violently. He could hear her heart going a mile a minute and beads of sweat dampened her forehead. The color of her complexion drained to a whiter shade of pale and she covered her mouth with her hand as she dry-retched.

"I would offer to stop the car but under the circumstances I—"

"Don't stop!" she screamed in response. "*Please*, don't stop."

"Not for anything, kitten." He promised as he floored the gas pedal while checking the rear view mirror. "Not for anything."

Chapter Nineteen

Meaghan accepted her second glass of whiskey and spoke for the first time since arriving home to her little cottage.

"I guess I have Anna to thank for your impeccably timed arrival?"

"You do indeed, but I wouldn't call my arrival impeccably timed." He examined Meaghan's shredded coat. "You barely made it out alive."

Meaghan took a big gulp of her whiskey and nodded. "I've never been so afraid in my life. What the hell was that thing anyway?"

"A hell-hound."

"Of course it was…" she agreed sarcastically. "What else would it be?" she finished the drink and held out her glass for a refill. "Just keep 'em coming."

David shook his head but refilled the glass. "I know you've had a shock but I think you should take it easy on the scotch otherwise you'll have one hell of a hang-over tomorrow."

"I don't care." She announced as she took a sip. The alcohol was beginning to soothe her fractured nerves. She planned on drinking until she passed out. "I'd rather deal with a hell of a hang-over than a hell of a hound any day."

"We'll see," David chuckled as he sat down on the settee beside her. "I have a feeling that you'll think differently in the morning."

"Nope, nope, nope." She insisted with a shake of her head. "Won't change my mind."

She leaned her head on David's shoulder and closed her eyes to stop the room from spinning. "David?"

"Yes, my love?"

"What is it like to be a vampire? Were you born a vampire? If you weren't born a vampire, did it hurt? Do you—"

"If we're to proceed with this interrogation, Officer Lamb. I request that you limit your questions to one at a time." He protested with a chuckle.

"Fine. How did you become a vampire?"

"A two-hundred-year-old woman got me drunk and had her wicked way with me."

Meaghan screwed up her face in disgust and shuddered. "Eww, gross. How could you … you know, get *it* up for a nasty old woman?"

"She didn't look like an old woman, Meaghan. Vampires don't age. She looked as young as she did when she died at the age of twenty-three."

"How old were you when you were … what's the word … turned?"

"Twenty-eight."

"And how long ago was that?" She held her breath in anticipation of his answer.

"Just over one hundred years."

"Wow. If someone had told me that my first time would be with a one-hundred-year old man, I never would have believed them."

"One hundred and twenty-eight," David corrected.

"Oh, thanks. That makes it sound so much better."

David drew her close to his chest as he told her. "I aim to please."

"And you do, you really do. But… I have a few more quest-io-ns."

"I think you need to go to bed."

"Mmmm." She smiled up at him. "That would be lov-el-y. But I need to ask you something first."

"Ask away."

"Did it hurt? I mean, becoming a vampire."

"A little."

"You're such a pain in my arse, David Corel. I want full disclosure. Tell me every little detail."

David smiled. "Well, at first I didn't understand what was happening. The sex was—"

"Ewww. I don't want to know about the sex. Not with that old lady anyway."

"Well it's a bit hard to leave out that part because we were ... you know ... at the time she sunk her fangs into my throat. At first I didn't notice the pain. By the time I realized that she was somehow draining my blood, I was too weak to fight her."

"And then you were a vampire?"

****

"No Meaghan, it isn't as easy as that." He lifted her chin with his index finger so he could be sure she was paying attention. Her beautiful pale eyes stared up at him. He knew that she was a stickler for details, there was no way he could betray her trust by fabricating a story. She had asked for the truth and he was going to tell her, despite realizing that it may cost him dearly. The reality was painful, cruel and undesirable. He was hesitant, afraid she may reject his way of life but he was determined to be honest.

"After she had drained me almost to the point of death, she bit her wrist and forced me to drink some of her blood..." He watched as the color drained from Meaghan's face and her mouth dropped open in shock.

"For a few moments, I lay there wondering what was going on. She told me that she'd given me a gift. When I glared at her, she laughed and told me I could thank her later. She informed me that, if I concentrated on the eyes of a potential victim, I could bend them to my will. I guess that's what she'd done to me. As I digested the information, I was hit by a wave of pain, worse than anything I'd ever experienced. My physical body was dying. Somehow I made it to the bathroom before I was violently ill. Imagine a terrible case of food-poisoning. My bowels and stomach heaved and clenched uncontrollably until all traces of my humanity were expelled. When I came back from the head, she was gone. She'd left me to suffer the pain of blood-lust without any assistance or guidance. The hunger I later experienced was almost as painful as my death."

Meaghan could taste the bile in her mouth. *Hunger for blood?* "Did you ever see her again?"

"No. I never saw her again. At first she connected with me psychically, explaining how I could use mind control in my favor."

She felt the sting of jealousy. "Does she still connect with you?"

"No. She was killed by the vampire council for neglecting her duties. It's an offense to abandon a fledgling, and, from what I've since heard, I was not the only vampire she deserted."

"Have *you* ever killed?"

"No. Not humans anyway. I've killed many rogue vampires but, only as part of my job as leader. Killing isn't something I take lightly, Meaghan."

"But you drink blood?"

"Yes, but it's not necessary to kill in order to feed, and I only take enough to survive. The donor feels no pain and doesn't remember the incident."

"But you drink blood?" Meaghan repeated. "You survive on blood?"

"I thought we established that, kitten. I told you I was a vampire. What did you think I drank?"

"Well … I saw you drinking wine…" Meaghan

insisted, "…I don't know David! I just got caught up in the romance. I guess I tried to push the blood part out of my mind."

"I think this is a conversation we should have when you are a little less … under the weather."

"You mean drunk," Meaghan corrected.

"You've had a traumatic experience, kitten. Have a good night's sleep and we'll discuss my lifestyle another time."

"No." She shook her head vehemently. "We will discuss this now! I let you tell me your story, now I want to share a story of my own. It's important, an insight into my reluctance to watch you feed."

David narrowed his eyes as he nodded his agreement. Part of him was reluctant to hear her story. He sensed the beginning of the end of their relationship but he was obliged to listen. He knew she'd grown up in an orphanage and had later become a police woman but he knew little else. He poured himself a scotch as she began her tale.

"By the time I was a teenager, there were only a few of us older kids left at the orphanage, me, Terry, and a girl named Clarissa. Terry and I were really close but Clarissa kept pretty much to herself after she was returned from her foster parents' home. She never spoke about why they brought her back. I think she blamed me."

"Why would she blame you?"

"Well, before she was fostered, we were sort-of friends. She was a bit high strung and could have moments of violent rages but she was my roommate since as long as I can remember. When they fostered her out and she went to her new home, I missed her. I wanted to know that she was happy so I focused on the photo Clarissa had given me and found myself at her new house."

"You mean your incorporeal self?"

Meaghan nodded. "I was very young and didn't realize what I was doing. Clarissa freaked out and started screaming about me being a ghost. I got such a shock I shot back into my body before anyone else saw me. After she came back to the orphanage, she never spoke to me again. She would just stare at me with hate in her eyes or ignore me completely. I tried to apologize but she refused to listen. She became sullen and completely anti-social, refusing to speak to anyone and one day..." She paused. "One day I went to use the bathroom and found her on the tiled floor. Her blood was … everywhere. Arterial spray up the walls, on the ceiling … everywhere. She had slit her wrists with a razor that she'd stolen from the caretaker's room."

"Did she survive?"

Meaghan shrugged. "I don't know. All they would tell me was that she wouldn't be coming back. I was barely a teenager. I thought that it was probably adult code for dead."

"That's possible. Death is hard to explain to a child."

"Since that day, I can't stand the sight of blood whether it's mine or someone else's. I can't stand the sight, smell or even the thought of blood. I get physically ill. I could never—not in a million years—entertain the thought of becoming a vampire. I'm sorry, David. I love you but I can't be with you."

David opened his mouth to protest but Meaghan touched his mouth with her fingers and shook her head as tears began to flow down her cheeks. "I know I'm drunk and not making any sense but I need you to leave now. Please, David."

****

After David left the cottage and she had dead bolted the front door, Meaghan flopped onto her bed and cried. Despite being exhausted, both physically and emotionally, her mind went on hyperdrive. She felt pain, anger, sorrow, dread and most of all … fear. That hellhound had come dangerously close to catching her and if it hadn't been for David … well, she shuddered to think what might have happened. She clutched her own arms, finding her hands a poor substitute for David's warm embrace and she suddenly wished that she had not sent him away. Her hands fumbled under her pillow and located her revolver. If that thing attacked again, this time she would be armed and ready. Terry's words echoed in her head. *Carry that gun with you at all times!* He'd warned her that she wasn't tough enough to be a cop and maybe he was right. Maybe the need to protect others wasn't enough. Even David knew that it was a mistake to confront Lilith and her friends alone and without her sidearm. *"How could you be so stupid?"*

Was he right? Had she grown careless or, had she always been careless and was only now recognizing her faults? Exhaustion closed her eyes but her mind continued to process the events of the evening. Humankind had its share of flesh and blood monsters … she could deal with them. But real monsters? Vampires and hell hounds? How was she supposed to cope with that?

****

Meaghan woke often during the night, sure that she had heard the familiar weird howling from her old neighborhood. Her hand slid under her pillow to retrieve her weapon. She wrapped her fingers around the trigger of her gun. *It's your imagination. You had too much to drink and your mind is playing tricks.* But, recent events had taught her that anything was possible and that there were dangers roaming around at night. Creatures born from nightmares, and at least one of them wanted her dead.

When sunlight illuminated her bedroom, she gave up on the idea of sleep. Yawning, she threw back the covers and headed to the kitchen to put on the kettle before assembling an outfit suitable for the day's work. While the kettle boiled, she wrapped her cast in plastic bags and climbed into the shower. The hot water eased some of the aches in her tired body but it was still a struggle to shampoo her hair. The pain in her wrist reminded her that—compared to the supernatural creatures that she had encountered—she was fragile and easily broken. David had not even intended to harm her but his superior strength had broken her wrist. *How much damage could the hell-hound do?* Meaghan remembered the training videos of the police dogs and how they'd been able to bring down full grown men using their fangs and claws. A mental vision formed. She saw herself being attacked by the hell-hound. Its fangs tore at her skin, gouging chunks of flesh from her bones, blood gushed from the wounds. She heaved and bolted from the shower to the toilet. Bile burned her throat and David's warning rang in her ears. "You should take it easy on the scotch otherwise you'll have one hell of a hang-over tomorrow." Damn you, David."

Somehow she managed to finish her shower and dress before returning to the kitchen. She chose to omit the usual splash of milk to her coffee, suspecting that it might upset her stomach but added a third spoonful of sugar to counteract the bitterness. As she drank, she counted her blessings. Being ambidextrous meant that her broken right hand only handicapped her a little. She could still maintain her independence. More importantly, she could still shoot. The long hours spent at the shooting range practicing with both hands had paid off. She was a crack shot with both, but, would that be enough? *Would a bullet stop the hell-hound?* And what about the demon? *If that thing became corporeal...*

****

During her research, her mobile phone rang. She picked it up on the second ring.

"Hello, Terry."

"Look, Megs. I'm sorry about last night. I was worried about you and ... well, I just lost it."

"I know, I'm sorry too. You know that I can never stay mad at you. I love you."

"I love you too. Actually, there's something I have been meaning to tell you for a long time, something that—"

"What? Yeah, sorry. Look, Terry, I'm in the campus library and I've just been shooshed."

"I can hardly hear you ... can you speak up?"

"No. I'm in a quiet zone. I have to go. Can we finish this discussion later? I'll call in to the station after I'm finished here."

"Yeah, sure. It's nothing that can't wait."

"Great, thanks. See you later."

She hung up the phone, mouthed an apology to the librarian and continued to search the computer as a smile spread across her face. *I must remember to take him a chocolate éclair later. That always cheers him up.*

She typed in the word demon which led her to an alternate spelling ... daemon. As she continued her search, it surprised her to discover that many cultures believed in the existence of these creatures whose name supposedly originated in Mesopotamia. The pinging of her phone attracted more angry glances so she mouthed another apology before reading the text from Terry.

Leaving the station to check out a lead. How about

185

meeting at my place around 7? I'll supply pizza.

Her first instinct was to decline. David would worry if she was late home but she couldn't use him as an excuse. Besides, Terry offered an olive branch. How could she refuse? She texted back.

I'll bring the wine. Is red okay? Send.

Ping. **You know it.**

Seven it is. Send.

With a sigh, she typed another message, this time addressed to David. **Having dinner with a friend. May be late home. Don't worry.**

"Excuse me." She looked up to see a rather irritated librarian scowling down at her. "There are students waiting to use this computer. If you are finished, please vacate this seat."

"I'm not finished with the computer," Meaghan told her. "And I promise that I won't be any more trouble. Look. No more interruptions." She turned the phone off and placed it in her handbag as she forced a smile.

With a huff, the librarian departed and Meaghan returned to her search in earnest. The faster she got out of the library, the better.

****

"Am I late?"

"Nope, right on time." Terry stepped aside and ushered Meaghan into his apartment. "The pizza guy just left."

"Smells good. My stomach was beginning to think that my throat had been cut."

Terry's laugh brought a smile to Meaghan's face. "It's been a while since I heard you laugh."

"It's been a while since we spent actual quality time together."

Meaghan nodded. "Too long." She handed him a

bag. "I brought two bottles, just in case."

"That's my girl. The pizza is on the table. Help yourself while I get the glasses."

"Only one pizza?"

"Geez, looking at you, no one would guess how much you like to eat. Don't worry, Miss Piggy. There is garlic bread on the table and dessert in the fridge."

Meaghan pulled a face and poked out her tongue. "Just for that ... I might keep the éclairs for myself." She dangled another bag in his face.

"Chocolate?" His eyes widened. He snatched bag from her hand and peeked inside. "I take back the Miss Piggy reference and will now refer to you as my goddess."

"That's better." She opened the pizza box and leaned in for a sniff. "Pepperoni heaven."

"Didn't they feed you at the mansion?" Terry placed the wine glasses on the dining table and pulled out a chair for Meaghan. "Sit. Or are you going to stand over the pizza box and eat the lot by yourself?"

Meaghan grabbed a slice of pizza before accepting the seat. With her mouth half-full, she answered. "Yes, they fed me very well and if you keep insulting me, I'm going home and taking the chocolate éclairs with me."

Terry raised his hands in surrender. "I'll be good." He put a slice of pizza on his plate and reached for the garlic bread, offering it to Meaghan. She reached out her hand but hesitated, then shook her head.
Vampires are allergic to garlic, aren't they?

"What? No garlic bread? Who are you and what have you done with Meaghan?"

"Just leaving room for dessert and besides, I wouldn't want garlic breath later..." She considered the implications and added, "It might make the chocolate taste funny."

Terry put down the bread without taking a piece. Instead, he took a gulp of wine.

"Hard day?"

He shrugged. "No more than usual." Between bites of pizza, he asked, "How was your excursion to the library?"

"Actually, very informative." She scoffed down her slice and grabbed another. "Did you know that Demons are mentioned in ancient texts from many cultures?"

"You don't *still* believe that you saw a demon? I thought I explained how—"

"Yes … you told me that the smoke could have contained some sort of hallucinates, but, I know what I saw."

"Meaghan—"

"Just hear me out, Terry."

"Fine. Spin me your yarn." He took another slice from the box, rolled it into a scroll and shoved half in his mouth, chewing noisily.

"Pretty." She rolled her eyes. "Look. Whether you believe in Demons or not … it doesn't matter. What matters is, the killers believe."

"Okay. You have my undivided attention." He took a sip of wine. Meaghan mirrored his actions.

"Bear with me while I try to explain. The ancient texts spoke about using daemons against their enemies. You know, like some evil genie."

"They grant wishes?"

"In a way. If someone had a problem, they might call upon a daemon to solve it."

"Sounds like a twisted, screwed up fairy god-mother to me."

"Yeah, I know, right?"

"How do they find these demons?"

"From what I read … they might use a curse tablet. They write their request on a piece of metal or pottery and leave it hidden. Sometimes they would put it under floors or even place it in a cemetery." She shuddered as she remembered her first encounter with the daemon.

"Are you okay? You just paled a shade."

"Yeah. I just remembered something that might be important."

Terry leaned back in his chair and clasped his hands behind his head. "Spill."

"Sacrifice was a big deal in antiquity, especially blood sacrifices."

Terry's hands dropped to his lap and he sat forward. "What about candles? Did your research say anything about black candles?"

"Candles and incense." She nodded. "More common in modern times."

"So, you're telling me that this is *still* practiced? This is the twenty-first century for fuck's sake."

"I believe that candles are for effect and the blood is usually from a small animal. The practitioners don't really believe that anything will happen. It's a bit of a game, like dungeons and dragons."

"But, you don't believe that our unsub is playing?"

She shook her head. "I believe that our *unsubs* are not pulling any punches. They're sacrificing humans in the hope of gaining something from a demon." She held her hand up, palm out. "Before you naysay my theory. It doesn't matter whether you believe or not. The perps will not stop killing until they get what they want."

"Then I guess we'd better figure out what that is."

****

"I don't trust him."

"Sit down, David. You've been pacing the room since you read that text. How do know that she's with this Terry Palmer guy?"

David plonked himself into the nearest chair. "Satisfied?"

"Yes, thank you. I was beginning to feel seasick just watching you. Now, did she say she was going out with her boss?"

"No. The text said that she was having dinner with a friend."

Derrick smirked. "I'm sure that she has more than one friend."

"You don't know her like I do. She was raised in an orphanage with Palmer. He has been her friend for her entire life."

"Then I don't see the problem."

"Well, you would if you'd been privy to his thoughts. When he interviewed me after one of the murders, he could barely take his eyes off her."

"He was probably keeping an eye on her. I imagine it was all very innocent."

David's mood darkened. "There was nothing innocent about the images in his head. He lusts after her. It was all I could do not to punch him in the mouth."

"Take a deep breath and calm down."

David rolled his eyes. "Really? You want me to take a deep breath? When was the last time you breathed?"

"Sorry, poor choice of words. Anyway, I meant it figuratively, not literally." He stood up and walked over to David, placing a hand on his shoulder. "If you plan on going after her, and I assume you are?" David nodded. "Then you had better calm down. Remember the last time you lost your temper with her?"

"I broke her wrist." He placed his forehead into his cupped hands and sighed. "I would give anything to take it back."

"Hindsight is 20/20. Just don't let it happen again, and make sure you stay out of sight." He gave his brother a playful slap across the cheek and began to walk away. "Anna and I are heading out to visit Sofie *if* she ever finishes getting ready!" he called up the stairs.

"Don't get your knickers in a knot," Anna complained as she made her way down the staircase. "I've been ready for ages."

"Sure she has," he whispered the words to David. Anna joined him and he wrapped his arm around her waist. As they reached the door, he called back… "I have my woman. Go get yours."

****

Meaghan picked up a tea towel and joined Terry in the kitchen as he washed the dishes. "I'm stuffed." She told him as she rubbed her belly. "Thanks for dinner."

"I've missed sharing meals with you, Megs. We should do it more often."

She nodded with a smile and put the last of the dishes away. "I should be going."

"Going? It's still early."

"I know, but I'm feeling tired and I should get home."

"Not yet." Terry grabbed her left hand and led her to the settee. "We haven't had a chance to talk."

She laughed as she plonked onto the couch. "We haven't stopped talking all night."

"Police stuff and small talk." He sat beside her, still holding her hand. "I have a proposition for you."

Meaghan tilted her head to the side, her eyebrows narrowed. "That sounds ominous."

"Actually, I think you'll find it practical." He

casually stroked her hand as he spoke, a gesture that did not go unnoticed. Meaghan stiffened in her seat feeling suddenly uncomfortable.

"I want you to move in here."

"I have a place Terry. I appreciate the offer but it's unnecessary."

"What place? Corel's place? He's dead, Megs."

"I'm well aware of that but I have been invited to stay. Derrick Corel says that the company will continue to fund my studies and they will even find me another teacher."

"But why stay there? Move in with me. We have fun together, don't we?"

"Yes, Terry but I'm settled in the cottage. You know I love you but—"

"I love you too, Meaghan. I always have."

"I know that Terry, I—"

His kiss came from left field. He lunged forward, cupping her head in his hand as he drew her in. There was no trace of brotherly love in the kiss, it was passionate, hard and unwelcome. She pushed him away and kept her palm to his chest as he pressed forward again, his arms crushing her to his body, his mouth bruising her lips. She slapped his face.

"Terry! What's gotten into you?"

He appeared shocked, cupping his hand to his reddened cheek. "I thought…"

Meaghan jumped to her feet, her own face hot with embarrassment. "I'm sorry if you misunderstood me, Terry. I meant that I love you like a brother."

"I want more." He stood up and took her hands in his. "I was afraid that you were falling for Corel especially after your reaction to the news of his death."

She opened her mouth to speak but he silenced her with a shake of his head.

"You recovered quickly. You couldn't have loved him. Not the way I love you. Give me some time to prove that we can work. Move in with me."

She shook her head. "You're wrong on so many levels. Moving in with you is a bad idea. And, Terry. As much as I hate to hurt you … I did love David. I still do. Nothing will change that."

He dropped her hands, flopped back onto the sofa and mumbled under his breath.

"How can I compete with a dead guy?"

"You can't and you shouldn't try. In your heart you know that we weren't meant to be together. It would never work out. We have too much history. You're my closest friend. Can't we stay as we are?"

"I don't need any more friends." He mumbled as he crossed his arms across his chest and stared down at his feet.

"I think I should go." She grabbed her bag from the kitchen table and marched towards the door. He remained in his seat but called after her.

"Fine. Go! Run back to your dead boyfriend's house but don't coming crawling back to me when you realize that you want a flesh and blood lover. Dead is dead, Meaghan, and I'm done waiting for you."

****

As she ran to the bus stop, blinding tears streamed down her face blurring her vision. She ran head-long into a wall. At least it felt like a wall. She looked up into familiar eyes and felt strong arms wrap around her as she dissolved into tears.

"Hush, kitten." He soothed as he stroked her hair. "Tell me what happened."

"Oh, David." She sobbed. "I've been selfish and blind. I've unintentionally led Terry on and now … our friendship is probably over."

"It's not your fault, Chérie. The heart wants what the heart wants. He'll get over it."

"He doesn't understand. He and I … we could never be more than friends."

"Because you think of him as a brother?"

"Yes and…"

"And?"

She gazed up into his eyes, her eyes filled with tears. "I have already given my heart to another."

His mouth dropped.

"I had hoped—"

She silenced him with a kiss.

"I love you, David."

"You don't know how long I have waited to hear those words from you." He drew her in and kissed her. His warm, soft lips welcoming. He whispered into her ear.

"I love you too, kitten. I always have."

A noise from the adjoining building broke the magic. They turned quickly, expecting danger. The elderly man shuffled past them, mumbling under his breath about his wife's nagging driving him from the house on such a cold night. He tipped his cap as he passed them.

Meaghan gasped. "David. You shouldn't be on the street. What if someone recognizes you?"

"I guess that would complicate matters." He grinned before kissing her again.

"Be serious, David. Terry could be watching from his window. If he sees you–"

"I know. It'll blow my cover." He took her by the hand. "My car is around the corner; we'd better get you home quickly."

Meaghan looked around suspiciously. "Why? Did you hear something? Do you suspect that something is going to happen?"

David's mouth widened into a grin before he leaned in and whispered into her ear. "I suspect that if I don't get you home soon, I'll be forced to make love to you ... here. Right on the sidewalk against this wall."

She returned the grin. "Then you'd better take me home now, Mr. Corel and don't spare the horses."

Chapter Twenty

"Tired?"

Meaghan fidgeted in her chair.

"I'm fine thanks, Anna." She moaned quietly as she adjusted her position on the lounge. Her body ached in places that she never knew existed. David's "lessons" were becoming strenuous. Strenuous, but exhilarating. Her skin still tingled from his touch and his close proximity was making her feel uncomfortably aroused. She turned to face him and was horrified to see him grinning like a Cheshire cat. She frowned and slapped his arm. Her facial expression only made him laugh.

She was about to reprimand him when her phone began to dance across the glass table. As she picked it up, she noticed that it was Terry and hesitated before announcing,

"Excuse me, I have to take this." As she walked out of the room, she pressed the answer icon. "Hello?"

"Oh, thank god you're okay. I thought ... I'm so sorry I let you walk home alone, Megs."

"I'm okay Terry. Why do you sound so breathless?"

"I called you last night, after ... I just wanted to apologize. I called every hour and left messages. At first I thought that you were ignoring me, which I completely understand. But then, I considered that you might have been attacked by the unsub..."

She heard a catch in his voice.

"I should never have let my ego put you in danger. If anything had happened to you Megs—"

"I'm sorry to have worried you, Terry. I was tired and put my phone on silent so I wouldn't be disturbed. I guess I forgot to turn it back on."

"I'm just grateful that you're okay." He sighed. "Do me a favor, Megs? Actually, more than one."

"Of course."

"Delete all the messages I left. I said a few things that I regret. I was drunk and hurt and acted like a real prick."

"No probs. What was the other favor?"

"Take the sick leave. I need some space until I can face you again. Please, Megs. Stay away from the station ... and the case. You know how I can be, and throwing myself into a case will give me time to move on. Do that for me."

Meaghan was tempted to argue. She opened her mouth to speak, let her shoulders drop as she sighed.

"All right Terry. I'll stay away ... for now."

"Thanks, Megs."

"Terry." She hesitated as she waited to see if he was still on the line.

"Yes."

"Friends?"

"Friends."

She heard the familiar sound of a dial tone as Terry hung up the call and wondered if he really meant what he'd said. He'd sounded sad, defeated.

"Is everything all right?" David asked when she joined the others in the living room.

She nodded and forced a smile before sitting beside him on the couch. "What did I miss?"

"Anna and Derrick were just telling me about their meeting with Sofie."

"Sofie?"

"The witch that I told you about."

"Oh, yes. I remember. The one who's teaching Anna."

"She has a store in town where she sells crystals

and does readings etc." Anna informed her. "We've been trying to work out who is blocking our powers."

"Any leads?"

"Not yet. It's very frustrating. "How about you?"

"I was talking with Terry last night…" her thoughts drifted back to the end of the evening but she blocked them out as she continued, "about demons."

Derrick sat forward in his seat. "He believed you?"

Meaghan shook her head. "Not about the demon, but I think I convinced him that whoever summoned the demon believes in demons."

"I imagine that he found it all a bit surreal."

"Yes, Derrick. Even as I told him, *I* could hardly believe what I was saying. I wish it wasn't true. It's hard to sleep knowing that there are creatures prowling the streets looking for blood." She realized her blunder. "No offense, you guys."

David placed his hands on her knee. "No offense taken. Besides, I don't prowl, I shop and evil is not confined to creatures of the night. Humans can be just as malevolent, maybe more. It's a fact of life, kitten. Since the dawn of time, good and evil have co-existed. You can't have one without the other."

"We're you lying about your age?" she teased. "Have you been around since the dawn of time?"

Derrick choked on his drink, spitting the wine across the table as he chortled. He wiped his nose with a handkerchief as Anna used a napkin to clean the table. "I like her, David. You should hang on to this one."

David wrapped an arm around her and squeezed. "I'm glad that I have your approval, brother, because I'm never letting her out of my sight."

"That's going to be difficult," Anna reminded him, "when you're asleep, she's getting up and vice-versa. Unless—"

"We haven't discussed that," David interrupted as he rose from his seat pulling Meaghan up with him. "If there isn't any more news pertaining to the murders, we'll be heading downstairs."

"David, I didn't mean anything by it. I just—"

David stopped her again. "It's all right, Anna. Goodnight." He hurried Meaghan down the stairs to the studio and led her towards the bed.

Meaghan stopped short of the bed. "What did Anna mean David?"

"How would I know," he teased as he attempted to nuzzle her neck. She pushed him away and held him at arm's length.

"What's the unless she mentioned? Is there a way for us to be together?"

"There is only one way for us to be together, kitten ,and I don't think that you'd consent. Let's forget about it for the moment and hop back into bed." He sat on the edge of his bed and patted the mattress.

"She was talking about making me into a vampire, wasn't she?"

David nodded. "She doesn't know about your hemophobia. There is no way she would have suggested it, had she known. It's my fault, I should have told them, warned them not to drink blood near you."

Meaghan sat down beside him. A chill ran down her spine. Even the thought of blood made her ill. "Is that likely to happen? The blood drinking, I mean."

"No. I'll make sure that they understand. Besides, Anna only drinks blood from David."

"How does that work?"

"Easy. He feeds … usually from a blood bag and then he feeds her."

Meaghan gasped and held her hand to her mouth.

"No, you goose." David laughed. "Not like a bird feeds its young."

"Then how?"

David's mouth twisted into a smile and Meaghan saw a twinkle of mischief in his eyes as he told her, "I'd rather show you. I promise that I won't bite." He moved his lips to her throat and ran his tongue over her carotid artery, his cool breath tickled her skin and she shivered. She touched his face.

"Your skin … it's so cold."

"I missed my dinner."

"But we ate less than an hour ago."

"I can consume human food, kitten, but it doesn't nourish me. I need blood to live. My body will continue to grow colder until I feed."

Meaghan gasped. "You'll die?"

He shook his head. "Basically, I'm already dead my love. I'd enter into a state of hibernation if I go without blood for a long period of time. Either that, or I'd turn feral."

"I don't like the sound of either of those choices."

"Then, I'd best be off to the upstairs refrigerator." He rose to leave the room but she reached for him and drew him back to the bed.

"Not so fast. I have more questions."

"Yes Officer Lamb. Fire away…" He held out his palm in mock horror. "Not literally of course. I haven't quite recovered from my last encounter with bullets."

Meaghan ran her hand over his chest. She could feel the slight impressions of the bullet holes that had torn through his body. She pictured the stake that barely missed his heart. She'd almost lost him.

"I've noticed that you and Derrick have a psychic connection. He and Anna seem to do the same. How does that work?"

"It's called a sire bond. When a vampire is turned, the victim is drained of blood, almost to the point of death."

"Almost? I thought … didn't you say that you *were* dead?"

"If you'll allow me to finish…"

"Go ahead."

"When the victim is close to death, the vampire opens a vein and forces the victim to drink." Meaghan could feel the bile rising. She held her hand to her throat and closed her eyes. David touched her hand.

"Are you sure that you want me to continue?"

She opened her eyes and nodded. "Yes. Go on. I want to know everything."

"After consuming the vampire's blood. The transformation begins. The human part dies and the vampire is born."

"And the psychic connection?"

"The new vampire will always remain connected to his or her sire and the sire has the ability to find the newborn whenever he is."

"So, if a human consumes vampire blood, he automatically becomes a vampire?"

"No. Only if he is drained. Why are you asking?"

"One more question. Does the connection work both ways? I mean, if we—for example—had a psychic link, could I contact you?"

David nodded. "Yes, most definitely. You and I already have a strong connection."

"I'd like to try."

"As much as I want to taste you kitten. I'm not sure if you're ready."

"Feed from me, David. I want to be the one who nourishes you but more than that, I want to feel you close to me when daylight keeps us apart."

"That *would* make things easier." He narrowed his eyebrows. "Especially when you take off to investigate on your own. But there is one, rather big problem."

"Being?"

"You do understand that the process involves the taking and giving of blood?"

Meaghan swallowed the lump that was caught in her throat. "Could you hypnotize me? Maybe you could knock me out?"

"Both those suggestions are abhorrent to me, kitten. I would never knock out a woman and I want you to be fully in control of your faculties when you accept my blood. I vowed that I'd never again…"

"What is it? Have you forced someone to drink your blood? Wait. Your connection with Derrick. Did you … are you Derrick's sire?"

David rose from the bed and walked to the liquor cabinet. He kept his back turned to her as he poured himself a scotch. "Yes, kitten. I sired Derrick. It wasn't by choice—his or mine—and he hated me for years. I found him beaten almost to death, our sister dead by his side. Her ruthless thug of a husband had killed her and his minions were still beating on Derrick when I arrived. I … dispatched them, and tried to help Derrick but he was already dying. I had no choice but to convert him." he turned to Meaghan with tears in his eyes. "I couldn't watch my brother die."

Meaghan felt his pain. She had witnessed the connection between the brothers first hand. She imagined how difficult a choice it had been.

"Your relationship seems all right now."

"I believe Anna deserves the credit for that. When Derrick converted her, it was under similar circumstances, so he was in a better position to understand my dilemma. Fortunately for him, she forgave him soon after."

"So, Anna didn't want to convert? Not even for Derrick?"

David made his way back to the bed with two whiskey glasses. He handed one to Meaghan. "No. She had her reasons. You'd have to discuss that with her."

Meaghan gulped her two fingers worth of scotch and took a deep breath. *You bet I will.*

"I haven't mentioned it before as I didn't want to worry you but, this demon. I think it saw me and I have been hearing howling outside my window since the first victim was found."

"Why didn't you tell me before? Did Palmer know?"

"Terry would have thought that I was losing my mind or else, he would have worried about me. Either way, I'd be pulled from the case." She held out the glass and smiled, indicating that she'd like a refill. "I didn't tell you because, well, as you know … until recently, I thought that you were the killer."

"That's fair enough," he told her as he handed her the fresh drink, "I suspected you too. On that subject, just a word of warning…you may want to avoid getting undressed in any room besides your bedroom and bathroom."

"You have me under surveillance?"

He shrugged and smiled awkwardly but his expression turned solemn when he told her. "I wish you'd told me about the howling. You need to take precautions."

"I am. I mean, I plan to. That's why I think it is necessary for us to have a psychic connection."

She held out her hand to stop him from objecting before she could finish. Her confidence was fading and she was afraid that she would change her mind. Her speech was as much for herself as it was for him.

"I can't function as well at night and there will be times when it is necessary to question suspects during daylight hours. I would feel safer knowing that I can contact you whenever I need you and it would be easier for me to think if I know you're safe."

"That suits me but, are you sure? I'll try and make this as pleasurable as possible but if you change your mind—"

"Do it now … before I change my mind."

She pulled her t-shirt over her head, exposing her throat but he seemed more interested in her bare breasts. His fangs sprung from his gums and he lowered his head to her chest to lick her nipple, lapping and sucking until it hardened in his mouth. She gasped when his lips moved over her breast, kissing and sucking while his hands fondled her, first her other breast then lower, until his hand was at her navel, unzipping her jeans, slipping inside her lace panties, his fingers working their magic between her legs. She wiggled under him, assisting him as he freed her of her jeans. Her own hands aided him as he tugged at his own pants and when his erection sprung into her palm, she stroked him.

Her damp entrance welcomed him and with a thrust of his hips, he simultaneously drove into her body while his teeth sunk into her breast. She threw back her head and groaned as he drove into her, her body thrusting against him as the pressure inside her intensified. The loss of blood left her light-headed, as though she would float away on a cloud of ecstasy. Her own heart-beat pounded in her ears. She closed her eyes, barely noticing when he ran his fingernail across his own chest, cupped her head in his hand and directed her mouth to the wound. An explosion of color skyrocketed behind her closed eyes. Her skin prickled with electricity. A voice called his name, begging him to do things that she would never have said aloud. Words that she would been embarrassed to use.

She screamed his name again as her body shattered into a million fragments and he groaned his own orgasm into her mouth. When he recovered, he rolled onto his back taking her with him. She lay across his chest, kissing his face, his neck. She raised her head, running her tongue over her lips as she prepared to thank him for another earth shattering orgasm, but, as her senses return, she recognized the thick, coppery taste as it assaulted her senses. Her stomach somersaulted. Her eyes sprung open. She tried to swallow down the last of the blood as it mixed with her own saliva but as she tore her gaze away from his face, she stared directly at the gash that was beginning to close on his chest. She turned her head away. Looked down. Her gaze found a new source of panic … the puncture wounds on her chest. Ringed with blood, the blue veins startlingly prominent on her fair skin. It was more than she could stand. She tried to push away from his body. Escape to the bathroom but the room began to spin. Her mouth filled with saliva. Her skin beaded with sweat and a violent tremor shook her body before darkness swallowed her whole.

****

"Meaghan. Meaghan, wake up." He shook her, lightly at first but firmer when she didn't respond. "Please, baby. Open your eyes."

Her eyelids fluttered open, shut, and then opened again. This time they remained open.

"What happened?"

"I made a mistake and you paid for it."

"Oh, my lord. I'm so embarrassed." She crossed

her arms over her face. "I can't believe that I fainted during … you know."

"I should have warned you that the effect of the blood exchange was heightened during sex. I'd hoped that it would take your mind off the—"

She placed her hand over his mouth. "Please don't say the word. I think I'll heave." She closed her eyes. "I'm afraid to look. My breast"

"Healed. And it's safe to look at my chest too."

She smiled as she opened her eyes. "It's never safe to look at your chest, David." She traced his pectorals with a feather-light touch sending ripples of desire soaring through his already electrified blood stream. He'd dreamed of her taste and the real experience was nothing short of spectacular. Had it not been for her dramatic reaction, he would be in heaven.

"Ditto." He said, returning the favor. His fingers brushed the point on her breast where he had fed. He longed to taste her again. She touched her fingers to her lips and even without the newly acquired mental connection, he knew what she was thinking.

"Not a trace left, kitten."

She gasped. Her lips formed a perfect O and she smiled. "You licked me?"

"Ah, you're a fast learner grasshopper." He said with a bow. "I needed a few attempts before I was able to create a connection with my sire. *We* aren't even sire bonded."

"About that…" she hesitated. He knew she'd made a decision but he couldn't stand to hear the words out loud. It was his turn to hold a finger to her lips, silence her words although he couldn't block her thoughts.

"A conversation for another time, love. Let's just enjoy the moment." He lay down beside her and slipped his arm under her shoulders, hugging her tight. A smile spread across his face as he sent her a mental push. A memory of their lovemaking. She covered her face with her hands but he could tell by the sound of her voice that she was blushing.

"I can't believe that I said those things."

"The euphoria lasts for several hours after, kitten," he informed her as his free hand began to explore her curves. "Let's see if I can entice you to say those things again."

Chapter Twenty-One

"Did you find anything?"

"No, kitten. Whatever it was, it's gone, but I did notice the distinct odor of sulfur."

"Demon?"

David stepped into the lounge room and locked the sliding door behind him. He pulled the drapes closed before informing her. "I think it was the hell-hound."

"Oh, that makes me feel a lot better." She groaned as she slumped onto the couch. "I'm sorry if I woke you. It sounded closer this time."

"I was rising anyway," he assured her. "And you were understandably upset. This is the third time this week isn't it."

"Fourth." She said as she held up four fingers. "It feels like whoever is controlling the hell hound is getting anxious to finish—" she raised her arms in the air— "whatever he has planned."

"He?"

"He, she, whatever." She leaned forward in the seat and rested her forehead in her hands. "I don't know any more David. I'm exhausted, I'm confused and to be totally honest … more than a little scared. I still have nightmares about that evening outside the station. If you hadn't shown up—"

"But I did."

"But if you hadn't…"

"I will always be there for you, Meaghan. That's a promise." He sat down beside her and she curled up with her head in his lap. He stroked her hair. "It's been a long week."

"Aha." She mumbled. "I can't seem to adjust to sleeping through the day. My mind is on auto pilot and I can't relax without you but lying next to you is torture. I just want to wake you and have my wicked way with you."

"Do you hear me objecting?"

"No, but we still have a murderer on the loose and the case won't be solved in your bedroom."

"Have you heard from Palmer?"

"No." Reluctantly, she lifted her head and forced herself to sit up. "He still isn't returning my calls or answering my texts. I know I promised to give him space, but, I keep hoping that he'll come around."

"He will. I'm sure that he just has a lot on his mind."

"I should be out there ... helping him with the case."

"He ordered you to stand down."

"I'm not good at following orders."

David laughed. "I noticed that." She felt the buzzing in his jeans moments before his phone rang so she lifted her head off his lap. He reached into his pocket as the sound of a coffin opening startled her.

"Dracula? Really David?"

David shrugged. "It seemed funny when I downloaded it." He pressed the answer icon. "Yes, Anna. What? Okay, what station?" He grabbed the remote and turned on the T.V.

The screen sprung to life with the scene of an angry riot before flashing back to the male newsreader who announced...

"Breaking news. What started as a peaceful protest rally has escalated to a riot outside the police station in the small town of Azure Waters. Protestors have clashed with police who tried to move them on. We will now cross live to our reporter Pamela Brookes. Pamela, what can you tell us?"

The scene changed back to the riot and a young woman who was standing beside the police station. Her eyes flittered nervously between the camera and the crowd. "Hello, Grant. Senior Detective Inspector Terry Palmer is about to hold a press conference…" She touched her hand to her earpiece. "Okay, let's hear what he has to say." She turned to face the group of officers standing meters away. The camera panned in on a familiar face and Meaghan gasped when she saw Terry appear on screen. He looked tired. Tired and anxious.

"Although we understand the concern of the students, we promise that we, the police, are doing all we can to guarantee their safety. We have a few suspects but until we find the perpetrator of these crimes, we urge everyone to stay in their homes after dark. If you must venture out for work, it is safer to travel in pairs. Until further notice, the campus will remain closed, including the library—"

"How are we supposed to study?" screamed a protestor from off screen.

"What don't you do your fucking jobs and catch the fucking creep, you cu—" the last expletive was bleeped from the broadcast as Terry continued.

"The police are doing all we can to catch the killer or killers. Please, stay in your homes and let the police do their jobs. Thank you."

He stepped away from the podium and the camera panned across the crowd where protestors were setting fire to garbage cans and hurling empty beer bottles at the riot police. Meaghan noticed that most of the crowd was wearing black clothing and the familiar piercings and tattoos of Lilith's crew. As if on cue, she spotted Lilith in the crowd, screaming abuse and obviously enjoying the notoriety. When the camera panned back, Meaghan froze. Menacing eyes stared back at her from the screen. It was a though the woman was staring into her soul. "That's her!" she told David. "That's the woman from the cafeteria, the one who followed me to the carpark. Lilith's friend."

"I remember her from your art class. Strange young woman. While the other students were painting images of the model, she seemed more focused on your side of the room. Her canvas was completely blank and I assumed that she wasn't sure how to start so, I offered my assistance."

"What did she say?"

David cleared his throat. "I was raised never to use such vulgar language in the presence of a lady."

Meaghan pointed to the screen. "Look, she's following Terry to the carpark."

"Perhaps she wants to share some information about the case?"

Meaghan narrowed her eyes.

"All right, I agree. It does look suspicious."

She grabbed her bag from the hall table and headed towards the door.

"Where are you going young lady?"

"Terry may be in trouble."

"You stay here. I'll check it out."

"I'm not afraid of her David. I'll take my gun this time." She grimaced when she remembered that her gun was still under the pillow.

He held her by the shoulders. "Are you afraid of the hell-hound? Don't forget, it was less than an hour ago that you heard it outside your window."

She thought for a minute. "Could I take your car? I promise to stick to the speed limit … unless of course that thing attacks again, then, all bets are off."

"I'll drive. If anything happens, I can—"

"Blow your cover by exposing yourself in

public?"

"Exposing myself? What did you have in mind Officer Lamb?"

"You have a very naughty mind Mr. Corel. You know very well what I mean. If Terry or any of the students see you—"

"I know. The reports of my death would appear highly exaggerated but, I have a better idea. Try ringing him before you go charging off to save him. He is probably more than capable of looking after himself."

She shrugged. "He hasn't answered my call so far, but…" She flipped open her phone and pressed his number. "I guess it's worth a try." The phone rang three times before it was answered.

"Yes, Meaghan?"

"Terry. Thank goodness you answered. I wanted to—"

"Hold on a minute, Megs."

She heard him move the phone away from his mouth. "Yes, can I help you?"

She held her breath as she listened to the sound of scuffling, the crack of something hitting the ground and then, a sharp intake of breath. She screamed his name into the phone and heard the faint reply. "Meaghan..."

The line went dead.

****

For the third time in half an hour, Meaghan checked the time on her wrist watch. *David should have been there by now. I should have insisted that he take me along. Where the hell are they?*

As if on cue, a voice in her head answered. *"I'm here, kitten, but there's no sign of Terry. Look, I don't mean to worry you but, there is a fair quantity of blood beside his car. I'm about to do a sweep of the area. Stay there. Derrick and Anna are home and I have explained the situation to them. If you need any help, call them first."*

Meaghan felt the tears swell and burn behind her eyes. Despite the calm in his voice, she could tell that David suspected the worst. The prospect of finding Terry alive didn't look good. *Find him, David. Please find him and bring him back.*

She felt him break the connection. It left her even more empty inside despite knowing that he did it for her protection. Thoughts of Terry flashed in her head and it broke her heart to think that their last moments together had ended with so much pain. She couldn't imagine a life without him. He was her brother, her confident and her protector for more years than she cared to remember. Without him, she would not have survived the lonely years in the orphanage or the difficult transition into the real world. They had to find him alive.

Briiiiing. The landline's ring shocked her out of her thoughts and it took a moment to realize where the noise was coming from. She lifted the receiver, wondering why David had chosen the outdated form of communication when it was easier to project his thoughts.

"David?"

"No, Meaghan … it's Anna."

"You sound flustered. Did David ask you to call me? Has he found Terry?"

"Sorry, Meaghan, but I haven't heard a thing. I know we promised David that we would stay home and look after you, but, there's been another attack. My friend Sofie was attacked in her store tonight and she's in intensive care. I hate to leave you, but her daughter lives in another state and I didn't want to leave Sofie alone in the hospital in case the attacker isn't finished with her.

Derrick is still at her store checking for clues and rounding up some of the coven members to help. You should be okay there. Just stay put. A couple of days ago, Sofie and I placed a protection spell around the cottage. Nothing supernatural, besides David of course, can get in."

"Of course I'll be fine. You stay with your friend. I hope that she'll recover soon."

"I can't believe anyone would want to hurt her. She's blind. What sort of animal would attack a blind woman? It looks like the doctor is coming back … I gotta go."

As she hung up the phone, Meaghan tried to clear her mind. *Think, Meaghan, what would be the point of these attacks?* She searched through her bag for her notebook and found her previous notes on the killer's modus operandi, preferring the written word to using technology. She read her list out loud.

- Killer has only attacked University students, as far as we know so far

- Victims strangled

- Killer has changed his MO. Now using a knife

- New suspect. David Corel. Artist/Model and billionaire playboy. Seems rather unlikely considering he is a chick magnet but Terry is convinced

- Covert operation. Lucky turn of events has put me in a position to watch Corel closely.

- Suspiciously, David has turned up at the murder sites before the police. Must work out how he does it.

- David Corel was shot dead tonight.

Feeling numb. I don't believe he was the killer but Terry believes that the case is now closed

- Witnessed a murder tonight. Poor young woman was sacrificed. Not sure if I believe my own eyes. Must find a way to convince Terry.

Terry. Please be alive. She shook her head. *This won't get you anywhere. Think Meaghan. What is the connection?* She picked up her pen and added to the list.

- Attacked by hell-hound outside police station

- Stalked by Lilith and friends
- Terry suddenly disappears
- Blind witch attacked in her store

She tapped her pen against her bottom lip as she considered the clues. *Why would the hell-hound be after me? Is it because the demon saw me at the ceremony? Why come after me at the police station, does the unsub know I'm a cop? Why the blind lady and Terry? Think, think, thi— Oh my gosh. I'm the connection. I was at the police station to see Terry and whoever has him must know that we are friends. No. That couldn't be it. I don't even know this, Sofie woman, she's Anna's friend ... who is working with Anna to break whatever spell was cast to block the killer. They must be making progress or else why would she be attacked.*

With notebook in hand, she rose from her seat and walked over to the large sliding door, carefully lifting the corner of the curtain to peer outside. The sky was cloudless and filled with stars. The moon hung low in the sky illuminating the huge estate. She could see all the way to the beach from her position but she knew that there were many dark corners that could conceal the hound or its master. The thought chilled her to the bone.

She felt confident enough to take on a flesh and blood killer but she now knew that there were things that lived for the darkness, things that could rip you to sheds, and she had no intention of becoming the next victim. It pained her to allow fear to keep her sequestered in her home while her loved ones were in danger. If it wasn't for her phobia, she could have helped David search for Terry. Her injured hand rendered her even more useless against an attacker.

"Some detective you are," she said aloud as she threw her notebook across the kitchen counter. It knocked the phone off the hook before skidding off the bench and onto the floor. "You should be at the station looking for Terry." If only she wasn't so scared of the hell-hound. If she could only find a way of … *idiot*! She slapped the side of her head with her palm. *Why didn't I think of that before?*

****

"Hello?"

"Hello, Evan. Listen, I'm sorry if I woke you up old man but I need your help."

"Of course, Master David. I wasn't asleep, just resting my eyes."

David knew that Evan was fibbing. The call had almost gone to voicemail before it was picked up. Poor Evan. Eighty years old and still refusing to retire.

"What can I do for you, Sir?"

"I've been trying to contact Meaghan at the cottage but she isn't answering her cell phone and the landline is busy. Could you do me a favor and check the surveillance camera from the study?"

"Certainly, Master David. Just give me a minute, if you will."

David's exceptional hearing picked up the sound of the contents of a bottle shaking and he heard water being poured from a jug. "Is everything all right, Evan? Are you ill?"

"No, sir. Just a slight headache. I'm just popping a paracetamol. Here I go ... off to the study."

Time dragged on as the old servant shuffled the length of the house to the study. David could hear the Evan's wheezing breaths as he made his way along the long corridors. He cursed himself for not forcing Evan to take retirement and go on a long cruise.

"I'm here, Master David." Evan gasped. "I can see Miss Lamb sitting in a chair with her back to the camera. I believe that she is asleep."

"Thank you, Evan. Once again, I'm so sorry to have disturbed you. You sound tired old man. When I get home, we need to have a serious discussion about your retirement."

"Master David?"

"Yes, Evan."

"I just wanted to take the opportunity to thank you and Master Derrick for all that you've done for me. I may never have had children of my own, but you've been like sons to me. God bless you both."

David felt uneasy. It was uncharacteristic of Evan to sound so maudlin.

"We could never manage without you, old man. You've been more of a father to us than our natural parent and that's why I will be forcing you to have a holiday. I'm worried about you. Are you sure that you feel all right, Evan?"

"Never better. Goodnight, sir."

"Good night, Evan."

"Master David, wait!" The old butler sounded panicked.

"Yes, Evan. What's the matter?"

"I can see someone entering Miss Lamb's

cottage. Two people, dressed in black and wearing masks. She doesn't seem to notice them. Oh, no. They've picked her up. I must do something…"

"Don't hang up, Evan. Stay on the phone."

He could hear the old man shuffling along. The sound of a door opening. The squeal of tires on the asphalt driveway. Evan's breathing became labored, thready.

"Evan! Are you all right? Are you still there, man?"

"They took her. Black panel van- sped- down-driveway. Couldn't stop them." He wheezed.

"Evan?"

"Master David. They to-ok her. They took Miss. La-amb." A tremor shook his voice as his words faded away.

"Evan? Are you still there?"

"B-lack van. No pl-ates. Two of them- dre-ssed in black. Aargh—"

"Evan. Stay where you are. I'll send an ambulance."

"It's … all right, Master David. It's … my time."

"No! Hold on. Please, Evan…" his voice broke as he felt his beloved friend slipping away. He could hear the erratic beating of Evan's heart as it slowed. "Don't leave us."

"Never leave you- always in my heart. My sons."

****

Despite being incorporeal, Meaghan could smell the blood even before she found Terry slumped against the alley wall. He wasn't moving. She gasped and edged closer, fighting the urge to flee the scene. The area reeked of blood and Terry's body sat in a puddle of the sticky mess. She swallowed down the bile and reached out to touch him. Her hand passed through him, barely causing a breeze to brush his skin. She tried again, concentrating her efforts as she touched his cheek with her fingers. Nothing. Aiming for his carotid artery, she reached out her hand but stopped when she saw the blood seeping from a wound to his stomach. Her incorporeal hand shook, almost fading into the ether. It took all her effort to hold herself together. *If the blood is still seeping, his heart must still be pumping.* She tried again. This time she could actually feel a pulse. His eyelids fluttered then slowly opened.

"Megs?" he moaned.

She nodded and smiled.

Terry's fear filled eyes motioned for her to look behind her. She turned to find Lilith and her group standing meters away. The strange girl with menacing eyes addressed her as if they were friends.

"Hello, Meaghan. Long time no see."

Meaghan tried to return to her body but something was wrong. She was stuck in the void. She closed her eyes and concentrated on her body but it was as if she never existed.

"Why are you doing this?" she directed her question to Lilith. "Terry and those other poor souls did nothing to you. Why did you target them?"

"Because we could," squawked one of the group. Meaghan recognized him as the belligerent male from the canteen. The others were there too.

"Lilith. I don't understand. Why are going along with this madness?"

"She promised me that I would get your talent."

"Who promised you?"

"Nemesis." She motioned to the ringleader who smiled menacingly but remained silent. "She's a powerful black witch and we've—"

"Shut up!" Nemesis ordered with a back hand to

Lilith's cheek. "She'll find out soon enough." She motioned for the others to pick Terry up. They carried him to a black van that was parked in front of the alley. When she turned back to face Meaghan, she smiled and casually asked, "Are you coming?"

"Do I have a choice?"

Nemesis shook her head. "I suggest that you take a look inside the van and see the answer for yourself."

Cautiously, Meaghan floated towards the back of the van where Terry had already been dumped onto an old, worn mattress. His blood soaked clothes beginning to soak through the fabric. Meaghan fought the urge the cover her mouth. She could see the two males sitting beside Terry and the three girls waiting outside the van, but someone else lay on the mattress behind Terry. She leaned closer for a better look and screamed. "No!"

****

"It doesn't seem right," Derrick told his brother as he accepted the glass of scotch. "We should call the funeral home and have him laid out properly."

"If we call the funeral home, there will be papers to fill out and the police may need to be called. We don't have time for this now, Derrick. We must find Meaghan."

"But, after all he's done for us over the years—"

"I know," he rested his hand on his brother's shoulder and squeezed, "and we will give him a fitting and proper send-off … later. He would understand."

Derrick nodded and sipped his drink. "Anna is devastated but can't leave Sofie. Not until we know she's safe. Have you been able to contact Meaghan telepathically?"

"No. I've been trying ever since I got the call from…" He swallowed the painful memory of Evan's last moments. "No, Derrick. Not yet."

"Well the surveillance tape wasn't a lot of help and Evan's description a little vague. Do you think that they somehow drugged her?"

"I don't see how. He said that she seemed to be asleep before they arrived. What I can't understand is … why didn't she wake up?" He took a few steps before slapping his forehead with his palm. "Of course. She didn't wake up because she wasn't in her body."

"She was astral travelling?"

"That little minx. I made her promise not to leave the house so she figured out another way."

"Where would she have gone?"

"My guess is she would look for Palmer."

"You were in the underground carpark. Didn't you see her?"

"No, but I saw a lot of blood. If Palmer is alive … he's in a bad way." He leaned against the kitchen counter, running his hands through his hair. "Whoever they are, they're not our kind. A vampire would never waste so much blood."

He turned to his brother. "Meaghan recognized a girl in the riot as being part of that cult who followed her on campus. She was worried that they were after Palmer … that's why she sent me to find him. If they *are* the people who took him, I suspect that they also took Meaghan."

"Dark clothes, dark van." Derrick agreed. "What do you think they want with them?"

David's eyes widened and his nostrils flared. "Every other victim was sacrificed."

Derrick rose from his seat and grabbed his brother by his upper arms. "Take it easy, David. You won't be able to help her if you lose control."

"I can't sense her, Derrick. She may already be dead." He threw his empty glass across the room, shattering it. "I've tried to contact her in my mind but I can't reach her."

"What if we try together?" David looked puzzled. Derrick offered an explanation.

"I will reach out to you and we will try to reach her as one."

David nodded and closed his eyes to concentrate. He could feel the second Derrick made the psychic connection and together they reached out for Meaghan. For a moment, he connected with her, sensed her distress but, no sooner had he bonded, he lost contact.

"Someone is blocking us," he told his brother.

"But she's alive, David. We could both feel her."

"Yes, but she's afraid. Afraid and in shock." He fisted his hair, squeezed his eyes tight shut as he told his brother, "I haven't had a chance to tell you but, Meaghan is deathly afraid of blood. The sight and smell repels her. It comes from a childhood experience and is a real phobia."

"That could be problematic."

"Not only that. Judging by the emotions I'm sensing … wherever she is … she is surrounded by blood."

****

"Where are you taking us?" Meaghan asked the unholy alliance as she hovered over her body.

"To the cemetery," Lilith answered with a smug expression that was soon disappeared when Nemesis glared at her.

"What? I don't see how telling her makes any difference now. It's not as if she can do anything about it. She can't even get back in her body."

"Yeah. How cool is that?" the other girl added in between puffs of the joint that she passed on. "You really did a number on her, Nemesis. I can't wait until the master gives me some of those powers."

"You'd better hope he isn't disappointed this time," Nemesis warned the girl before directing her gaze to Lilith. "If you lied—"

"No. No, Nemmy. I'm sure it'll work this time."

"I've told you a million times you stupid bitch, don't call me Nemmy!"

"Okay. Don't have a cow." She snatched the joint from the other Goth and blew the smoke in Terry's face. He coughed and then groaned from the pain that obviously resulted from the sudden movement.

"Won't be long now pig." She turned to Meaghan's incorporeal form and smiled. "Who'd 'ave thought you're virginitis would be so profitable for me." She giggled and took another drag. "The master will be very pleased this time."

"You'd better hope that you haven't stuffed up again, Lilith." One of the others warned her. "I thought he'd skin us alive when he realized that the last one wasn't pure."

"She was a Sunday school teacher. You'd think that she'd have been as pure as driven snow."

"You haven't tasted the yellow snow," the argumentative male informed her and the others joined him as he laughed. "She must've tasted like piss too cause the master spat her out."

"You're all scum. Do'you know that?" Meaghan cursed. "Whatever it is that you think he'll give you. He's lying." She tried again to return to her body but it was as though a barrier was around it. She couldn't break through.

"You can try all you like but you won't get back in." Nemesis informed her with a chuckle. "You say he's lying to us? Well, how do you think I was able to block you out of your body? *He* gave me the power. We've had a partnership, him and I, for years now. He even gave me a little pet … I think you've met Fido." She smirked as she looked from Meaghan to Terry then back. "By the way, if I'd wanted Fido to kill you, you'd be dead. We were playing a little game of cat and mouse with you, keeping you up at night, weakening you."

"He was trying to do more than weaken me when he attacked me outside of the police station."

"You know how wild things can be … a little uncontrollable sometimes. He would have been severely punished if he had killed you. That pleasure is to be mine."

"Why? I've never done anything to you. We've barely spoken. Why would you want to torment and kill me?"

"You still don't know who I am, do you?" she mumbled to herself as though she was arguing with internal voices. "I can't believe that I've spent most of my adult life hating you and you don't even remember me. You lousy bitch!" She flicked the lit joint at Meaghan's body. It left a small burn mark on her bare arm but she felt nothing. "All I ever wanted was to be part of a family but you couldn't bear for me to find happiness, could you? You had to show up and ruin everything."

Meaghan gasped as Nemesis smiled. "Oh, so you do remember? Which part stands out for you the most, Meaghan? The part where you flew in through my bedroom window and convinced me that you were a ghost or the part where you found me half-dead on the bathroom floor?"

When Meaghan grimaced she laughed.

"Ah, the bathroom floor. I thought that might jog your memory." She unfastened the leather bracelets from her wrists and held out her hands, palms up to show the thin pale scars. "At the time, I didn't realize that it would have been more effective to slice down the vein instead of across. So much blood wasn't there, but not enough to kill me."

"I never meant to hurt you Clarissa, I—"

"Clarissa is gone. I killed her off along with those do-gooders who couldn't wait to get rid of me. They thought I was crazy. Even called me that to my face … until they saw the knife in my hand. You see, they wanted a perfect little girl. A clever, talented girl. If they'd seen you first, they'd have chosen you but we all make mistakes…" She glared at Lilith, "And we learn from them. It took me a while to track you both down. She flicked her head in Terry's direction. "But I was pleasantly surprised to find that you're still friends. It worked well with my plans. Two for the price of one."

"Leave Terry out of this. He never did anything to you."

"That's right. He never did anything. He never paid any attention to me because he was so in love with you. You had each other … I was alone."

Terry groaned and turned to Nemesis. "We tried to be friends with you, Clarissa—"

"Nemesis!"

He coughed and a trickle of blood ran down his chin. "Sorry. Nemesis. You shut us out. We would have—"

"No. When she was around you didn't see anyone else but I bet you see me now. And when the master devours her, you can have a front row seat. You see, it's a win/win situation for me. I tracked down this group of idiots when I heard about the first murder." She scoffed as she looked her group over. "Amateurs. They were trying to conjure a demon by strangling their victims. Even when I explained how the process works, they still managed to stuff up. I admit I needed their help to find sacrifices for my master." She shook her head. "You'd think that virgins would be easier to find but, I guess not. When I saw you at one of the murder scenes, I upped the ante, hoping that I could trap you outside of your body. The master promised that if your incorporeal self was in the area when I summoned him, he could kill your corporeal body and trap you in the ether forever. Unfortunately, these fuckers stuffed so he refused to pay up. Who'd have thought that the very person I planned on killing would turn out to be the sacrifice? What a joke."

Meaghan tried again to enter her body to no avail. She tried to leave the van and will herself to wherever David was but that didn't work either. She was trapped outside her body, waiting to watch herself die, knowing that her soul would be doomed to float around in the ether. Her thoughts turned to David. Would he still be able to see her? How awful, if they could see each other but never touch, never make love. She suppressed a sob, not wanting Nemesis to see how much pain she caused. She didn't want her to have the satisfaction of knowing that she'd won. She bit her bottom lip, hard. A droplet of blood reached her tongue and she pushed down the wave of nausea as she remembered her last encounter with blood. *She and David had mind bonded.* An idea popped into her head offering a flicker of hope. If she couldn't go to him, maybe she could call him to her?

****

When Anna entered the lounge room, both brothers rushed to her.

"What's going on? Why did you call me back from the hospital?"

"Someone stole Meaghan's body from the cottage while she was astral travelling and we can't communicate with her. Someone or something is blocking us. We almost got through but it failed. Derrick thought that we should all try together. Maybe your power will be the key."

"Do you think that it was the same group who attacked Sofie?"

"I'd bet my life on that." He grimaced. "Well, you know what I mean."

"It makes sense. The only way that they could have entered the cottage was if the protection spell was broken. Sofie and I cast that spell together. They must have gone after her first."

Derrick grabbed his wife by the shoulders. "That means they'll be coming for you next." He turned to David. "We need to finish this … now!"

"How do you propose we do this, Anna?"

Anna thought for a moment. "Come with me."

She led them to the dining room table and motioned for them to sit. "I think that we should hold hands, like a séance, only, instead of me, David will lead us."

"I don't know how to run a séance."

"Just think of Meaghan. We'll concentrate our energy on you while you try to communicate with her. Both of you, close your eyes and focus on Meaghan."

David closed his eyes and tried to connect. Something fluttered in his mind, he heard the tinkling sound of glass shattering and then he heard her.

"David, is that you?"

"Meaghan! Oh, kitten, it's so good to hear your voice. How—"

"I don't have much time. I'm trapped outside my body. Terry and I are in a van travelling, I think, to the cemetery. They plan to sacrifice us to the demon I saw but it won't work. The believe me to be a virgin so when the demon discovers their mistake, all hell will break loose. Terry is in a really bad way; I don't think he'll make it. David, if I don't survive this—"

"Don't talk like that. We'll get to you in time, I promise."

"The killer calls herself Nemesis but her real name is Clarissa. She's the girl from the orphanage. The one who tried to kill herself. She blames me for her problems but I don't believe that she will stop killing after I'm dead."

"If she does anything to hurt you, I will end her and all her friends."

"Just promise me that you'll stop them. And, David?"

"Yes, kitten."

"Whatever happens tonight, I need you to know—"

"You can tell me in person my love."

"David, we seem to be stopping. I can't…"

"Meagan? Meaghan!"

"We've lost communication, David." Anna informed him. "They must be moving her."

David sprung to his feet and slammed his fist onto the glass table. His chair clattered to the floor as he turned to his brother. "I'm going to the cemetery, are you coming?"

"Wait!" Anna grabbed her husband by his shirt sleeve. "You're not prepared to face a demon. You must have a plan."

"I plan to kill the bastard."

"David, think for a minute. Do you even know how to kill a demon?"

"I think ripping its head off will be a good start. What do you think Derrick?"

"Sounds like a plan."

"And how do you plan on doing that? Until it's made corporeal, there is nothing to kill."

"She's right, David. It would be akin to fighting a cloud."

"They're going to kill her if we don't do something. We must act now!"

"What do you suggest?" Derrick asked his wife who was chewing on her fingernails.

She looked up from her hands and her eyes widened. "The girl that Meaghan mentioned. This … Nemesis. She's the key. She controls the hell-hound and she is the one who summons the demon. If you destroy her, the demon will never return."

"What about the hell-hound?"

"Have you seen it?"

"Meaghan and I were chased by it and it howled outside her window but, we never actually saw it. Why?"

David turned to his wife. "Yes, what difference would that make?"

Anna sighed. "Thank goodness. From what I've read, the hell-hound drags a soul to hell after it has shown itself to that person three times. I don't think it can hurt you … yet."

"That's a useful piece of information and I thank you but we're wasting time. How do we save Meagan and Palmer?"

Anna's shoulders slumped but her facial expression hardened as she told him, "You have to kill Nemesis."

Chapter Twenty-Two

Meaghan watched her body get dragged through the long grass and rubble towards a group of head stones. She considered herself lucky that she was unable to feel the pain of the bruises and scrapes that were coloring her skin black and blue. She tried to ignore the blood as it seeped through the open wounds and concentrate on Terry who was beginning to turn a shade of gray. His lips going blue. He'd passed out in the van and she hoped that he would remain unconscious throughout the ordeal to come. Nemesis would delight in torturing him and—as he would never beg for mercy—his punishment would be prolonged. She raised her head to the sky and silently prayed. *If you plan on taking him tonight, please, do it now.*

"Here!" Nemesis ordered as she pointed to a patch of loose dirt. "There should be powerful magic over this fresh grave."

The men threw Terry onto the ground. He groaned and opened his eyes in time to see Meaghan's body dumped beside him. He looked past the body to Meaghan's incorporeal spirit. "Hey … Megs. Sorry, I must have taken a little nap."

She forced a smile. "Rest, Terry. Close your eyes and sleep. You don't want to be awake for this."

"We made a promise to each other, back in the orphanage, do you remember?"

"Yes, I remember. We promised to stick together."

"Well, I intend to keep that promise, kiddo. Together to the end."

"Very touching," Nemesis interrupted. She turned to her cloaked companions and ordered, "Strip her."

"No!" Meaghan screamed as she watched the women remove her clothes. "Please Nemesis, why can't you leave me with some dignity?"

"Do you think the mental asylum treated *me* with any dignity? I want you to suffer as I suffered. Besides, when I bleed you, I want you to see every drop as the blood stains your skin crimson." She leaned in towards Meaghan. "I want you to smell the blood on my master's breath as he licks your skin, I want you to—"

"That's enough!"

Meaghan turned to Terry who was trying to keep his face turned away from her. She knew he was trying to protect her modesty. "Close your eyes, Megs, close your eyes and block it out. From what you told me of the last sacrifice, it will be over soon."

"Slight change of plans." Nemesis informed them as the others lifted Meaghan's body into a sitting position against the newly carved headstone. "Cutting your throat will kill you too fast and we can't have that." She motioned for the others to light the black candles and gather around. She accepted the sacrificial knife from Lilith and lifted it to admire the long, serrated blade before slicing it across Meaghan's cast-less wrist. "This way I get to enjoy watching you as you go into shock."

Meaghan gasped and held her hand to her mouth. She couldn't feel the pain of her bleeding wrist, but she could see and smell the blood as it oozed out of the cut and ran down into her open palm. Nemesis placed a cup under the wrist and collected some of the blood while she chanted in Latin. The others joined the chant and squealed with delight when Nemesis sliced through Meaghan's other wrist. She caught some of the blood then left both hands resting on Meaghan's legs so that the blood could drain out. It trickled down Meaghan's fingers, snaked down her thighs and began to pool on the ground around her. She dry heaved as tears streamed down her ethereal face. She felt helpless. Helpless to save Terry. Helpless to save herself. The smell of the blood overwhelmed her senses and, through the rapidly forming fog, she could see the demon taking shape. Nemesis and her coven dropped to their knees before him and kept her head down as she addressed him.

"Master. I have, at last, delivered you a virgin sacrifice. Take her and grant me what you have promised."

"Do not presume to make demands of me, human. I have not yet tasted the blood." His gaze drifted over Meaghan's naked body and he sniffed the air. "I approve of this one. She is quite beautiful. I may keep her in your stead."

"No!" Nemesis's head shot up and she stared defiantly into the demon's flaming red eyes. "You promised that if I made you corporeal, that you would send her soul into the ether and give me her gift of astral projection."

He smiled and bared his fangs. "We shall see." The demon ignored the extended chalice and lapped the blood from Meaghan's thigh. He turned back to Nemesis. His eyes blazing as he roared. "What-is-this? You continue to try my patience!"

Meaghan watched as color rushed to Nemesis's cheeks. "I don't understand, I—"

"This woman is not pure. She has known a man. You have dared to deceive me again."

Nemesis turned to Lilith. "You told me that she was still a virgin."

"She is … was … she told me—"

The punch caught Lilith off-guard. She held her hand to her cheek as it began to bruise and glared at Meaghan. "You told me that you hadn't done the dirty with Spartan boy. Why would you lie?"

Meaghan didn't answer. She couldn't answer even if she'd wanted to. Her body and corporeal body in shock from blood loss. As her body began to die, she felt her spirit drifting away. She stared at the blood, unable to think, unable to care what was going on around her. Blood surrounded her. Her own blood, Terry's blood. It was more than she could bear.

"She is dying," the demon announced. "And when she is dead, I will allow her to join with her body and I will take her with me."

"No!" Nemesis screamed. "You are to send her soul into the ether. You promised me. You said that you would do this if I supplied you with blood sacrifices."

"Stupid girl. You *offered* me those sacrifices and I agreed to take them. I never promised to *give* you *anything*. I was promised the blood of a virgin and you tricked me. I will take this woman and punish you for your deceit. You will be stripped of all the powers that you were given." He waved his hand, first over Nemesis and the Meaghan. Nemesis fell to her knees and pounded the ground with her fists.

"You bastard. You promised!"

The demon laughed and turned his attention to Meaghan. She felt the familiar tug of her body and found herself hurtling back. Once joined, the smell of the blood overpowered but she was too weak to vomit. She gagged and slumped back against the grave stone as the demon leaned in towards her.

"It's nearly time to go little one."

"Over my dead body!"

Meaghan recognized the voice immediately and weakly cried out. "David."

"Corel? How is that even possible?" Terry tried to raise his head but didn't manage it.

Clarissa's crew scattered in all directions.

"It's a long story, Palmer." David turned to face the demon. "This is not your world. You have no power here."

"So, she is *your* woman, vampire."

Terry turned to Meaghan. "Did he say vampire?"

She nodded weakly as she listened to the conversation going on beside her.

"Yes. She's mine. Go back to your dimension and take your hell-hound with you."

"I will go … this time, but my pet has unfinished business." He glanced at Meaghan, "I suspect we will meet again my lovely." In a puff of smoke, he disappeared.

David tore off his jacket and wrapped it around Meaghan. "Hold on, kitten."

"Corel. You must get her to a hospital. She's—"

Derrick suddenly appeared before him. "What the fuc—"

"Terry Palmer. I'd like you to meet my brother Derrick."

"Sorry to startle you, Detective Palmer. David, I have four of them tied up in their own van. Looks like they were trying to escape. How is Meaghan?"

David shook his head.

Terry struggled to sit up. "No. She can't die. You have to do something, Corel. If you and your brother really are vampires, surely you can help her."

"I want to, but it would mean turning her and—"

"You're concerned about her phobia?"

"I don't know if she would be able to cope."

"She's a lot stronger than we give her credit for, Corel. If you love her, you have to at least try."

"I concur, David." Derrick told him as he knelt down beside them. "We'll all help her to manage her phobia."

****

David gazed down at Meaghan's face. The color all but gone and dark shadows were beginning to form under her eyes. He whispered, "Forgive me, kitten," and as he gently cradled her in his arms, he drank from her. When her heart slowed to almost a stop, he opened a vein on his wrist and put it to her lips. She lay still. He had expected her to gag or at least pull away but she remained motionless as the blood filled her mouth and dribbled down her chin.

"You're too late." Nemesis's face twisted into a smirk. "I'm glad that she's dead."

David's first reaction was to tear the smirk from her face but Derrick's expression reminded him that it was against their code to kill a human, even if it had been their intention. The demon was not likely to return. The police could deal with the Clarissa.

He stared down at Meaghan and noticed her eyelashes subtly flutter. It was barely a movement, but it was there. Again. He looked across to Derrick.

"Yes, I saw that too."

"You saw what?"

"She moved her eyes." Derrick told Terry. "The blood seems to be taking affect."

David leaned close to Meaghan's ear. "Come on, kitten, you can do it, I know you can."

Nemesis balled her hands into tight fists and screamed. "No. It's not fair. She was supposed to suffer and die. She can't—" suddenly she stopped talking and looked around before asking, "Did you hear that?"

Derrick stood up. "I heard a howl." He paused to listen. "Yes, there it is again. Definitely a howl."

Terry groaned as he tried to raise his head. "I didn't hear anything."

Nemesis smiled. "At least I get to watch the four of you die. He's coming for you. My hound will gnaw off your limbs and eat you slowly. I can't wait to see the look on your faces when you see him. He's fucking big and his fangs could tear through a rhino hide. He looks like a friggin' nightmare."

"You've seen the hound?" David asked as the significance of her brag became clear to him.

"Of course I've seen him. He belongs to me. What a stupid question."

"How many times have you seen him?"

"Twice." She motioned with a flick of her head as she looked over their shoulders. A twisted smile wrinkled her nose. "Correction, three times."

David and Derrick shared a look. David rose to his feet keeping Meaghan tight to his chest. David nodded his understanding of their telepathic conversation and helped Terry to his feet and then lifted him over his shoulders. Together they started walking towards David's car which was parked beside the black van. Terry strained his neck to look in the direction of Nemesis's gaze.

"I don't see a thing."

"Don't look back," Derrick told him. "No matter what you hear, don't look back."

"Wait! Stop! What are you doing?" the woman screamed as a throaty growl pierced the silence followed by a roar and the crunch of shattering bones. A blood curdling scream tore from her throat. Then the sickening sound of tearing flesh dulled the scream. She gurgled as her mouth filled with blood. Then, nothing.

****

Pain surged through her body and Meaghan clutched her stomach as she dashed for her bathroom, slamming the door behind her.

"Oh god, these cramps are unbearable, I feel like I'm dying," she called out to the man in the other room.

"You *are* dying, kitten. At least your body is."

Meaghan rested her forehead on the cold marble of the vanity and contemplated what David had said. She remembered the events of the previous night. Nemesis had cut her left wrist. The wound had been deep enough to slice through her vein. She had lost a copious quantity of blood. Blood. She waited for the nausea to overwhelm her but while she experienced the familiar quickening of her heartbeat, she discovered that she could not only tolerate the thought of blood, she suddenly craved it. Opening the bathroom door slightly, she poked her head out and saw David sitting at the foot of her bed.

"David. What happened to me last night? What do you mean by saying that my body is dying?" Before he could answer, the realization hit her. "I'm becoming a vampire?"

With a single nod of his head, David confirmed her suspicion. She wasn't sure whether to laugh or cry. Pain shot through her like a bolt of electricity and she slammed the door shut as she rushed for the toilet. When the pain eased, she called out.

"How much longer will I feel like this?"

"Not long to go now." He waited for a response. Nothing. Minutes passed before he called to her.

"Meaghan?"

She stepped into the bedroom wearing a cotton bathrobe she had thrown on to warm herself while the convulsions shook her body but she found that her body had stopped shivering. She held out her right hand to show him that the cast was gone and she waved her hand around, drawing patterns in the air with her fingers. "My wrist … it's completely healed and David … I tore off the cast with my teeth."

"One of the perks of being a vampire, my love. We heal very quickly and we have very strong fangs."

She smiled coyly. "For someone recently deceased, I feel surprisingly alive. Actually, I feel pretty wonderful." She opened the curtains and stared out at the stars. "Even the stars seem brighter."

"You will discover that everything is a little brighter, my love. Colors are more vibrant and your hearing will become exceptional."

"What else?" She asked as she bounced on the balls of her feet. "What else can I do?"

"You will be stronger … as strong as ten men. Faster than a car—"

Striking an arrogant pose, she laughed. "Just wait until I show those macho men at the station. There are a couple of guys that I would like to put on their arse. Wait until the next time they challenge me in the gym, I'll show—"

"You can't go back to work, Meaghan. Not as a police officer anyway."

Meaghan's shoulder's dropped and her expression turned solemn. "I guess that it would be hard explaining why I can't work the day shift?"

David nodded. "If it makes you feel any better, at least you can join the company firm."

Tilting her head to one side, she asked, "And what does the company firm do?"

"I guess you would call us private investigators. It should be right up your alley."

"At least that'll make Terry happy. He's been trying to talk me out of being a cop for years. He'll … oh, my god. I completely forgot about Terry. Did you turn him too?"

"Derrick took him to the hospital last night."

"Is he okay?"

"He's in surgery now. There was a lot of damage to his internal organs and he lost a lot of blood. Derrick compelled one of the officers to call him as soon as they have any news. All we can do now is wait."

Memories of the previous evening came flooding back. The attack on Terry. The demon. The last thing she remembered was the demon leaning over her and the overpowering smell of blood. Her stomach rumbled in response.

"What happened to Nemesis?"

"Who?"

"Clarissa."

David sat down on the end of the bed and took her hand. "Have you heard the expression … you reap what you sow?"

"Y-e-s."

"Well, let's just say that she got a taste of her own medicine."

"You mean … she's dead?"

"She may have believed that the hell-hound was a pet but, like any wild animal, he's a natural born killer and serves no master. Derrick and I recently learned that they are sent to deliver an evil person to hell. They stalk their victims and on the third visit, they kill them."

Meaghan sighed. "Despite all that she's done … I can't help but feel sorry for her."

David cupped the back of her head and kissed her gently on her forehead. "You have a kind heart, Chérie. Few people could find it in their hearts to forgive someone who attempted to take their life."

"I doubt that I'd have been as forgiving if she had killed Terry." She paused before asking, "David, he is going to be all right, isn't he?"

"We'll go to the hospital as soon as you have fed. It wouldn't be safe for anyone there if you suddenly decided to snack."

"Fed? As in, eaten *blood*?"

"It's the final part of the transformation. If you don't consume blood—"

"I'll die for good?"

He nodded. "I know that the last time we tried, it didn't work out very well."

"Oh, I'd say it worked fine if the objective was to make me puke and pass out."

"At least you have retained your sense of humor."

"I don't see that I have much choice. Besides…"

"Besides?"

"I can't believe that I'm going to say this, but, I'm kinda hungry."

David undid the buttons on his white silk shirt, exposing his chest. He dragged a fingernail across the side of his neck, the skin opened and blood began to trickle from the wound. Meaghan licked her lips. Her newly formed fangs shot through her gums with such force, she heard them snap as they broke the skin. She lunged forward, knocking him onto his back as she straddled his waist and sunk her fangs into his neck without hesitation. She gripped his shoulders, digging her long nails into his flesh as she siphoned the warm liquid from his veins. Her taste buds danced as the thick, coppery fluid ran across her tongue and down her throat, igniting every nerve ending in her body.

He sat up, lifted her, her legs still wrapped around his body as he unzipped his jeans, allowing them to drop to his knees. He untied her robe and threw it across the room as he positioned her over his lap. She felt a wave of pleasure as he entered her, filled her with moist, solid heat. She rode him, keeping a tight grip on his shoulders, lapping every drop of blood as it oozed from his neck. The taste tantalizing, deliciously decadent. She craved more. They came together in an explosion of sensations … passion, urgency, ecstasy. He flipped her onto her back and pulled free of her fangs as he pinned her to the bed by her shoulders. She tried to sit up, she reached for the blood, needed more but he held her fast.

"You'll bleed me dry kitten. As it is, I may need to feed again before we go to the hospital."

She gasped, suddenly aware of what she'd done. David's face had turned deathly pale and dark circles formed under his eyes.

"David. I'm so sorry. I couldn't stop."

"Don't be sorry my love." He leaned down and caught one of her nipples in his teeth. He tugged gently and she bucked beneath him ready to continue their lovemaking.

The sound of David's phone broke the mood. She pouted as he released her nipple and eased himself from her in order to reach the phone. He laughed at her pout but his expression hardened as he turned to her. "It's Derrick. Palmer is out of surgery but it doesn't look good. The doctor says that he isn't likely to last the night."

Meaghan sprung from the bed and rushed to her wardrobe. She threw on a pair of jeans and a t shirt and searched for a pair of boots. Combing her fingers through her bed-tussled hair, she secured her unruly locks into a ponytail with a rubber band and turned to David.

"Show me how to get to the hospital in the shortest time possible."

****

"You must concentrate on keeping to a human speed," David informed Meaghan as they left the underground parking station. "I know that you're anxious to get to Palmer, but, we mustn't draw attention to ourselves."

"I'm sure we could have been here much faster if we'd run." She bypassed the elevator and ran up the stairs in a blur of speed that would have gone undetected by the human eye. At the top floor, she paused. "No one would have seen me."

"It's not the running that causes humans alarm, it's the sudden appearance when you stop."

"There wouldn't have been any cause to stop. If we hadn't been in your car, we wouldn't have been held up in traffic and at the red lights."

"There is a downside to being a vampire, kitten."

Meaghan pushed open the exit door, almost breaking it off its hinges. She cringed and checked to see if anyone saw her grand entrance before turning to David. "Is that one of the downsides? Super strength?"

"Among other things."

"Such as…"

"Such as our 'allergy' to the sun."

Meaghan screwed up her face as she pointed out, "It's the middle of the night David."

"At present. But we don't know how long we'll be here. If we'd run here and the sun came up before we leave, we would have been stranded. The car has specially tinted windows and the underground parking protects us as we leave."

"What about the windows in the rooms?"

"Taken care of." David slipped his arm around her in order to slow her down as they made their way to the Intensive Care Unit. "Slowly, kitten, slowly."

"*How* is it taken care of?"

"After an incident last year when Anna was admitted to hospital—prior to her conversion—we realized there was a need to protect ourselves so we could enter the wards. Derrick and I paid to have all the windows in the hospital replaced with treated glass."

"Didn't the board question your agenda?"

He shook his head. "We've always generously sponsored the hospital so they had no reason to suspect any ulterior motives. We told them that it was a safety precaution and they were happy to comply."

"Meaghan!" A young police officer rushed towards them. "I'm so glad you're here."

"David, this is Adam." She instantly realized her mistake. David was believed to be dead. She turned to David with wide eyes but he merely smiled and offered his hand. If Adam understood the connection, he didn't react.

The men shook hands and Adam hugged Meaghan. "You look pale. I heard that the scum that attacked Detective Palmer also hurt you. Are you okay?"

She nodded. "Fine now. How is he?"

Adam bit his lip. His expression spoke volumes and tears rimmed his lower lashes. He shook his head but choked when he tried to speak. Meaghan hugged him again. "I'll stay with him for a while. You go and have a coffee. You look as though you need it."

"Will you call me if…" A sob caught in his throat.

"The moment there is any change."

Adam forced a smile and headed towards the cafeteria. They watched as he walked away, his shoulders slumped, his head down.

"Palmer seems to mean a lot to him."

"He means a lot to everyone at the precinct." She stepped inside the room and gasped. Terry was hooked up to an intravenous drip and transfusion bags. His complexion ashen and dark circles defined his eyes. She hurried to his side and lifted his hand. "He feels so cold. Isn't there something we can do?"

"He may not want our help, kitten."

"Why wouldn't he? He's not like me. He doesn't have a problem with blood."

"If I turn him, he won't be able to return to the force. All those people who you said look up to him and rely on him for support would lose him."

"The force is my life…" Terry's voice was barely above a whisper. "But I see that being dead agrees with you, Megs. You look completely healed."

She hugged him as gently as she could but he still groaned under the pressure of her embrace. "Trying to hasten my death, Officer Lamb?"

"Let us help you, Terry."

"No, Megs. It's like Corel said. I would have to give up the force and I can't do that. It's my life."

"No, Terry. It's your death!" She dropped his hand and walked to the window. "You are so pig-headed! Let us save you. We can work out the consequences later."

Terry looked into David's eyes. "I know that you could overpower me and turn me into whatever the hell you are, Corel, but, you seem to be an honorable man. Promise me that you won't let her talk you into it. Give me your word."

"You have it, Palmer. It is not something that I do lightly."

"Well I'm not prepared to lose you." Meaghan flew at him, fangs bared and ready to attempt a conversion despite having no idea what to do. David intercepted her and held her firmly.

"Do you have any idea what you're doing?"

"No, but I don't care," she sobbed as she struggled in his arms. "I have to try."

"Please, Meaghan," Terry mumbled. "Just let me go in peace."

David saw the look of desperation on his love's

face and felt his own heart break. "There may be something…"

She grabbed his forearms. "Whatever it is, please try."

"Palmer. What if we were able to save you but you would be forever linked to us? Could you handle that?"

"Would I be undead?"

"That depends on how you look at it, old man." David laughed. "You would be alive, so technically you would be undead but not in the same sense as us."

Terry smiled at Meaghan. "I'm already forever linked with you, Megs, have been since the orphanage, so I may as well make it official." He questioned David. "In what way linked?"

"A telepathic bond. You will be able to communicate across long distances telepathically." When Terry turned his attention back to Meaghan, David instantly regretted his idea. Despite Meaghan's rejection, Palmer still loved her.

"So, we've come to an agreement?"

"Yes. I accept those terms. How is this done? I'm not sure if I have enough blood for you to take, Meaghan."

"There's no need for the taking of your blood, Palmer, but, I hope that you're not squeamish."

"You mean…"

"Just close your eyes and pretend that you're drinking a warm milkshake laced with pennies."

Chapter Twenty-Three

"So, this is the Corel Detective agency."

"What do you think, Terry?" Meaghan ushered her friend inside the building and showed him to her office where she pointed to the chair beside the large mahogany desk. He flopped into the large leather chair and surveyed the room.

"Not too shabby, Megs. Not too shabby." He glanced around the room. "Where's Corel?"

"He's on the phone in the other room, finalizing details for our honeymoon."

"Oh, yeah. I forgot. How many weeks till the big day?"

"You know very well that it's three weeks until the wedding, Terry Palmer. You'd better not let me down. I couldn't go through with it without you by my side."

"And miss the opportunity to remind Corel that *I* am the best man … not a chance. Besides, if you change your mind at the last minute, I'll be there to help you escape."

You are walking a very fine line, Palmer. Must I remind you that I have access to your thoughts and I am very close to ripping your head off. That is my fiancé you are lusting after.

"Damn, Megs!" Terry cursed as he looked over his shoulder. "Why did it have to be him to give me blood? Why couldn't you do it?"

"I had every intention of giving you my blood but David insisted. I think that he decided I was too new at being a vampire."

We both know that's not true, don't we, Corel?
No, it did play a small part in my decision.

Terry could hear the laughter in David's voice as he continued.

Meaghan might not appreciate some of the thoughts that pop into your head while you're staring at her and besides, I think I'm going to enjoy knowing what's going on in that stubborn head of yours. What was it Meaghan called you ... pig-headed. He laughed again.

Why don't you shut the fu—

Now, now, Palmer. No need for profanities.

Well ... it goes both ways you know. I will be able to—

Sorry old man but it doesn't work that way unless I allow it. I can listen to your thoughts anytime I want but you can only hear me when I need to contact you.

Meaghan cleared her throat. "I hate to interrupt this male bonding but we have business to discuss."

"Sorry, my love." David entered the room and gave Terry a slap on the back as he passed the chair. "Palmer and I were just having a little man to man talk." He leaned down to kiss her forehead before sitting on the edge of the desk beside her. "So, Palmer. What do you think of our little business venture?"

"I can see at least one major problem." He rose from the chair and walked to the window. "Most people do business in the daylight hours. How do you propose to deal with that?"

"The windows are tinted." Meaghan informed him with a huge grin. "David has the glass made specially. As long as we don't follow the clients outside, we should be fine."

"How do you propose to follow wayward husbands and tail criminals? Not all evil deeds are performed at night."

"I may have risen up the food chain but I still

have my old talents, Terry. I can astral travel during the day. If you remember, it's a safer way to stalk unsubs anyway."

"Well, you seem to have everything sorted out. Looks like you're still chasing bad guys, Megs."

"And she's developing quite a following as an artist," David added, with a proud grin on his face.

"Good for you." Terry helped Meaghan to her feet. David stepped forward, but allowed Terry to give her a congratulatory hug.

"Everything is coming up roses for you kid. I couldn't be happier." He reached out his hand to David. "I don't think I've thanked you yet, Corel. You saved my life … twice. First when you found us at the cemetery and then when you gave me your blood. I'm in your debt."

"I believe that you paid your debt in full when you not only helped Meaghan and I obtain our licenses but also when you had me officially declared alive."

"That one was the hardest to pull off. Explaining your demise at the University wasn't too hard. The powers that be believed that you were working undercover for me and that, somehow, we used theatrical makeup and special effects to fake your death. The coroner was harder to convince. He swears that he remembers cremating you."

"Derrick has a gift for planting suggestions. It appears as though he did a thorough job with the coroner. I might ask him to pay the poor man another visit and clear things up."

"Good idea." Terry headed towards the door then paused. "Maybe you could have a word with the officers who examined the cemetery for evidence too? They're all getting counselling for recurring nightmares. It took days to find all of Clarissa and the parts that they found were not pretty." He shook his head. "I wish we could have helped her."

"You can't save everyone, Palmer. But, on that note, we would like to make you an offer."

Terry's eyes narrowed. "I'm listening."

"We were hoping we might enlist your help."

Terry raised one eyebrow at Meaghan, then answered David. "Yeah. In what way?"

"Meaghan tells me that you're passionate about keeping the streets safe. David and I share your desire. Perhaps you'd be willing to join our agency?"

He nodded. "I'll give it some thought." And waved his hand as he prepared to leave almost walking into Derrick who stood in the doorway of the office.

"You Corels are a stealthy lot." He held his hand to his chest. "You almost gave me a heart attack."

"Good to see you too, Palmer." Derrick shook Terry's hand and introduced Anna. "I don't believe you've met my wife."

"Hi. I'm Anna." She offered her hand. "And this is my friend Susie."

"Terry. Terry Palmer." He took her hand and left it extended for Susie who remained behind Anna. She offered a quiet "hello" but kept her eyes down and ignored his gesture.

****

Terry glanced in David's direction.

David shook his head and answered the unspoken question telepathically.

Susie has recently been through a traumatic experience. We're taking her home to live with us for a while.

She's beautiful, Corel.

He turned back to face Susie who chewed nervously on her fingernails. Dark yellow smudges stained her arms. Scabs were forming in the shape of teeth marks on her skin.

Who did this to her?

It's a long story, best kept for another time.

Did you get the bastard?

Yes. We got all of them.

Terry gasped. *All of them?*

He shook his head and let out a deep breath before addressing the group. "Well, it was great meeting you lovely ladies. I'd best get back to work." He headed back towards the front door.

"Get back to me soon about that offer," David called after him.

Terry stopped, took another look at Susie and told David. "Consider me in. I'll get the paperwork started and let you know when it's approved."

He left the building but maintained his psychic connection with David.

They really did a number on her, didn't they?

Yes, Palmer. It's going to take a while for her to trust any man. Her body is healing but emotionally she's still quite fragile.

Okay. I get your drift. Kid gloves right?

Right.

I hate to admit this, Corel, but, you're not such a bad guy after all.

David's chuckle sounded in Terry's ears. *That must have been hard to say.*

You don't know the half of it. And, David. Susie ... she's really special, isn't she?

Probably better than you deserve, but, I think you might be good for her, if you give her time to get to know you.

Thanks, Corel. I owe you one.

David broke the mental connection and turned his

attention back to his family.

"What was that about?" Derrick asked.

Anna answered for him. "He's been making a point of teasing Terry every chance he gets."

Derrick scowled. "Give him a break. He's been through a lot lately."

"Thanks for the lecture little brother, but Palmer and I are actually getting on rather well. He's a pretty nice guy." He hooked his arm around his fiancé. "So, now that you've collected Susie from the hospital, where are we going for dinner?"

Susie blushed and chewed her bottom lip. Her downcast eyes informed him that dinner was off.

"We decided to order take-away." Anna told them. "It's been a long day for Susie so we're taking her straight home for a rest."

Derrick answered David's silent question with a slight nod of his head before the newlyweds took their friend home.

****

"What did Derrick tell you?" Meaghan asked as they drove towards home.

"He and Anna are concerned that Susie is teetering on the edge. She had a panic attack in the carpark of the hospital. One of her male gym clients touched her shoulder and she collapsed in a screaming heap. The poor guy was a shocked as she was."

"Do you think that she'll cope at the house, surrounded by vampires?"

"It's either that or they'll have her committed. She's been crying out in her sleep about being attacked. David compelled the hospital staff to forget but it's only a matter of time before someone reports it."

"Does Anna think she can help?"

"At the very least, we can look after her at home.

Derrick had a special watch made for her with an alert button to push if she's afraid and so he can monitor her blood pressure. That way she can contact us during daylight hours. At night, she can sleep in the knowledge that she had four vampires to protect her."

Meaghan shrugged. "I hope we can help her. She looks like a frightened rabbit."

"I guess we'll find out soon enough." David pulled up at the large metal gates at the entrance of the estate and pressed the numerals on the keypad. As the gates opened, he drove through. "By the way, we owe her thanks for getting Palmer to join the team."

"Aah. *That's* what the secret conversation was about."

"I think he's smitten."

"Smitten? You're beginning to sound like an old man. Fortunately, I find old men very sexy."

David parked the car in the driveway and opened the passenger door, pulling Meaghan into his arms. She flung her arms around his neck as he took possession of her mouth. Her lips parted. He tasted her sweetness.

"You're pretty damned sexy yourself." He scooped her up in his arms and bounded up the stairs two at a time. Once inside, he called out to his brother. "Sorry guys, skipping dinner tonight."

"Lost your appetite?" Meaghan asked, a sly grin spreading her lips.

"Not in the least," he informed her. "Which brings us to lesson five."

"Lesson five? I'm almost afraid to ask what that involves."

"It involves stripping you naked, covering every inch of your body with kisses while reminding you—with every kiss—how much I love."

Anna giggled. A blush spread across her chest,

neck and cheeks.

"I like the sound of lesson five. How long does the class last?"

"For the rest of our eternal lives, kitten." His lips claimed hers again. "For the rest of our lives."

The End

ANNIE HARLAND CREEK

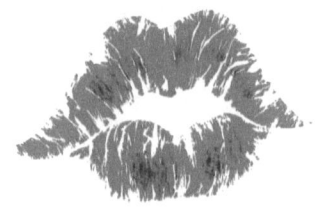

EVERNIGHT PUBLISHING ®

www.evernightpublishing.com